Julia Quinn started writing her first book one month after finishing university and has been tapping away at her keyboard ever since. The No. 1 *New York Times* bestselling author of more than two dozen novels, she is a graduate of Harvard and Radcliffe Colleges and is one of only sixteen authors ever to be inducted in the Romance Writers of America Hall of Fame. She lives in the Pacific Northwest with her family.

Please visit Julia Quinn online:

www.juliaquinn.com
www.facebook.com/AuthorJuliaQuinn
@JQAuthor

D1152103

By Julia Quinn

Everything and the Moon

Julia Quinn

PIATKUS

PIATKUS

First published in the US in 1997 by Avon Books,
An imprint of HarperCollins, New York
First published in Great Britain in 2008 by Piatkus
This paperback edition published in 2021 by Piatkus

1 3 5 7 9 10 8 6 4 2

A CIP catalogue record for this book
is available from the British Library

ISBN 978-0-349-43060-7

Typeset by Action Publishing Technology Ltd, Gloucester
Printed and bound in Great Britain by
Clays Ltd, Elcograf S.p.A.

Papers used by Piatkus Books are from well-managed forests
and other responsible sources.

Piatkus
An imprint of
Little, Brown Book Group
Carmelite House
50 Victoria Embankment
London EC4Y 0DZ

An Hachette UK Company
www.hachette.co.uk

www.littlebrown.co.uk

For Lyssa Keusch, my most excellent editor
and protector of all things chartreuse, puce,
and brackish green. This paint chip's for you!

And for Paul, even though he wants me
to call the sequel *Everything and Baboon*.

Dear Reader,

I'm going to admit something that no romance novelist should ever say in public: I don't believe in love at first sight. The first date, maybe, but first sight? Please.

But when I started writing *Everything and the Moon*, I resolved to try something new, and when I realized that the heroes and heroines of my three previous novels had required considerably more than a single glance to find true bliss, I decided to go for it, and I sent my hero tumbling headlong into love in the very first sentence.

And once I did, it was magic. Never before had I written a scene that felt so heady, so full of that elusive enchantment we've all felt while falling in love. My fingers tingled as I typed, and I couldn't seem to wipe the loopy grin off my face as the words poured forth. By the time I reached the end of chapter one, I, the non-believer, believed that Robert and Victoria were truly, madly, and deeply in love, and, if it weren't for two meddling fathers, would have lived happily ever after from that moment on.

So I'll ask the question of you: Do you believe in love at first sight? Yes? No? Never mind, it doesn't matter. Because I promise you this: For the next 372 pages, you will.

Best wishes,

Julia Q.

Chapter 1

Kent, England
June, 1809

Robert Kemble, Earl of Macclesfield, had never been given to flights of fancy, but when he saw the girl by the lake, he fell instantly in love.

It wasn't her beauty. With her black hair and pert nose she was certainly attractive, but he'd seen women far more beautiful in the ballrooms of London.

It wasn't her intelligence. He had no reason to believe that she was stupid, but as he hadn't shared two words with her, he couldn't vouch for her intellect either.

It *certainly* wasn't her grace. His first glimpse of her came as she flailed her arms and slipped off a wet rock. She landed on another rock with a loud thump, followed by an equally loud "Oh, *bother*" as she stood and rubbed her sore backside.

He couldn't put his finger on it. All he knew was that she was perfect.

He moved forward, keeping himself hidden in the trees. She was in the process of stepping from one stone to another, and any fool could see that she was going to slip, because the stone she was stepping onto was slick with moss, and—

Splash!

"Oh dear oh dear oh dear oh dear!"

Robert couldn't help but grin as she ignominiously hauled herself to the shore. The hem of her dress was soaked, and her slippers had to be ruined.

He leaned forward, noticing that her slippers were sitting in the sun, presumably where she'd left them before hopping from stone to stone. Smart girl, he thought approvingly.

She sat down on the grassy bank and began to wring out her dress, offering Robert a delicious view of her bare calves. Where had she stashed her stockings, he wondered.

And then, as if guided by that sixth sense only females seemed to possess, she jerked her head up sharply and looked about. "Robert?" she called out. "Robert! I know you're there."

Robert froze, certain that he'd never met her before, certain they'd never been introduced, and even more certain that even if they had, she'd not be calling him by his given name.

"Robert," she said, fairly yelling at him now. "I insist you show yourself."

He stepped forward. "As you wish, my lady." He said this with a courtly bow.

Her mouth fell open. She blinked and scrambled to her feet. Then she must have realized that she was still holding the hem of her dress in her hands, baring her knees for all the world to see. She dropped the dress. "Who the devil are you?"

He offered her his best lopsided smile. "Robert."

"You are *not* Robert," she spluttered.

"I beg to differ with you," he said, not even trying to contain his amusement.

"Well, you're not *my* Robert."

An unexpected surge of jealousy raced through him. "And who is your Robert?"

"He's . . . He's . . . I fail to see how that is your concern."

Robert cocked his head, pretending to give the matter ample thought. "One might be able to broach the argument that since this is *my* land and your skirts are soaked with water from *my* pond, then it is indeed *my* concern."

The color drained from her face. "Oh, dear Lord, you're not his lordship."

He grinned. "I'm his lordship."

"But, but his lordship is supposed to be old!" She looked most perplexed and rather distraught.

"Ah. I see our problem. I'm his lordship's son. The other his lordship. And you are . . . ?"

"In big trouble," she blurted out.

He took her hand, which she had not held out to him, and bowed over it. "I am extremely honored to make your acquaintance, Miss Trouble."

She giggled. "My name is Miss *Big* Trouble, if you please."

If Robert had had any doubts about the perfection of the woman standing before him, they melted away under the force of her smile and obvious sense of humor. "Very well," he said. "Miss Big Trouble. I shouldn't want to be impolite and deprive you of your full name." He tugged on her hand and led her back to the bank. "Come, let us sit awhile."

She appeared hesitant. "My mother, bless her soul, passed on three years ago, but I have a feeling she would have told me that this is a most inadvisable idea. You look as if you might be something of a rake."

This caught his attention. "And have you met many rakes?"

"No, of course not. But if I were to meet one, I should think he would look rather like you."

"And why is that?"

She quirked her lips in a rather knowing expression. "Come now, are you looking for compliments, my lord?"

"Absolutely." He smiled over at her, sat down, and patted the ground next to him. "There is no need to worry. My reputation is not so very black. More of a charcoal gray."

She giggled again, causing Robert to feel as if he must be King of the Universe.

"My name is actually Miss Lyndon," she said, sitting beside him.

He leaned back, resting on his elbows. "Miss Big Trouble Lyndon, I presume?"

"My father certainly thinks so," she replied pertly. Then her face fell. "I really should go. If he caught me here with you . . ."

"Nonsense," Robert said, suddenly desperate

to keep her there beside him. "There is no one about."

She sat back, her manner still somewhat hesitant. After a long pause she finally said, "Is your name truly Robert?"

"Truly."

"I imagine the son of a marquess would have a long list of names."

"I'm afraid so."

She sighed dramatically. "Poor me. I have but two."

"And they are?"

She looked sideways at him, the expression in her eyes most definitely flirtatious. Robert's heart soared.

"Victoria Mary," she replied. "And you? If I may be so bold to ask."

"You may. Robert Phillip Arthur Kemble."

"You forgot your title," she reminded him.

He leaned toward her and whispered, "I didn't want to scare you."

"Oh, I'm not *that* easily frightened."

"Very well. Earl of Macclesfield, but it's only a courtesy title."

"Ah, yes," Victoria said. "You don't get a real title until your father dies. Aristocrats are an odd lot."

He raised his brows. "Such sentiments could probably still get one arrested in some parts of the country."

"Oh, but not here," she said with a sly smile. "Not on *your* land, by *your* lake."

"No," he said, staring into her blue eyes and finding heaven. "Certainly not here."

Victoria appeared not to know how to react to

the pure hunger in his gaze, and she looked away. There was a full minute of silence before Robert spoke again.

"Lyndon. Hmmm." He cocked his head in thought. "Why is that name so familiar?"

"Papa is the new vicar of Bellfield," Victoria replied. "Perhaps your father mentioned him."

Robert's father, the Marquess of Castleford, was obsessed with his title and his lands, and frequently lectured his son on the importance of both. Robert had no doubt that the new vicar's arrival had been mentioned as a part of one of the marquess's daily sermons. He also had no doubt that he hadn't been listening.

He leaned toward Victoria interestedly. "And do you enjoy life here in Bellfield?"

"Oh, yes. We were in Leeds before this. I do miss my friends, but it's much lovelier in the country."

He paused. "Tell me, who is your mysterious Robert?"

She cocked her head. "Are you truly interested?"

"Truly." He covered her small hand with his. "I should like to know his name, since it appears I may have to do him bodily harm if he ever again attempts to meet you alone in the woods."

"Oh, stop." She laughed. "Don't be silly."

Robert lifted her hand to his lips and placed a fervent kiss on the inside of her wrist. "I'm deadly serious."

Victoria made a feeble attempt to pull her hand back, but her heart wasn't in it. There was something about the way this young lord was staring at her, his eyes flashing with an intensity that scared and excited her. "It was Robert Beechcombe, my lord."

"And does he have designs on you?" he murmured.

"Robert Beechcombe is eight years old. We were to go fishing. I suppose he bowed out. He did say that his mother might have some chores for him to do."

Robert suddenly laughed. "I am beyond relieved, Miss Lyndon. I detest jealousy. It's a most unpleasant emotion."

"I-I can't imagine what it is you would feel jealous about," Victoria stammered. "You have made no promises to me."

"But I intend to."

"And I have made none to you," she said, her tone finally growing firm.

"A situation I will have to rectify," he said with a sigh. He lifted her hand again, this time kissing her knuckles. "For example, I should very much like your promise that you will never again even so much as look at another man."

"I don't know what you're talking about," Victoria said, utterly bewildered.

"I shouldn't like to share you."

"My lord! We have only just met!"

Robert turned to her, the levity leaving his eyes with astounding swiftness. "I know. I know in my brain that I only just laid eyes on you ten minutes ago, but my heart has known you all my life. And my soul even longer."

"I-I don't know what to say."

"Don't say anything. Just sit here beside me and enjoy the sunshine."

And so they sat on the grassy bank, staring at

the clouds and the water and each other. They were silent for several minutes until Robert's eyes focused on something in the distance, and he suddenly jumped to his feet.

"Don't move," he ordered, a silly grin stealing the sternness from his voice. "Don't move an inch."

"But—"

"Not an inch!" he called over his shoulder, dashing across the clearing.

"Robert!" Victoria protested, completely forgetting that she should be calling him "my lord."

"I'm almost done!"

Victoria craned her neck, trying to make out what he was doing. He'd run off to a spot behind the trees, and all she could see was that he was bending down. She looked at her wrist, almost surprised to see that it wasn't burning red where he had kissed her.

She had felt that kiss throughout her entire body.

"Here we are." Robert emerged from the forest and swept into a courtly bow, a small bouquet of wild violets in his right hand. "For my lady."

"Thank you," Victoria whispered, feeling tears sting her eyes. She felt unbelievably moved, as if this man had the power to carry her across the world—across the universe.

He released all but one of the violets into her hand. "This is the real reason I picked them," he murmured, tucking the last flower behind her ear. "There. Now you are perfect."

Victoria stared at the bouquet in her hand. "I've never seen anything so lovely."

Robert stared at Victoria. "Neither have I."

"They smell heavenly." She leaned down and took another sniff. "I adore the smell of flowers. There is honeysuckle growing just outside my window at home."

"Is there?" he said absently, reaching out to touch her face, but catching himself just in time. She was an innocent, and he didn't want to scare her.

"Thank you," Victoria said, suddenly looking up.

Robert jumped to his feet. "Don't move! Not an inch."

"Again?" she burst out, her face erupting into the widest of smiles. "Where are you going?"

He grinned. "To find a portrait artist."

"A *what?*"

"I want this moment captured for eternity."

"Oh, my lord," said Victoria. Her body shook with laughter as she rose to her feet.

"Robert," he corrected.

"Robert." She was being dreadfully informal, but his given name fell so naturally from her lips. "You are so amusing. I cannot remember the last time I laughed so much."

He leaned down and laid another kiss upon her hand.

"Oh dear," Victoria said, glancing up at the sky. "It's grown so late. Papa might come looking for me, and if he found me alone with you—"

"All he could do is force us to marry," Robert interrupted with a lazy grin.

She stared at him. "And that isn't enough to send you scurrying off to the next county?"

He leaned forward and brushed the softest of kisses against her lips. "Shhhh. I've already decided that I'm going to marry you."

Her mouth fell open. "Are you mad?"

He drew back, regarding her with an expression that hovered somewhere between amusement and amazement. "Actually, Victoria, I don't think I have ever been saner than I am at this very moment."

Victoria pushed open the door to the cottage she shared with her father and younger sister. "Papa!" she called out. "I'm sorry I'm late. I was out exploring. There is still so much of the area I have not seen."

She poked her head into his study. Her father was seated behind his desk, hard at work on his next sermon. He waved his hand in the air, presumably signaling to her that all was well and he did not wish to be disturbed. She tiptoed from the room.

Victoria made her way to the kitchen to prepare the evening meal. She and her sister Eleanor took turns making supper, and Victoria was on duty that night. She tasted the beef stew she had put on the stove earlier that day, added a bit of salt, then sank down into a chair.

He wanted to *marry* her.

Surely she had been dreaming. Robert was an earl. An earl! And he would eventually become a marquess. Men of such lofty titles didn't marry vicar's daughters.

Still, he had kissed her. Victoria touched her lips, not at all surprised to see that her hands were trembling. She couldn't imagine that the kiss had been as meaningful to him as it had been to her—he was, after all, many years older than she was. He had surely kissed dozens of ladies before her.

Her fingers traced circles and hearts on the wooden tabletop as her mind dreamily recounted the afternoon. Robert. Robert. She mouthed his name, then wrote it on the table with her finger. Robert Phillip Arthur Kemble. She traced all his names out.

He was terribly handsome. His dark hair had been wavy and just a touch too long for fashion. And his eyes—one would have expected such a dark-haired man to have dark eyes, but his had been clear and blue. Pale blue, they should have looked icy, but his personality had kept them warm.

"What are you doing, Victoria?"

Victoria looked up to see her sister in the doorway. "Oh, hello, Ellie."

Eleanor, younger than Victoria by exactly three years, crossed the room and picked Victoria's hand up off the table. "You're going to give yourself splinters." She dropped Victoria's hand and sat down across from her.

Victoria looked at her sister's face but saw only Robert. Finely molded lips, always ready with a smile, the vague hint of whiskers on his chin. She wondered if he had to be shaved twice a day.

"Victoria!"

Victoria looked up blankly. "Did you say something?"

"I was asking you—for the second time—if you wanted to come with me tomorrow to bring food to Mrs. Gordon. Papa is sharing our tithe with her family while she is ill."

Victoria nodded. As vicar, her father received a tithe of one-tenth of the area's farm produce. Much of this was sold to care for the village church, but there was always more than enough food for the Lyndon family. "Yes, yes," she said absently. "Of course I'll go."

Robert. She sighed. He had such a lovely laugh.

". . . more in?"

Victoria looked up. "I'm sorry. Were you speaking to me?"

"I was saying," Ellie said with a decided lack of patience, "that I tasted the stew earlier today. It needs salt. Would you like me to put more in?"

"No, no. I added a bit a few minutes ago."

"Whatever is wrong with you, Victoria?"

"What do you mean?"

Ellie exhaled in an exasperated gesture. "You haven't heard two words of what I've said. I keep trying to talk to you, and all you do is gaze out the window and sigh."

Victoria leaned forward. "Can you keep a secret?"

Ellie leaned forward. "You know I can."

"I think I'm in love."

"I don't believe that for one second."

Victoria's mouth fell open in consternation. "I just told you that I have undergone the most life altering transformation in a woman's life, and you don't believe me?"

Ellie scoffed. "*Who* in Bellfield could you possibly fall in love with?"

"Can you keep a secret?"

"I already said I could."

"Lord Macclesfield."

"The marquess's son?" Ellie fairly yelled. "Victoria, he's an earl."

"Keep your voice down!" Victoria looked over her shoulder to see if they had caught their father's attention. "And I am well aware that he is an earl."

"You don't even know him. He was in London when the marquess had us up to Castleford."

"I met him today."

"And you think you're in love? Victoria, only fools and poets fall in love at first sight."

"Then I suppose I'm a fool," Victoria said loftily, "because Lord knows I am no poet."

"You are mad, sister. Utterly mad."

Victoria lifted her chin and looked down her nose at her sister. "Actually, Eleanor, I don't think I've ever been saner than I am at this very moment."

It took Victoria hours to fall asleep that night, and when she did she dreamed of Robert.

He was kissing her. Gently on the lips and then traveling along the planes of her cheek. He was whispering her name.

"Victoria . . ."

"Victoria . . ."

She came suddenly awake.

"Victoria . . ."

Was she still dreaming?

"Victoria . . ."

She scrambled out from under her covers and peered out the window that hung over her bed. *He* was there.

"Robert?"

He grinned and kissed her nose. "The very one. I cannot tell you how glad I am that your cottage is only one story tall."

"Robert, what are you doing here?"

"Falling madly in love?"

"Robert!" She tried to keep herself from laughing, but his good spirits were infectious. "Really, my lord. What are you doing here?"

He swept his body into a gallant bow. "I've come to court you, Miss Lyndon."

"In the middle of the night?"

"I cannot think of a better time."

"Robert, what if you had gone to the wrong room? My reputation would be in tatters."

He leaned against the windowsill. "You mentioned honeysuckle. I sniffed about until I found your room." He sniffed in demonstration. "My olfactory senses are quite refined."

"You're incorrigible."

He nodded. "That, or perhaps merely in love."

"Robert, you cannot love me." But even as she said the words, Victoria heard her heart begging him to contradict her.

"Can't I?" He reached through the window and took her hand. "Come with me, Torie."

"N-no one calls me Torie," she said, trying to change the subject.

"I'd like to," he whispered. He moved his hand to her chin and drew her toward him. "I'm going to kiss you now."

Victoria nodded tremulously, unable to deny herself the pleasure she'd been dreaming about all evening.

His lips brushed hers in a feather-light caress. Victoria shivered against the tingles that shot down her spine.

"Are you cold?" he whispered, his words a kiss against her lips.

Silently, she shook her head.

He drew back and cradled her face in his hands. "You're so beautiful." He pinched a lock of her hair between his fingers and examined its silkiness. Then he moved his lips back to hers, brushing against them back and forth, allowing her to accustom herself to his nearness before he moved in closer. He could feel her trembling, but she made no move to pull away, and he knew that she was as excited by the encounter as he was.

Robert moved his hand to the back of her head, sinking his fingers into her thick hair as he darted out his tongue to trace the outline of her lips. She tasted like mint and lemons, and it was all he could do not to pull her through the window and make love to her right there on the soft grass. Never in his twenty-four years had he felt this particular brand of need. It was desire, yes, but with a stunningly powerful rush of tenderness.

Reluctantly he drew away, aware that he wanted far more than he could ask her for that evening. "Come with me," he whispered.

Her hand flew to her lips.

He took her hand again and pulled her toward the open window.

"Robert, it's the middle of the night."

"The best time to be alone."

"But I'm—I'm in my nightdress!" She looked

down at herself as if only then realizing how indecently attired she was. She grabbed her blankets and tried to wrap them around her body.

Robert did his best not to laugh. "Put on your cloak," he gently ordered. "And hurry. We've much to see this evening."

Victoria wavered for but a second. Going with him was the height of nonsense, but she knew that if she closed her window now she would wonder for the rest of her life what might have happened this full-mooned night.

She rushed off her bed and pulled a long dark cloak from her closet. It was far too heavy for the warm weather, but she couldn't very well traipse around the countryside in her nightdress. She buttoned the cloak, climbed back onto her bed, and with Robert's help crawled through the window.

The night air was crisp and laden with the scent of honeysuckle, but Victoria only had time to take in one deep breath before Robert yanked on her hand and took off at a run. Victoria laughed silently as they raced across the lawn and into the forest. Never had she felt so alive and free. She wanted to shout her glee to the treetops, but was mindful of her father's open bedroom window.

In a few minutes they emerged into a small clearing. Robert stopped short, causing Victoria to stumble into him. He held her firmly, the length of his body indecently pressed against hers.

"Torie," he murmured. "Oh, Torie."

And he kissed her again, kissed her as if she

were the last woman left on the earth, the only woman ever born.

Eventually she pulled away, her dark blue eyes flustered. "This is all so very fast. I'm not sure I understand it."

"I don't understand it, either," Robert said with a happy sigh. "But I don't want to question it." He sat down on the ground, pulling her along with him. Then he lay down on his back.

Victoria was still crouching, looking at him with a trace of hesitancy.

He patted the ground next to him. "Lie down and look at the sky. It's spectacular."

Victoria looked at his face, alight with happiness, and lowered herself onto the ground. The sky seemed enormous from her vantage point.

"Are the stars not the most amazing thing you've ever seen?" Robert asked.

Victoria nodded and moved closer to him, finding the heat of his body oddly compelling.

"They're there for you, you know. I'm convinced that God put them in the sky just so you could watch them this very evening."

"Robert, you're so fanciful."

He rolled to his side and propped himself up on his elbow, using his free hand to brush a lock of hair from her face. "I was never fanciful before this day," he said, his voice serious. "I never wanted to be. But now . . ." He paused, as if searching for that impossible mix of words that would precisely convey what was in his heart. "I can't explain it. It's as if I can tell you anything."

She smiled. "Of course you can."

"No, it's more than that. Nothing I say sounds odd. Even with my closest friends I cannot be completely forthcoming. For example—" He suddenly jumped to his feet. "Don't you find it astounding that humans can balance on their feet?"

Victoria tried to sit up, but her laughter forced her back down.

"Think about it," he said, rocking from heel to toe. "Look at your feet. They're very small compared with the rest of you. One would think we would topple over every time we tried to stand."

This time she was able to sit up, and she looked down at her feet. "I suppose you're right. It is rather amazing."

"I've never said that to anyone else," he said. "I've thought it all my life, but I never told anyone until now. I suppose I worried people would think it was stupid."

"I don't think it's stupid."

"No." He crouched next to her and touched her cheek. "No, I knew you wouldn't."

"I think you're brilliant for having even considered the idea," she said loyally.

"Torie. Torie. I don't know how to say this, and I certainly don't understand it, but I think I love you."

Her head whipped around to face him.

"I *know* I love you," he said with greater force. "Nothing like this has ever happened to me, and I'll be damned if I let myself be ruled by caution."

"Robert," she whispered. "I think I love you, too."

He felt the breath leave his body, felt himself overtaken by such powerful happiness that he couldn't keep still. He pulled her to her feet. "Tell me again," he said.

"I love you." She was grinning now, caught up in the magic of the moment.

"Again."

"I love you!" The words were mixed with laughter.

"Oh, Torie, Torie. I'll make you so happy. I promise. I want to give you everything."

"I want the moon!" she shouted, suddenly believing that such fancies were actually possible.

"I'll give you everything *and* the moon," he said fiercely.

And then he kissed her.

Chapter 2

Two months passed. Robert and Victoria met on every occasion, exploring the countryside, and whenever possible, exploring each other.

Robert told her of his fascination with science, his passion for racehorses, and his fears that he would never be the man his father wanted him to be.

Victoria told him of her weakness for romantic novels, her ability to stitch a seam straighter than a yardstick, and her fears that she would never live up to her father's strict moral standards.

She loved pastries.

He hated peas.

He had the appalling habit of putting his feet up when he sat down—on a table, a bed, whatever.

She always planted her hands on her hips when she was flustered, and never quite managed to look as stern as she hoped.

He loved the way her lips pursed when she was annoyed, the way she always considered the

20

needs of others, and the mischievous way she teased him when he acted too self-important.

She loved the way he ran his hand through his hair when he was exasperated, the way he liked to stop and examine the shape of a wildflower, and the way he sometimes acted domineering just to see if he could rile her.

They had everything—and absolutely nothing—in common.

In each other they found their own souls, and they shared secrets and thoughts that had heretofore been impossible to express.

"I still look for my mother," Victoria once said.

Robert looked at her oddly. "I beg your pardon?"

"I was fourteen when she died. How old were you?"

"I was seven. My mother died in childbirth."

Victoria's already gentle face softened even more. "I'm so sorry. You barely had a chance to know her, and you lost a sibling as well. Was the baby a brother or a sister?"

"A sister. My mother lived just long enough to name her Anne."

"I'm sorry."

He smiled wistfully. "I remember what it felt like to be held by her. My father used to tell her that she was coddling me, but she didn't listen."

"The doctor said my mother had a cancer." Victoria swallowed painfully. "Her death wasn't peaceful. I like to think that she's somewhere up there"—she waved her head toward the sky—"where she isn't in any pain."

Robert touched her hand, deeply moved.

"But sometimes I still need her. I wonder if we ever stop needing our parents. And I talk to her. And I look for her."

"What do you mean?" he asked.

"You'll think I'm silly."

"You know I would never think that."

There was a moment of silence, and then Victoria said, "Oh, I say things like, 'If my mother is listening, then let the wind rustle the leaves of that branch.' Or, 'Mama, if you're watching, make the sun go behind that cloud. Just so I know you're with me.'"

"She's with you," Robert whispered. "I can feel it."

Victoria settled into the cradle of his arms. "I've never told anyone about that. Not even Ellie, and I know she misses Mama just as much as I do."

"You'll always be able to tell me everything."

"Yes," she said happily, "I know."

It was impossible to keep their courtship a secret from Victoria's father. Robert called at the vicar's cottage nearly every day. He told the vicar that he was teaching Victoria to ride, which was technically the truth, as anyone who watched her limp about the house after a lesson could attest.

Still, it was obvious that the young couple shared deeper feelings. The Reverend Mr. Lyndon vehemently disapproved of the match, and told Victoria as much on every possible occasion.

"He will never marry you!" the vicar boomed,

using his best sermon voice. Such a tone never failed to intimidate his daughters.

"Papa, he loves me," Victoria protested.

"It doesn't matter if he does or doesn't. He won't marry you. He's an earl and will someday be a marquess. He won't marry a vicar's daughter."

Victoria took a deep breath, trying not to lose her temper. "He is not like that, Father."

"He is like any man. He will use you and discard you."

Victoria blushed at her father's frank language. "Papa, I—"

The vicar jumped on top of her words, saying, "You are not living in one of your silly novels. Open your eyes, girl."

"I am not as naive as you think."

"You are seventeen years old!" he yelled. "You couldn't be anything *but* naive."

Victoria snorted and rolled her eyes, aware that her father hated such unladylike mannerisms. "I don't know why I bother to discuss this with you."

"It is because I am your father! And by God, you will obey me." The vicar leaned forward. "I have seen the world, Victoria. I know what's what. The earl's intentions cannot be honorable, and if you allow him to court you further, you will find yourself a fallen woman. Do you understand me?"

"Mama would have understood," Victoria muttered.

Her father's face turned red. "What did you say?"

Victoria swallowed before repeating her

words. "I said that Mama would have understood."

"Your mother was a God-fearing woman who knew her place. She would not have crossed me on this measure."

Victoria thought about how her mother used to tell silly jokes to her and Ellie when the vicar wasn't paying attention. Mrs. Lyndon hadn't been as serious and grave as her husband had thought. No, Victoria decided, her mother would have understood.

She stared at her father's chin for a long moment before finally lifting her eyes to his and asking, "Are you forbidding me to see him?"

Victoria thought her father's jaw might snap in two, so tense was his facial expression. "You know I cannot forbid it," he replied. "One word of displeasure to his father, and I will be tossed out without a reference. *You* must break it off."

"I won't," Victoria said defiantly.

"You must break it off." The vicar showed no sign of having heard her. "And you must do it with supreme tact and grace."

Victoria glared at him mutinously. "Robert is calling on me in two hours. I shall go walking with him."

"Tell him you cannot see him again. Do it this afternoon, or by God I'll make you sorry."

Victoria felt herself grow weak. Her father had not struck her for years—not since she was a child—but he looked furious enough to lose his temper completely. She said nothing.

"Good," her father said in a satisfied manner, mistaking her silence for acquiescence. "And be sure to take Eleanor with you. You are not to leave this house in his company without the accompaniment of your sister."

"Yes, Papa." On that measure, at least, Victoria would obey. But only that.

Two hours later Robert arrived at the cottage. Ellie swung open the door so quickly he didn't even manage to bring the knocker down for a second rap.

"Hello, my lord," she said, her grin just a bit cheeky. And no wonder—Robert had been paying her a full pound for every outing on which she managed to make herself disappear. Ellie had always believed wholeheartedly in bribery, a fact for which Robert was undyingly grateful.

"Good afternoon, Ellie," he replied. "I trust your day has been pleasant."

"Oh, very much, my lord. I expect it to grow even more pleasant very shortly."

"Impertinent baggage," Robert muttered. But he didn't really mean it. He rather liked Victoria's younger sister. They shared a certain pragmatism and a penchant for planning for the future. If he'd been in her position, he'd have been demanding *two* pounds per outing.

"Oh, you're here, Robert." Victoria came bustling into the hall. "I didn't realize you had arrived."

He smiled. "Eleanor opened the door with remarkable alacrity."

"Yes, I suppose she did." Victoria shot her sister a slightly waspish look. "She is always very prompt when you are calling."

Ellie lifted her chin and allowed herself a half smile. "I like to look after my investments."

Robert burst out laughing. He extended his arm to Victoria. "Shall we be off?"

"I just need to get a book," Ellie said. "I have a feeling that I will have a great deal of time to read this afternoon." She darted down the hallway and disappeared into her chamber.

Robert gazed at Victoria as she fastened her bonnet. "I love you," he mouthed.

Her fingers fumbled over the bonnet's strings.

"Should I say it louder?" he whispered, a wicked grin crossing his face.

Victoria shook her head vehemently, her eyes darting over to the closed door of her father's study. He had said that Robert didn't love her, said that he *couldn't* love her. But her father was wrong. Of that Victoria was certain. One had only to look at Robert's twinkling blue eyes to know the truth.

"Romeo and Juliet!"

Victoria blinked and looked up at the sound of her sister's voice, thinking for a moment that Ellie had been referring to her and Robert as those ill-fated lovers. Then she saw the slim volume of Shakespeare in her sister's hand. "Rather depressing reading for such a sunny afternoon," Victoria said.

"Oh, I disagree," Ellie replied. "I find it most romantic. Except for the bit about everyone dying at the end, of course."

"Yes," Robert murmured. "I can see where one wouldn't find that bit romantic."

Victoria grinned and nudged him in the side.

The threesome made their way outside, crossing the open field and heading into the forest.

After about ten minutes Ellie sighed and said, "I suppose this is where I leave off." She spread a blanket on the ground and looked up at Robert with a knowing smile.

He tossed her a coin and said, "Eleanor, you have the soul of a banker."

"Yes, I do, don't I?" she murmured. Then she sat down and pretended not to notice when Robert grabbed Victoria's hand and dashed out of sight.

Ten minutes later they arrived at the grassy shore of the pond where they'd first met. Victoria barely had time to spread out a blanket before Robert had pulled her down to the ground.

"I love you," he said, kissing the corner of her lips.

"I love you," he said, kissing the other corner.

"I love you," he said, yanking off her bonnet.

"I love—"

"I know, I know!" Victoria finally laughed, trying to stop him from pulling out all of her hairpins.

He shrugged. "Well, I do."

But her father's words still echoed in her head. *He will use you.* "Do you truly?" she asked, staring intently into his eyes. "Do you truly love me?"

He grasped her chin with uncharacteristic force. "How can you even ask that?"

"I don't know," Victoria whispered, reaching up to touch his hand, which immediately gentled its hold. "I'm sorry. I am so sorry. I know you love me. And I love you."

"Show me," he said, his voice barely audible.

Victoria licked her lips nervously, then moved her face across the inch that separated them.

The moment her lips touched his, Robert was on fire. He sank his hands in her hair, locking her against him. "God, Torie," he rasped. "I love the feel of you, the smell of you. . . ."

She responded by kissing him with renewed fervor, tracing his full lips with her tongue as he had taught her to do.

Robert shuddered, feeling white-hot need rock through him. He wanted to sink himself into her, wrap her legs around his waist, and never let go. His fingers found the buttons on her dress, and he began to undo them.

"Robert?" Victoria pulled away, startled by this new intimacy.

"Shhh, darling," he said, passion making his voice rough. "I just want to touch you. I have been dreaming of nothing else for weeks." He cupped her breast through the thin fabric of her summer dress and squeezed.

Victoria moaned with pleasure and relaxed, allowing him to complete his task.

Robert's fingers were shaking with anticipation, but somehow he managed to open enough buttons to let her bodice fall open. Victoria's hands immediately flew up to cover her nakedness, but he gently pushed them away. "No," he whispered. "They're perfect. *You're* perfect."

And then, as if to illustrate his point, he brought his hand forward and grazed the tip of her breast with his palm. Round and round he went, moving his hand in tiny circles, sucking in his breath as her nipple tightened into a hard bud. "Are you cold?" he whispered.

She nodded, then shook her head, then nodded again, saying, "I don't know."

"I'll warm you." He cupped his hand and wrapped it around her breast, branding her with the heat of his skin. "I want to kiss you," he said hoarsely. "Will you let me kiss you?"

Victoria tried to moisten her throat, which had gone quite dry. He had kissed her a hundred times before. A thousand, possibly. Why was he suddenly asking her permission?

When his tongue drew a lazy circle around her nipple, she found out. "Oh, my God!" she burst out, barely able to believe what he was doing. "Oh, Robert!"

"I need you, Torie." He buried his face between her breasts. "You don't understand how I need you."

"I-I think we must stop," she said. "I can't do this. . . . My reputation . . ." She had no idea how to put her thoughts into words. Her father's warning rang ceaselessly in her ears. *He will use you and discard you.*

She saw Robert's head at her breast. "Robert, no!"

Robert inhaled raggedly and pulled her gaping bodice together. He tried to redo the buttons, but his hands were trembling.

"I'll do it," Victoria said quickly, turning so that he would not see the red shame on her face. Her fingers were shaking, too, but they proved more nimble than his, and eventually she managed to right her appearance.

But he saw her pink cheeks, and it nearly killed him to think that she was ashamed of her behavior. "Torie," he said softly. When she didn't turn around he used two fingers to gently prod her chin until she faced him.

Her eyes were bright with unshed tears.

"Oh, Torie," he said, wanting desperately to haul her into his arms, but settling for touching her cheek. "Please don't berate yourself."

"I shouldn't have let you."

He smiled gently. "No, you probably shouldn't have. And I probably shouldn't have tried. But I'm in love. It's no excuse, but I couldn't help myself."

"I know," she whispered. "But I shouldn't have enjoyed it so much."

At that Robert let out a bark of laughter so loud that Victoria was sure Ellie would come crashing through the woods to investigate. "Oh, Torie," he said, gasping for air. "Don't ever apologize for enjoying my touch. Please."

Victoria tried to shoot him an admonishing glance, but her eyes were far too warm. She allowed her good humor to rise back to the surface. "Just so long as you don't apologize for enjoying mine."

He grabbed her hand and pulled her to him in the breadth of an instant. He smiled seductively, looking rather like the rake Victoria had once accused him of being. "That, my darling, has never been a danger."

She laughed softly, feeling her earlier tension slip from her body. She shifted position, settling her back against his chest. He was absently toying with her hair, and it felt like sheer heaven.

"We'll be married soon," he whispered, his words coming with an urgency she hadn't expected. "We'll be married soon, and then I will show you everything. I'll show you how much I love you."

Victoria shivered with anticipation. He was speaking against her skin, and she could feel his breath near her ear.

"We'll be married," he repeated. "Just as soon as we can. But until then I don't want you to feel ashamed of anything we have done. We love each other, and there is nothing more beautiful than two people expressing their love." He turned her around until their eyes met. "I didn't know that before I met you. I—" He swallowed. "I had been with women, but I didn't know that."

Deeply moved, Victoria touched his cheek.

"No one will strike us down for loving before we are married," he continued.

Victoria wasn't certain whether "loving" referred to the spiritual or the physical, and all she could think to say was, "No one except my father."

Robert closed his eyes. "What has he said to you?"

"He said I must not see you anymore."

Robert swore softly under his breath and opened his eyes. "Why?" he asked, his voice coming out a bit harsher than intended.

Victoria considered several replies but finally opted for honesty. "He said you won't marry me."

"And how would he know that?" Robert snapped.

Victoria drew back. "Robert!"

"I'm sorry. I didn't mean to raise my voice. It's just— How could your father possibly know my mind?"

She placed her hand on his. "He doesn't. But he thinks he does, and I'm afraid that is all that matters just now. You are an earl. I am the daughter of a country vicar. You must admit that such a match is most unusual."

"Unusual," he said fiercely. "Not impossible."

"To him it is," she replied. "He'll never believe your intentions are honorable."

"What if I speak with him, ask him for your hand?"

"That might appease him. I have told him that you want to marry me, but I think he thinks I'm making it up."

Robert rose to his feet, drawing her up with him, and gallantly kissed her hand. "Then I shall have to formally ask him for your hand tomorrow."

"Not today?" Victoria asked with a teasing glance.

"I should inform my father of my plans first," Robert replied. "I owe him that courtesy."

Robert hadn't yet told his father about Victoria. Not that the marquess could forbid the match. At four and twenty Robert was of an age to make his own decisions. But he knew that his father could make life difficult with his disapproval. And considering how often the marquess urged Robert to settle down with the daughter of this duke or that earl, he had a feeling that a vicar's daughter wasn't quite what his father had in mind for him.

And so it was with firm resolve and some trepidation that Robert knocked on his father's study door.

"Enter." Hugh Kemble, the Marquess of Castleford, was seated behind his desk. "Ah, Robert. What is it?"

"Have you a few moments, sir? I need to talk with you."

Castleford looked up with impatient eyes. "I'm quite busy, Robert. Can it wait?"

"It is of great import, sir."

Castleford set down his quill with a gesture of annoyance. When Robert did not start speaking immediately, he prompted, "Well?"

Robert smiled, hoping that would set his father's mood aright. "I have decided to marry."

The marquess underwent a radical transformation. Every last touch of irritation disappeared from his expression, replaced by pure joy. He jumped to his feet and clasped his son into a hearty hug. "Excellent! Excellent, my boy. You know I have wanted this—"

"I know."

"You are young, of course, but your responsibilities are grave. It would be the end of me if the title passed out of the family. If you do not produce an heir . . ."

Robert declined to mention that if the title passed out of the family, his father would already be dead, so he would not know of the tragedy. "I know, sir."

Castleford sat down against the edge of his desk and crossed his arms genially. "So, tell me.

Who is it? No, let me guess. It's Billington's daughter—the blond gel."

"Sir, I—"

"No? Then it must be Lady Leonie. Smart pup, you are." He nudged his son. "Old duke's only daughter. She'll come into quite a portion."

"No, sir," Robert said, trying to ignore the avaricious gleam in his father's eye. "You are not acquainted with her."

Castleford's face went blank with surprise. "I'm not? Then who the devil is she?"

"Miss Victoria Lyndon, sir."

Castleford blinked. "Why is that name familiar?"

"Her father is Bellfield's new vicar."

The marquess said nothing. Then he burst out laughing. It was several moments before he was able to gasp, "Good God, son, you had me going there for a moment. A vicar's daughter. Quite beyond anything."

"I'm quite serious, sir," Robert ground out.

"A vicar's . . . heh heh— *What* did you say?"

"I said I'm quite serious." He paused. "Sir."

Castleford took stock of his son, desperately searching for a hint of jest in his expression. When he found none he fairly yelled, "Are you mad?"

Robert crossed his arms. "I'm utterly sane."

"I forbid it."

"Begging your pardon, sir, but I don't see how you *can* forbid it. I'm of age. And," he added as an afterthought, hoping to appeal to his father's softer side, "I'm in love."

"Goddamn it, boy! I'll disinherit you."

Apparently his father didn't *have* a softer side.

Robert raised an eyebrow and practically felt his eyes turn from light blue to steely gray. "Go ahead," he said nonchalantly.

"Go ahead?!" Castleford spluttered. "I'll turn you out on your ear! Cut you off without a farthing! Leave you to—"

"What you'll do is leave yourself without an heir." Robert smiled with a hard determination he had never known he possessed. "How unfortunate for you that Mother was never able to present you with another child. Not even a daughter."

"You! You!" The marquess began to turn red with rage. He took a few deep breaths and continued in a calmer fashion. "Perhaps you have not reflected adequately upon the unsuitability of this girl."

"She is entirely suitable, sir."

"She won't—" Castleford broke off when he realized that he was yelling again. "She won't know how to fulfill the duties of a noblewoman."

"She is quite bright. And one could find no fault with her manners. She has received a gentle education. I am certain she will make an excellent countess." Robert's expression softened. "Her very nature will bring honor to our name."

"Have you asked her father yet?"

"No. I thought I owed you the courtesy of informing you of my plans first."

"Thank God," Castleford breathed. "We still have time."

Robert's hands curled into harsh fists, but he held his tongue.

"Promise me you won't ask for her hand yet."

"I will do no such thing."

Castleford regarded the firm resolve in his son's eyes and met it with a harsh stare. "Listen to me well, Robert," he said in a low voice. "She cannot love you."

"I fail to see how you could know that, sir."

"Goddamn it, son. All she wants is your money and your title."

Robert felt a rage welling up within him. It was unlike anything he had ever known. "She loves me," he bit out.

"You will never know if she loves you." The marquess slammed his hands down on his desk for emphasis. "Never."

"I know it now," Robert said in a low voice.

"What is it about this girl? Why her? Why not one of the dozens you have met in London?"

Robert shrugged helplessly. "I don't know. She brings out the best in me, I suppose. With her by my side, I can do anything."

"Good God," his father snapped. "How did I raise a son who spouts such romantic drivel?"

"I can see that this conversation is pointless," Robert said stiffly, taking a step toward the door.

The marquess sighed. "Robert, don't leave."

Robert turned back around, quite unable to show his father the disrespect of countermanding a direct request.

"Robert, please listen to me. You must marry within your own class. That is the only way you will ever be sure that you were not married for your money and position."

"It has been my experience that women of the

ton are quite interested in marrying for money and position."

"Yes, but it is *different*."

Robert thought that this was a rather weak argument, and he said so.

His father raked his hand through his hair. "How can this girl know what she feels for you? How could she help but be dazzled by your title, your wealth?"

"Father, she is not like that." Robert crossed his arms. "And I *will* marry her."

"You will be making the biggest—"

"Not another word!" Robert exploded. It was the first time he had ever raised his voice to his father. He turned to leave the room.

"Tell her I've cut you off without a farthing!" Castleford yelled. "See if she'll have you then. See if she loves you when you have nothing."

Robert turned, his eyes narrowing ominously. "Are you telling me that I have been disinherited?" he asked, his voice chillingly soft.

"You're perilously close to it."

"Have I or have I not?" Robert's tone demanded an answer.

"You may very well be. Do not cross me on this measure."

"That isn't an answer."

The marquess leaned forward, his eyes steady on Robert's. "If you were to tell her that marriage to her would almost certainly result in a vast loss of fortune, you would not be lying."

Robert hated his father in that moment. "I see."

"Do you?"

"Yes." And then almost as an afterthought, he added, "Sir." It was the last time he addressed his father with that title of respect.

Chapter 3

Tap. Tap tap tap.

Victoria slammed awake, sitting bolt upright in the space of a second.

"Victoria!" came the hissed whisper from her window.

"Robert?" She crawled down the bed and peered out.

"I need to talk with you. It's urgent."

Victoria glanced around the room, quickly judged that the household was fast asleep, and said, "Very well. Come in."

If Robert thought it was odd that she was inviting him into her room—something she had never before done—he did not mention it. He climbed through the window and sat down on her bed. Oddly he made no attempt to kiss her or pull her into his arms—his usual methods of greeting her when they were alone.

"Robert, what is wrong?"

He didn't say anything at first, just stared out the window at the north star.

She put her hand on his sleeve. "Robert?"

"We must elope," he said baldly.

"What?"

"I have analyzed the situation from every direction. There is no other solution."

Victoria touched his arm. He always approached life so scientifically, treating every decision as a problem to be solved. Falling in love with her was probably the only illogical thing he'd ever done in his life, and it made her love him all the more. "What is wrong, Robert?" she asked softly.

"My father has cut me off."

"Are you certain?"

Robert looked into her eyes, stared into those fabulous blue depths, and then made a decision he wasn't proud of. "Yes," he said, "I'm certain," neglecting to mention that his father had only said, "Almost certainly." But he had to be sure. He didn't think it was possible, but what if Victoria really was more dazzled by the possessions than she was by the man?

"Robert, that is unconscionable. How could a father do such a thing?"

"Victoria, you must listen to me." He grabbed her hands in his, clutching them with a ferocious intensity. "It doesn't matter. You are more important to me than the money. You are everything."

"But your birthright . . . How can I ask you to give that up?"

"It is my choice to make, not yours, and I choose you."

Victoria felt tears stinging her eyes. She had never dreamed that she might cause Robert to lose so much. And she knew how important the respect of his father was to him. He had worked his whole life to impress him, always trying and always coming up just a little bit short. "You must promise me one thing," she whispered.

"Anything, Torie. You know I would do anything for you."

"You must promise me that you will try to make amends with your father after the marriage. I—" She swallowed, hardly able to believe that she was putting a condition on her acceptance of his proposal. "I won't marry you unless you do. I couldn't live with myself knowing that I was the cause of your rift."

A strange expression crossed Robert's face. "Torie, he is most stubborn. He—"

"I didn't say you have to succeed," she said quickly. "Just that you have to try."

Robert lifted her hands to his lips. "Very well, my lady. I give you my vow."

She offered him a smile that pretended to be stern. "I'm not 'your lady' yet."

Robert only grinned and kissed her hand again. "I would leave with you tonight if I could," he said, "but I will need a bit of time to amass some funds and supplies. I don't intend to drag you across the countryside with nothing but the clothes on our backs."

She touched his cheek. "You're such a planner."

"I don't like leaving anything to chance."

"I know. It's one of the things I love best about you." She smiled sheepishly. "I'm forever forgetting things. When my mother was alive she always said that I would forget my head if I weren't in possession of a neck."

That prompted a smile. Robert said, "I'm glad you have a neck. I'm rather fond of it."

"Don't be silly," she said. "I was merely trying to say that it is nice to know that I'll have you to keep my life in order."

He leaned forward and brushed the gentlest of kisses on her lips. "It's all I want to do. Just keep you happy."

Victoria looked up at him with damp eyes and curled her face into the crook of his shoulder.

Robert let his chin rest on the top of her head. "Can you be ready in three days time?"

Victoria nodded, and they spent the next hour making plans.

Robert shivered against the night wind, checking his pocket watch for what must have been the twentieth time. Victoria was five minutes late. Nothing to be alarmed about; she was terribly disorganized and was frequently five or ten minutes late for their outings.

But this was no ordinary outing.

Robert had planned their elopement to the last detail. He'd taken his curricle from his father's stables. He would have preferred a more practical vehicle for the long journey to Scotland, but the curricle belonged to him, not his father, and Robert didn't want to feel beholden.

Victoria was to meet him here, at the end of the road leading to her cottage. They had decided that she would have to slip out on her own. It would be far too noisy if Robert drove the curricle to her house, and he didn't want to leave it unattended. It would only take five minutes for

Victoria to make her way to him, and the area had always been quite safe.

But damn it, where was she?

Victoria scanned her room, checking for any last item she might have missed. She was running late. Robert expected her five minutes ago, but at the last minute she decided that she might need a warmer dress, so she had to repack her bag. It wasn't every day a young woman left home in the middle of the night. She ought to at least be certain that she packed the right belongings.

The miniature! Victoria smacked herself on her forehead as she realized that she couldn't possibly leave without the small painting of her mother. Mrs. Lyndon had had two done, and Mr. Lyndon had always said that Victoria and Ellie would each take one when they married so they would never forget their mother. They were tiny paintings; Victoria's fit in the palm of her hand.

Still clutching her satchel, Victoria tiptoed out of her room and into the hall. She made her way to the sitting room, silently crossing the rug to the end table where the small portrait sat. She snatched it up, stuffed it into her bag, and then turned around to go back to her room, where she planned to leave through the window.

But as she turned, her bag connected with a brass lamp, sending it crashing to the floor.

Within seconds the Reverend Mr. Lyndon came storming through the doorway. "What the devil is going on here?" His eyes took in Victoria, who was frozen with fright in the middle of the sitting room. "Why are you awake, Victoria? And why are you dressed?"

"I . . . I . . ." Victoria shook with fear, unable to force a word from her mouth.

The vicar spied her bag. "What is that?" In two steps he crossed the room and snatched it from her. He yanked out clothing, a Bible. . . . And then his hand rested on the miniature. "You're running away," he whispered. He looked up at her, staring at her as if he could not believe that one of his daughters would possibly disobey him. "You're running away with that man."

"No, Papa!" she cried. "No!"

But she had never been a very good liar.

"By God!" Mr. Lyndon shouted. "You'll think twice before you disobey me again."

"Papa, I—" Victoria couldn't finish the sentence, for her father's hand had come across her face with such blinding force that she was knocked to the ground. When she looked up she saw Ellie, standing motionless in the doorway, her expression petrified. Victoria shot her sister an entreating look.

Ellie cleared her throat. "Papa," she said in a gentling tone. "Is something amiss?"

"Your sister has chosen to disobey me," he snarled. "Now she will learn the consequences."

Ellie cleared her throat again, as if that were the only way she could summon the courage to speak. "Papa, I'm sure there has been a grave misunderstanding. Why don't I take Victoria to her room?"

"Silence!"

Neither girl made a sound.

After an interminable pause, the vicar grabbed Victoria's arm and roughly hauled her to her feet. "You," he said with a vicious yank, "are not going anywhere tonight." He dragged her into her room and shoved her onto her bed. Ellie followed fearfully behind, hovering in the corner of Victoria's chamber.

Mr. Lyndon poked his finger at Victoria's shoulder and growled, "Do not move." He took a few steps toward the door, and that was all the time Victoria needed to make a mad dash for the open window. But the vicar was fast, and his strength was fueled by rage. He threw her back down on the bed, giving her face another vicious slap. "Eleanor!" he barked. "Get me a sheet."

Ellie blinked. "I-I beg your pardon?"

"A sheet!" he bellowed.

"Yes, Papa," she said, scurrying off to the linen closet. In a few seconds she emerged, carrying a clean white sheet. She handed it to her father, who then began to methodically tear it into long strips. He bound Victoria's ankles together, then tied her hands in front of her. "There," he said, surveying his handiwork. "She won't be going anywhere this evening."

Victoria stared at him mutinously. "I hate you," she said in a low voice. "I will hate you forever for doing this."

Her father shook his head. "You'll thank me someday."

"No. I won't." Victoria swallowed, trying to work the quiver out of her voice. "I used to think that you were second only to God, that you were all that was good and pure and kind. But now—

Now I see that you are nothing but a small man with a small mind."

Mr. Lyndon shook with rage, and he raised his hand to strike her again. But at the last moment he brought it back down to his side.

Ellie, who'd been chewing on her lower lip in the corner, stepped timidly forward and said, "She'll catch a chill, Papa. Just let me cover her." She pulled the blankets up over Victoria's shaking body, leaning down to whisper, "I'm so sorry."

Victoria shot her sister a grateful look, and then rolled herself over so she was facing the wall. She didn't want to give her father the satisfaction of seeing her cry.

Ellie sat on the edge of the bed and looked up at their father with what she hoped was a gentle expression. "I'll just sit with her, if you don't mind. I don't think she should be alone just now."

Mr. Lyndon's eyes narrowed suspiciously. "Oh, you'd like that, wouldn't you?" he said. "I'll not leave you to untie her and let her run off to that lying bastard." He yanked on Ellie's arm and pulled her to her feet. "As if he would ever marry her," he added, shooting a scathing glance at his elder daughter.

Then he pulled Ellie from the room and proceeded to tie her up, too.

"God*damn* it," Robert bit out. "Where the hell is she?"

Victoria was now more than an hour late. Robert imagined her raped, beaten, killed—all of which were extremely unlikely to have occurred on her short walk down the road, but his heart was still icy with fear.

Finally he decided to throw caution to the wind, and he left his curricle and belongings unattended as he ran up the road to her house. The windows were dark, and he crept alongside the outer wall to her window. It was open, its curtains ruffling gently in the breeze.

A sick sensation formed in his stomach as he leaned forward. There, in the bed, was Victoria. She was facing away from him, but there was no mistaking that glorious black hair. Cozily bundled beneath her quilts, she appeared to be asleep.

Robert sank to the ground, landing in a silent heap.

Asleep. She'd gone to bed and left him waiting in the night. She hadn't even sent a note.

He felt something turn in his gut as he realized that his father must have been right all along. Victoria had decided that he wasn't such a catch without his money and title.

He thought about the way she'd pleaded with him to make amends with his father—amends that would surely result in the restoration of his fortune. He thought she'd asked that out of concern for his well-being, but now he realized she'd never been concerned with anyone's well-being but her own.

He'd given her his heart, his soul. And it wasn't enough.

Eighteen hours later, Victoria was racing through the woods. Her father had kept her prisoner through the night and morning and well into the afternoon. He had untied her with a stern lecture about behaving herself and honoring her father, but she let only twenty minutes go by before she climbed through her window and ran off.

Robert was going to be frantic. Or furious. She didn't know which, and she was more than a little apprehensive about finding out.

Castleford Manor came into view, and Victoria forced herself to slow down. She had never been to Robert's home; he had always come to call at her cottage. She realized now, after the marquess's vehement opposition to their betrothal, that Robert had been afraid his father would treat Victoria rudely.

With a trembling hand she knocked on the door.

A liveried servant answered, and Victoria gave him her name, telling him that she wished to see the Earl of Macclesfield.

"He is not here, miss," was the reply.

Victoria blinked. "I beg your pardon."

"He left for London early this morning."

"But that's not possible!"

The servant gave her a condescending look. "The marquess did ask to see you, should you call."

Robert's father wanted to speak with her? That was even more unbelievable than the fact that Robert had left for London. Numbly Victoria let herself be led through the great hall and into a small sitting room. She glanced around her surroundings. The furnishings were far more opulent than anything she and her family had ever owned, and yet she knew instinctively that she had not been shown to the best sitting room.

A few minutes later the Marquess of Castleford appeared. He was a tall man and looked very much like Robert, except for the little white frown lines around his mouth. And his eyes were different—flatter, somehow.

"You must be Miss Lyndon," he said.

"Yes," she replied, holding herself tall. Her world was falling apart, but she wasn't going to let this man see it. "I'm here to see Robert."

"My son has left for London." The marquess paused. "To look for a wife."

Victoria flinched. She couldn't help it. "He told you this?"

The marquess didn't speak, preferring to take a moment to assess the situation. His son had admitted to him that he had planned to elope with this girl, but that she had proven false. Victoria's presence at Castleford, combined with her almost desperate demeanor, seemed to point to the contrary. Obviously Robert had not been in possession of the full facts when he had wildly packed his bags and vowed never to return to the district. But the marquess was damned if he was going to let his son throw his life away over this little nobody.

And so he said, "Yes. It is high time he married, don't you think?"

"I cannot believe you're asking me that."

"My dear Miss Lyndon. You were nothing but a diversion. Surely you know that."

Victoria said nothing, merely stared at him in horror.

"I don't know whether my son managed to have his fun with you or not. Frankly I don't particularly care."

"You can't speak to me like that."

"My dear girl, I can speak to you any way I damn well please. As I was saying, you were a diversion. I cannot condone my son's actions, of course; it is a touch unsavory to go about deflowering the daughter of the local vicar."

"He did no such thing!"

The marquess looked at her with a condescending expression. "However, it is your job to keep your virtue intact, not his. And if you failed in that endeavor, well, then that is your problem. My son made you no promises."

"But he did," Victoria said in a low voice.

Castleford cocked a brow. "And you believed him?"

Victoria's legs went instantly numb, and she had to clutch the back of a chair for support. "Oh, my good Lord," she whispered. Her father had been right all along. Robert had never meant to marry her. If he had he would have waited to see why she had not been able to meet him. He probably would have seduced her somewhere on the way to Gretna Green, and then. . . .

Victoria didn't even want to think about the fate that had almost befallen her. She remembered the way Robert has asked her to "show him" how she loved him, how earnestly he'd tried to convince her that their intimacies were not sinful.

She shuddered, losing her innocence in the space of a second.

"I suggest you leave the district, my dear," the marquess said. "I give you *my* word that I shan't speak of your little affair, but I cannot promise that my son will be as closelipped as I."

Robert. Victoria swallowed. The thought of seeing him again was agony. Without another word she turned and left the room.

Later that night she spread a newspaper open across her bed, scanning the advertisements for positions. The next day she posted several letters, all applying for the post of governess.

Two weeks later, she was gone.

Chapter 4

⌒⌒ꝏ⌒⌒

Norfolk, England
Seven years later

Victoria chased the five-year-old across the lawn, tripping over her skirts so frequently that she finally snatched them up in her hands, not caring that her ankles were bared for the world to see. Governesses were supposed to behave with the utmost decorum, but she had been chasing the tiny tyrant for the better part of an hour, and she was about ready to give up on propriety altogether.

"Neville!" she yelled. "Neville Hollingwood! Stop your running this instant!"

Neville didn't show the least inclination of slowing down.

Victoria rounded the corner of the house and halted, trying to discern which way the child had run.

"Neville!" she called out. "Neville!"

No answer.

"Little monster," Victoria muttered.

"What did you say, Miss Lyndon?"

52

Victoria swung around to face Lady Hollingwood, her employer. "Oh! I beg your pardon, my lady. I did not realize you were here."

"Obviously," the older lady said acidly, "or you wouldn't have called my son such filthy names."

Victoria didn't much think that "little monster" qualified as filthy, but she bit down her retort and instead replied, "I meant it as an endearment, Lady Hollingwood. Surely you must know that."

"I do not approve of sarcastic endearments, Miss Lyndon. I suggest that you spend your evening reflecting upon the presumptuousness of your ways. It is not your place to assign nicknames to your betters. Good day."

It was all Victoria could do not to gape as Lady Hollingwood turned on her heel and swept away. She didn't care if Lady Hollingwood's husband was a baron. There was no way in this world that she would ever think of five-year-old Neville Hollingwood as her better.

She gritted her teeth and yelled, "Neville!"

"Miss Lyndon!"

Victoria groaned inwardly. Not again.

Lady Hollingwood took a step toward her, then stopped, lifting her chin imperiously in the air. Victoria had no choice but to walk over to her and say, "Yes, my lady?"

"I do not approve of your uncouth yelling. A lady never raises her voice."

"I am sorry, my lady. I was only trying to find young Master Neville."

"If you had been watching him properly, you would not find yourself in this situation."

It was Victoria's opinion that the boy was as slippery as an eel and that Admiral Nelson himself couldn't have held on to him for more than two minutes, but she kept these thoughts private. Finally she said, "I am sorry, my lady."

Lady Hollingwood's eyes narrowed, clearly indicating that she didn't for one minute believe that Victoria's apology was sincere. "See that you behave with more decorum this evening."

"This evening, my lady?"

"The house party, Miss Lyndon." The older woman sighed as if it were the twentieth time she'd had to explain this to Victoria, when in truth she'd never before mentioned it. And the lower servants never spoke to Victoria, so she was rarely privy to gossip.

"We will be entertaining guests for the next few days," Lady Hollingwood continued. "Very important guests. Several barons, a few viscounts, and even an earl. Lord Hollingwood and I move in lofty circles."

Victoria shivered as she remembered the one time she had had occasion to brush shoulders with the nobility. She hadn't found them particularly noble.

Robert. His face came unbidden to her mind.

Seven years and she could still remember every detail. The way his eyebrows arched. His laugh lines when he smiled. The way he had always tried to tell her he loved her when she least expected it.

Robert. His words had been proven false, indeed.

"Miss Lyndon!"

Victoria snapped out of her reverie. "Yes, my lady?"

"I would prefer it if you would endeavor not to cross paths with our guests, but if that proves impossible, do try to conduct yourself with the appropriate decorum."

Victoria nodded, really wishing that she didn't need this job so badly.

"That means you mustn't raise your voice."

As if anyone other than nasty Neville ever gave her cause to raise her voice. "Yes, my lady."

Victoria watched as Lady Hollingwood stalked off again, making sure that she was well out of sight. Then, as she resumed her search for Neville, she took great pleasure in saying, "I'm going to find you, you bloody little beast."

She tramped into the west garden, each step she took punctuated by a mild mental curse. Oh, if her father could hear her thoughts! Victoria sighed. She hadn't seen her family in seven long years. She still corresponded with Eleanor, but she'd never returned to Kent. She couldn't forgive her father for tying her up that fateful evening, and she couldn't bear to face him, knowing that he had been correct in his judgment of Robert.

But governessing had not proven easy, and Victoria had held three positions in the past seven years. It seemed most ladies didn't like their children's governesses to have silky sable hair and dark blue eyes. And they certainly didn't like them to be quite so young and pretty. Victoria had become quite adept at fending off unwanted attentions.

She shook her head as she scanned the lawn for Neville. In that measure, at least, Robert had not proven any different from the other young men of his class. All they seemed to be interested in was luring young women to their beds. Especially young women whose families were not powerful enough to demand marriage after the act.

The Hollingwood position had seemed a godsend. Lord Hollingwood wasn't interested in anything besides his horses and hounds, and there were no older sons to plague her on their visits home from university.

Unfortunately there was Neville, who had been a little terror from the first day. Spoiled and ill-mannered, he practically ruled the household, and Lady Hollingwood had forbidden Victoria from disciplining him.

Victoria sighed as she walked across the lawn, praying that Neville hadn't gone into the hedgerow maze. "Neville!" she called out, trying to keep her voice down.

"In he-ere, Lyndon!"

The little wretch always refused to call her *Miss* Lyndon. Victoria had brought the matter up with Lady Hollingwood, who had only laughed it off, remarking on how original and clever her son was.

"Neville?" Please, not the maze. She'd never learned her way around it.

"In the maze, you clodhead!"

Victoria groaned and muttered, "I hate being a governess." And it was true. She hated it. Hated every second of this beastly subservience, hated having to pander to spoiled children. But most of all she hated the fact that she'd been forced into this. She'd never been given a choice. Not really. She hadn't believed for one moment that Robert's father wasn't going to spread vicious gossip about her. He wanted her out of the district.

It was governessing or ruin.

Victoria entered the maze. "Neville?" she asked cautiously.

"Over here!"

It sounded like he was to her left. Victoria took a few steps in that direction.

"Oh, Lyndon!" he shrieked. "I bet you can't find me!"

Victoria ran around a corner, and then another, and another. "Neville!" she yelled. "Where are you?"

"Here I am, Lyndon."

Victoria nearly screamed with frustration. It sounded as if he was straight through the hedge to her right. The only problem was that she had no idea how to get to the other side. Maybe if she went around that corner . . .

She made a few more twists and turns, wretchedly aware that she was completely lost. Suddenly she heard an awful sound.

Neville's laugh. "I'm free, Lyndon!"

"Neville!" she yelled, her voice growing shrill. "Neville!"

"I'm going home now," he taunted. "Have a nice night, Lyndon!"

Victoria sank down onto the ground. When she made her way free, she was going to *kill* that boy. And she was going to enjoy doing it.

* * *

Eight hours later Victoria still hadn't found the exit. After two hours of searching, she finally sat down and cried. Tears of frustration were becoming increasingly common these days. She couldn't imagine that the household had failed to note her absence, but she rather doubted that Neville had confessed to leading her into the maze. The wretched boy had probably sent whomever was looking for her in the exact opposite direction. Victoria would be lucky if she only had to spend *one* night outside.

She sighed and looked up at the sky. It was probably nine in the evening, but twilight still hung in the air. Thank goodness Neville hadn't thought to play his prank in the winter, when the days were short.

The tinkle of music floated through the air, a sign that the festivities of the house party had begun, obviously without a thought to the missing governess.

"I hate being a governess," Victoria muttered for about the twelfth time that day. It didn't make her feel better to say it out loud, but she did so anyway.

And then finally, after she had begun to fantasize about the scandal that would ensue once the Hollingwoods found her dead body in the maze three months hence, Victoria heard voices.

Oh, thank the heavens. She was saved. Victoria jumped to her feet and opened her mouth to shout out a greeting.

Then she heard what the voices were saying.

She shut her mouth. Oh, *blast.*

"Come here, you big stallion," a female voice giggled.

"You're always so original, Helene." The male voice epitomized civilized boredom, but he did sound slightly interested in what the lady had to offer.

Oh, this was just her luck. Eight hours in the maze and the first people to join her were a pair of trysting lovers. Victoria rather doubted they would be pleased to learn of her presence. Knowing the nobility, they would probably find some way to make this awkward situation look as if it were *her* fault.

"I hate being a governess," she breathed hotly, sitting back down on the ground. "And I hate the nobility."

The female voice interrupted its giggles long enough to say, "Did you hear something?"

"Shut up, Helene."

Victoria sighed and clapped her hand to her forehead. The couple was beginning to sound quite amorous, despite the man's somewhat lazy rudeness.

"No, I'm sure I heard something. What if it's my husband?"

"Your husband knows what you are, Helene."

"Did you just insult me?"

"I don't know. Did I?"

Victoria could just imagine the man crossing his arms and leaning against the hedgerow.

"You're very naughty, did you know that?" Helene said.

"You certainly like to remind me of it."

"You make me feel naughty, too."

"I don't think you've ever needed assistance in that endeavor."

"La, sir, I'm going to have to punish you."

Oh, *please*, Victoria thought, sliding her hand to cover her eyes.

Helene let out another trill of high-pitched giggles. "Catch me if you can!"

Victoria heard the rhythm of running feet and sighed, thinking that she would be trapped in the maze with this couple for an extremely awkward amount of time. Then the footsteps came closer and closer. Victoria looked up just in time to see a blond woman come tearing around the corner. She didn't even have time to yell out before Helene tripped over her and landed ungracefully on the ground.

"What the *hell?*" Helene screeched.

"Now, now, Helene," came the male voice from around the corner. "Such language is unbecoming to your pretty mouth."

"Shut up, Macclesfield. There is a *girl* here. A girl." Helene turned to Victoria. "Who the devil are you? Did my husband send you?"

But Victoria didn't hear her. Macclesfield? *Macclesfield?* She shut her eyes in agony. Oh, dear Lord. Not Robert. Please, anyone but Robert.

Heavy, booted footsteps rounded the corner. "Helene, what the hell is going on?"

Victoria slowly looked up, her blue eyes huge and terrified.

Robert.

Her mouth went dry. She couldn't breathe. Oh, God. Robert. He looked older. His body was still rock hard and powerful, but there were lines on his face that hadn't been there seven years ago, and his eyes looked forever grim.

He didn't see her at first, his attention still on the fuming Helene. "She's probably that misplaced governess Hollingwood was talking about." He turned to look at Victoria. "Been missing since—"

The blood drained from his face. *"You."*

Victoria swallowed nervously. She'd never thought to see him again, had never even tried to prepare herself for how she might feel if she did. Her body felt strange, rather queer, and she wanted nothing more than to dig a hole in the ground and bury herself in it.

Well, that was not entirely true. Part of her wanted very much to scream out her fury and rake her nails across his cheeks.

"What the hell are you doing here?" he bit out.

Victoria gathered up her pride and looked back at him defiantly. "I am the misplaced governess."

Helene kicked Victoria in the hip. "You'd better call him 'my lord' if you value your position, girl. He is an earl, and you would do well not to forget it."

"I am well aware of what he is."

Helene flicked her head in Robert's direction. "Do you know this girl?"

"I know her."

It took all of Victoria's will not to cringe at the ice in his voice. She was wiser now than she'd been seven years ago. And stronger, too. She rose to her feet, stood straight, looked him in the eye, and said, "Robert."

"That's a fine greeting," he drawled.

"What's the meaning of this?" Helene demanded. "Who is she? What are you—" Her head swung from Victoria to Robert. "Did she call you *Robert?*"

Robert didn't once take his eyes off Victoria. "You'd better leave, Helene."

"I most certainly will not." She crossed her arms.

"Helene," he repeated, his voice laced with low warning.

Victoria heard the veiled fury in his voice, but apparently Helene did not, because she said, "I can't imagine what you would have to say to this . . . this governess person."

Robert turned to Helene and roared, "Leave us!"

She blinked. "I don't know the way out."

"A right, two lefts, and another right," he bit out.

Helene opened her mouth as if to say more, then obviously thought better of it. With one last nasty glance in Victoria's direction, she quit the scene. Victoria was more than half inclined to follow her. "A right, two lefts, and another right," she breathed to herself.

"You're not going anywhere," Robert barked.

His imperious tone was just enough to convince Victoria that there was no use even attempting to make polite conversation with him. "If you'll excuse me," she said, stalking past him.

His hand landed on her arm like a thunderstorm. "Get back here, Victoria."

"Don't give me commands," she burst out,

whirling to face him. "And don't speak to me in that tone of voice."

"Goodness," he mocked. "Such demands for respect. Most odd coming from a woman whose idea of faith—"

"Stop!" she yelled. She wasn't certain what he was talking about, but she couldn't bear to listen to his scathing tone of voice. "Just stop! Stop!"

Amazingly, he did. He looked rather shocked by her outburst. Victoria wasn't surprised. The girl he'd known seven years ago had never screamed like that. She'd never had cause to. She tugged at her arm and said, "Please leave me alone."

"I don't want to."

Victoria's head snapped up. "What did you say?"

He shrugged a shoulder and assessed her rudely. "I find myself rather interested in what I missed seven years ago. You're quite beautiful."

Her mouth fell open. "As if I would—"

"I wouldn't be so hasty to refuse me," he interrupted. "Of course you couldn't possibly hope for marriage, but there is no longer any threat of my being disinherited. I, my dear, am appallingly wealthy."

His father had called her "my dear." And he'd used that same condescending tone. Victoria swallowed down the urge to spit in his face and said, "How perfectly lovely for you."

He continued as if he hadn't heard her. "I must say, I never thought I'd meet you again under these circumstances."

"I had hoped *I* never would," she retorted.

"The governess," he said, using an oddly

thoughtful tone of voice. "What an interesting and precarious position she holds in a household. Neither family nor servant."

Victoria rolled her eyes. "I rather doubt you're as well acquainted as I with the 'interesting position' of the governess."

He cocked his head in a deceptively friendly manner. "How long have you been doing this? I find it rather amusing that England's elite is trusting *you* with their children's moral education."

"I could certainly do a better job of it than *you*."

He let out an abrupt laugh. "But then I never pretended to be good and true. I never pretended to be a young man's dreams." He leaned forward and stroked her cheek with the back of his hand. His touch was chillingly gentle. "I never pretended to be an angel."

"Yes," she choked out. "You did. You were everything I dreamed of, everything I'd ever wanted. And all you wanted—"

His eyes glittered dangerously as he pulled her closer. "What did I want, Victoria?"

She twisted her head to the side, refusing to answer him.

He let her go abruptly. "I suppose there is no point in reiterating all my foolish hopes."

She laughed hollowly. "*Your* hopes? Well, I'm so sorry you weren't able to get me into bed with you. That must have certainly broken your heart."

He leaned forward, his eyes menacing. "It's never too late to dream, is it?"

"That is one dream you will never see fulfilled."

He shrugged, his expression telling her that he didn't much care one way or the other.

"God, I meant so little to you, didn't I?" she whispered.

Robert stared at her, unable to believe her words. She had meant everything to him. Everything. He'd promised her the moon, and he'd meant it. He had loved her so much—he would have found a way to pull that sphere from the sky and hand it to her on a platter if she'd only demanded it.

But she'd never really loved him. She'd only loved the idea of marrying a wealthy earl. "Torie," he said, preparing to give her a blistering setdown.

She never gave him the opportunity. "Don't call me Torie!" she burst out.

"I seem to recall that I was the one to give you that particular nickname," he reminded her.

"You gave up all rights to it seven years ago."

"I gave up all rights?" he said, barely able to believe that she was trying to pin blame on him. Memories of that pathetic night flashed through his mind. He'd waited for her in the chilly night air. Waited for more than an hour, every fiber of his being alive with love, desire, and hope. And she'd simply gone to sleep. Gone to sleep without a single care for him.

Fury exploded in his body, and he pulled her closer, his hands biting into her flesh. "You seem to have conveniently forgotten the facts of our relationship, Torie."

She yanked her arm free with a strength that surprised him. "I said *don't* call me that. I am not her anymore. I haven't been for years."

His lips twisted humorlessly. "And who are you, then?"

She stared at him for a moment, obviously trying to decide whether or not to answer his question. Finally she said, "I am Miss Lyndon. Or these days I am more commonly just Lyndon. I am not even Victoria anymore."

His eyes swept over her face, not quite recognizing what he saw there. There was a certain strength to her that she hadn't possessed at seventeen. And her eyes held a steeliness that unnerved him. "You're right," he said with a purposefully bored shrug. "You're not Torie. You probably never were."

Victoria pursed her lips and refused to reply.

"And for that I thank you," he continued in a mockingly grand voice.

Her eyes flew to his face.

He raised his hand as if making a toast. "To Victoria Mary Lyndon! For providing me with an education no man should lack."

Victoria's stomach grew queasy and she took a step back. "Don't do this, Robert."

"For showing me that women are useless and vain—"

"Robert, no."

"—that they serve one purpose only." He drew his thumb across her lips with agonizing slowness. "Although I must say they perform that duty exceedingly well."

Victoria stood stock still, trying so hard not to

let her heart leap at the feel of his fingers on her lips.

"But most of all, Miss Victoria Lyndon, I must thank you for showing me the true measure of the heart. The heart, you see, isn't what I thought it was."

"Robert, I don't want to hear this."

He moved with startling speed, grabbing her brutally by the shoulders and pinning her against the hedge. "But you *will* hear this, Victoria. You will hear everything I have to say to you."

Because she could not shut her ears, she shut her eyes, but this did little to block his overwhelming presence.

"The heart, I have learned, exists only for pain. Love is a poet's dream, but pain—" His fingers tightened around her shoulders. "Pain is so very, very real."

Without opening her eyes, she whispered, "I know more about pain than you will ever learn."

"Pain that you failed to snag yourself a fortune, Victoria? That's hardly what I'm talking about. But—" He lifted his hands off her with a flourish. "I no longer feel pain."

Victoria opened her eyes.

He stared at her face. "I no longer feel anything."

She stared back, her eyes every bit as hard as his. This was the man who had betrayed her. He'd promised her the moon, and instead stolen her soul. Perhaps she wasn't such a noble person, because she was *glad* that he'd grown so bitter, glad that his was an unhappy life.

He no longer felt anything? She said exactly what she felt. "Good."

He raised a brow at the malicious pleasure in her voice. "I can see I did not misjudge you."

"Good-bye, Robert." A right, two lefts, and another right. She turned on her heel and stalked away.

Robert stood in the maze for an hour, his eyes unfocused, his body slack.

Torie. Just the sound of her name in his mind made him shake.

He'd lied to her when he told her he no longer felt anything. When he'd first seen her, impossibly sitting there in the maze, he'd felt such a rush of pleasure and relief—as if she could fill the emptiness that had engulfed him these past seven years.

But of course she was the one who'd carved his heart hollow.

He had tried to erase her memory with other women—although never, to his father's great dismay, the sort one might consider marrying. He'd consorted with widows, courtesans, and opera singers. He'd even sought out companions with Victoria's unique coloring, as if thick black hair and blue eyes could mend the rift in his soul. And sometimes, when the ache in his heart was particularly strong, he forgot himself and called out her name in the heat of passion. It was embarrassing, but none of his mistresses were indiscreet enough to mention it. They always received an extra token of gratitude when it happened, and they merely redoubled their efforts to please him.

But none of these women had made him forget. Not a day had gone by when Victoria didn't dance through his brain. Her laughter, her smiles.

Her betrayal. The one thing he could never forgive.

Torie. That thick black hair. Those bright blue eyes. Age had only made her more beautiful.

And he wanted her.

Lord help him, he still wanted her.

But he also wanted revenge.

He just didn't know which he wanted more.

Chapter 5

Victoria awoke the next morning with only one thought in her head: she wanted to stay as far away from Robert Kemble, Earl of Macclesfield, as possible.

She didn't want revenge. She didn't want an apology. She just didn't want to see him.

She rather hoped Robert felt the same way. Lord knew he had seemed uncommonly angry with her the previous night. She shrugged, not quite certain why he would have been quite so furious. She supposed she had pricked his male ego. She was probably his only failure at seduction.

Victoria dressed quickly, mentally preparing herself for breakfast with Neville, which was always an unpleasant chore. That boy had learned how to complain from a master—his mother. If the eggs weren't too cold, then the tea was too hot, or the—

A sharp rap sounded at the door, and Victoria whirled around, her heart suddenly pounding triple-time. Surely Robert wouldn't have the audacity to approach her in her room. She caught her lower lip between her teeth, remembering his surly attitude. He probably *would* go ahead and do such a foolish thing.

Fury rose within her. Such behavior could cost her her position, and unlike Robert *she* was not appallingly wealthy. She crossed the room in quick strides and yanked open the door with an angry, "What?"

"I beg your pardon, Miss Lyndon."

"Oh, Lady Hollingwood, I'm so sorry. I thought you were . . . That is to say . . ." Miserably, Victoria let her words trail off. At this rate she wouldn't need Robert to lose her position for her. She was doing a good job of it all by herself.

Lady Hollingwood inclined her head imperiously and entered the room without waiting for an invitation. "I am here to talk with you about your unfortunate disappearance last evening."

"Master Neville led me into the maze, my lady. I could not find my way out."

"Do not try to force a boy of only five years to accept the blame for your actions."

Victoria fisted her hands at her sides.

"Do you realize," Lady Hollingwood continued, "the extent to which you inconvenienced me? I had a house full of guests to attend to, and I was forced to take time away from them to put my son to bed. You should have been there to do it."

"I would have been, my lady," Victoria said, trying not to clench her teeth. "But I was trapped in the maze. Surely you—"

"You may consider this your final warning, Miss Lyndon. I am most displeased with your performance. One more mishap and I shall be forced to toss you out." Lady Hollingwood whirled on her heel and stalked back into the hall. Then she turned around to say, "Without a reference."

Victoria stared at the open doorway for several seconds before finally letting out a deep breath. She would have to find a new position. This was unacceptable. Unbearable. It was—

"Victoria." Robert's frame filled the doorway.

"As if the day could get any worse," she muttered.

Robert raised an insolent brow, glancing at the clock on her bedside table. "Really now, how bad could your day possibly be at this time in the morning?"

She tried to brush past him. "I have to get to work."

"And feed young Neville?" His hand closed around her arm, and he kicked the door shut behind him. "Not necessary. Neville has gone riding with my good friend Ramsay, who has graciously volunteered to entertain the little brat all morning."

Victoria shut her eyes for a moment and exhaled, a rush of memory overwhelming her. He had always been so organized, always attending to the smallest of details. She should have known he'd find a way to occupy Neville if he wanted to see her alone.

When she opened her eyes he was idly examining a book on her bedside table. "No more romantic novels?" he asked, holding up the book, a rather dry discussion of the study of astronomy.

Her chin lifted a fraction of an inch. "I don't enjoy romantic novels any longer."

Robert continued to flip through the pages of the book. "I had no idea you so enjoyed astronomy."

Victoria swallowed, not about to tell him that the moon and stars made her feel closer to him. Or rather, closer to the person she'd thought he'd been. "My lord," she said with a sigh. "Why are you doing this?"

He shrugged and sat on her small bed. "Doing what?"

"This!" She threw up her arms. "Coming to my room. Sitting on my bed." She blinked, as if just realizing what he was doing. "You're on my bed. For God's sake, get off my bed."

He smiled slowly. "Make me."

"I am not so infantile that you can rile me with such a challenge."

"No?" He leaned back against her pillows and crossed his ankles. "Don't worry. My boots are clean."

Victoria's eyes narrowed, and then she picked up the basin full of water she used for washing and dumped it on his head and chest. "I take that back," she said acidly. "I can be quite childish when the occasion warrants."

"Good Christ, woman!" Robert sputtered, leaping off the bed. Water ran in rivulets down his face, soaking his cravat and shirt.

Victoria leaned against the wall and crossed her arms, quite pleased with her handiwork.

"Do you know," she said with a satisfied smile, "but I think that all might be right with the world after all."

"Don't you dare," he roared, "try a stunt like that again!"

"And do what? Impugn your honor? I wasn't aware you had any."

He advanced on her with menacing steps. Victoria probably would have taken the cowardly way out and retreated, but her back was already up against the wall. "You," he said savagely, "are going to be extremely sorry you did that."

Victoria couldn't help it. She giggled. "Robert," she said, lapsing into the familiar. "Nothing could ever make me sorry I did that. For the rest of my life I will treasure this moment. *Treasure* it. In fact, this may very well be the one thing I am *least* sorry—"

"Victoria," he said, his voice deadly. "Shut up."

She did, but she didn't stop smirking.

He closed the space between them until he was just a heartbeat away. "If you are going to get me wet," he said, his voice dropping into a husky murmur, "then you are damn well going to dry me off."

Victoria scooted to the side. "Perhaps a towel . . . I'd be happy to lend you mine."

He moved so that he was right in front of her again, and touched her chin with his fingers. His body was hot, but his eyes were even hotter. "I've waited a lifetime for this," he whispered, pressing his body against hers.

The water from his clothing soaked into Victoria's dress, but she didn't feel anything but the heat from his body. "Don't," she whispered. "Don't do this."

His eyes held a strange desperation. "I can't help it," he said hoarsely. "God help me, I can't help it."

His lips came down toward hers with agonizing slowness. He hovered for a moment when he was just a hairbreadth away, as if he was trying to hold himself back at the last moment. Then, with stunning swiftness, his hands left her arms and moved to the back of her head, binding her lips to his.

Robert planted his hands into her thick hair, unmindful of the way her hairpins were clattering to the floor. It felt just the same—silky and heavy, and the scent of it was enough to drive him wild. He murmured her name over and over, forgetting for a moment that he hated her, that she'd abandoned him years ago, that she was the reason his heart had been dead for seven long years. He relied on instinct alone, and his body could do nothing but recognize that she was his Torie, and she was in his arms, and she belonged there.

He kissed her savagely, trying to drink in enough of her essence to make up for all their lost years. His hands clutched at her, roving over her body, trying to remember and memorize each curve.

"Torie," he murmured, trailing his lips down the line of her neck. "I've never . . . No other woman . . ."

Victoria let her head loll back, all reason

having fled with the first touch of his lips. She'd thought she'd forgotten what it felt like to be held in his arms, to feel the touch of his lips on her skin.

But she hadn't. Every touch was achingly familiar and startlingly exciting. And when he lowered her onto her bed, she couldn't even think to protest.

The weight of his body pressed her into the mattress, and one of his hands wrapped around her calf, squeezing and caressing its way up past her knee.

"I'm going to love you, Torie," Robert said fiercely. "I'm going to love you until you can't move. I'm going to love you until you can't think." His hand traveled ever higher, reaching the hot skin of her upper thigh where her stockings ended. "I'm going to love you the way I should have before."

Victoria groaned with pleasure. She'd spent seven long years without so much as a hug, and she was starved for physical affection. She had known what it was like to be touched and kissed, and she had no idea how much she'd missed it until that very moment. His hand moved, and she dimly realized that he was fumbling with his breeches, opening them and—

"Oh, God, no!" she cried out, pushing at his shoulders. In her mind's eye she could see them from above. Her legs were open, and Robert was settled between them. "No, Robert," she said again, wriggling out from beneath him. "I can't."

"Don't do this," he warned, passion still glazing his eyes. "Don't tease me and—"

"This is all you ever wanted, isn't it?" she demanded, darting off the bed. "All you ever wanted from me."

"It was certainly one thing," he muttered, looking as if he were in pain.

"God, I'm so stupid." She crossed her arms across her chest in a defensive maneuver. "One would think I'd have learned my lesson by now."

"As one would think I'd have learned mine," he said bitterly.

"Please go."

He stopped on his way to the door, just to be contrary. "Please? Such nice manners."

"Robert, I'm asking you as politely as I know how."

"But why ask me to leave?" He stepped toward her. "Why fight it, Torie? You know you want me."

"That's not the point!" Horrified, Victoria realized what she'd just revealed. She wasn't sure how she managed to get the words out, but she forced herself to lower her voice and said, "For the love of God, Robert, do you understand what you're doing? I am within an inch of being dismissed from this post. I cannot afford to lose it. If you were to be found in my room, I would be tossed out on my ear."

"Really?" He looked intrigued by the prospect.

She spoke slowly, carefully measuring her words. "I realize that you do not harbor any wealth of good feelings toward me. But for the sake of common decency, please leave!" She hated that she sounded as if she was begging, but she had no choice. At the end of the house party, Robert would leave and resume his life. This *was* her life.

He leaned forward, his blue eyes sharp and intent. "Why do you care? You can't possibly love this position so much."

Victoria snapped. She just snapped. "Of course I don't love this position. Do you think I enjoy attending to the needs of the world's most monstrous five-year-old? Do you think I enjoy being spoken to as if I were a dog by his mother? Use your brain, Robert. What there is of it, at least."

Robert ignored her insult. "Then why stay?"

"Because I don't have any choice!" she burst out. "Do you have any idea what it is like not to have any choices? Do you? No, of course you don't." She turned her back to him, unable to face him while she was shaking with emotion.

"Why don't you marry?"

"Because I—" She swallowed. How could she say that she had never married because she knew no man could ever live up to him? Even if his entire courtship of her had been false, it had been perfect, and she knew that she would never find anyone who could make her as happy as she'd been those two short months.

"Just go," she said, her words barely audible. "Go."

"This isn't over, Torie."

She ignored his pointed use of her nickname. "It has to be over. It should never have begun."

Robert stared at her a full minute. "You're different," he finally said.

"I am not the same girl you tried to take advantage of, if that is what you mean." She stood straight and tall. "It has been seven years, Robert. I am a different person now. As, apparently, are you."

Robert left the room without another word, swiftly making his way from the servants' quarters to the guest wing where he'd been given a room.

What the hell had he been thinking?

He hadn't been. That could be the only explanation. Why else would he arrange for Victoria's charge to be entertained all morning and then steal into her room?

"Because she makes me feel alive," he whispered to himself.

He couldn't remember the last time his senses were so finely tuned, the last time he'd felt such an exquisitely heady rush.

No, that wasn't entirely true. He remembered all too well. It had been the last time he'd held her in his arms. Seven years ago.

It was some consolation to learn that those years had not brought her happiness, either. She had been a scheming adventuress, intent upon marrying into a fortune, but all she had found was a miserable position as a governess.

Circumstances had certainly brought her low. He might be dead inside, but at least he had the freedom to do what he wanted when he wanted to do it. Victoria was desperately trying to hold on to a livelihood she hated, always fearing that she'd be tossed out without a reference.

That was when it occurred to him. He could have her and his revenge, too.

His body sang at the thought of holding her in his arms, of kissing every inch of that delectable body.

His mind raced at the idea that they might be discovered by Victoria's employers, who would then never allow her to watch over their precious Neville.

Victoria would be cut adrift. He doubted she would return to her father. She had too much pride for that. No, she would be all alone, with no one to turn to.

Except him.

He would need a very good plan this time.

Robert had spent two hours lying motionless on his bed, ignoring knocks on the door, ignoring the clock that told him that breakfast was no longer being served. He'd simply put his hands behind his head, looked up at the ceiling, and started to scheme.

If he was going to woo Victoria into his bed, he would have to charm her there. This was not a problem. Robert had spent the last seven years in London, and he certainly knew how to be charming.

He was, in fact, widely reputed to be one of the most charming men in all Britain, which was why he'd never lacked for female companionship.

But Victoria presented a new challenge. She was vastly distrustful of him and seemed to think that all he wanted was to seduce her. Which wasn't far from the truth, of course, but it would not aid his cause to let her continue to believe that his motives were so impure.

He would have to win back her friendship first. The concept was oddly appealing, even as his body hardened at the mere thought of her.

She would try to push him away. He was certain of that. Hmmm. He would have to be charming *and* persistent. In fact, he would probably have to be more persistent than charming.

Robert bounded out of bed, splashed some very cold water on his face, and left the room with only one aim.

Finding Victoria.

She was sitting under a shady tree, looking heartbreakingly lovely and innocent, but Robert tried to ignore the latter. Neville was some twenty yards away, screaming about Napoléon and slashing a toy saber wildly through the air. Victoria had one eye on the boy and one eye on a small notebook in which she was slowly writing.

"This doesn't seem like such a dreadful job," Robert said, lowering himself to the ground next to her. "Sitting under a shady tree, enjoying the afternoon sunshine . . ."

She sighed. "I thought I told you to leave me alone."

"Not precisely. I believe you told me to leave your room. Which I did."

She stared at him as if he were the world's biggest fool. "Robert," she said, not needing to finish the sentence. Her beleaguered tone said it all.

He shrugged. "I missed you."

At that, her mouth fell open. "Do try to come up with something even slightly believable."

"Enjoying the country air?" He leaned back and supported himself with his elbows.

"How can you come here and make polite conversation?"

"I thought that was what friends did."

"We are *not* friends."

He grinned rakishly. "We could be."

"No," she said firmly. "We couldn't."

"Now, now, Torie, don't work yourself into a snit."

"I am *NOT*—" She broke off, realizing that she was working herself into a snit. She cleared her throat and then forced her voice into carefully modulated tones. "I am not working myself into a snit."

He smiled at her in an annoyingly condescending manner.

"Robert—"

"I do like the sound of my given name on your lips." He sighed. "Always have."

"My lord—" she ground out.

"That's even better. It implies a certain subservience that is most appealing."

She gave up trying to communicate and turned her entire body away from him.

"What are you writing?" he asked, directly over her shoulder.

Victoria stiffened at the feel of his breath on her neck. "Nothing of interest to you."

"Is it a diary?"

"No. Go away."

He gave up on charm in favor of persistence

and craned his head to get a better view. "Are you writing about me?"

"I said it's not a diary."

"I don't believe you."

She whirled around. "Would you cease pestering—" Her words stopped short when she found herself nose to nose with him. She pulled back.

He smiled.

She pulled back farther.

He smiled wider.

She pulled back even farther. She fell over.

Robert immediately jumped to his feet and offered her his hand. "Would you like some assistance?"

"*NO!*" Victoria pulled herself upright, grabbed her blanket, and stalked over to another tree. She settled back down, hoping he would take the hint, but doubting he actually would.

He didn't, of course. "You never did tell me what you were writing," he said as he sat down beside her.

"Oh, for goodness' sake!" She thrust the notebook into his hands. "Read it if you must."

He scanned the lines and cocked a brow. "Lesson plans."

"I *am* a governess." It was perhaps the most sarcastic tone she'd ever used.

"You're quite good," he mused.

She rolled her eyes.

"How does one know how to be a governess?" he asked. "It isn't as if one can attend governess school."

Victoria closed her eyes for a moment, trying

to fight back a wave of nostalgia. That was exactly the sort of question Robert would have asked when they were younger. "I don't know how others do it," she finally replied. "But I try to emulate my mother. She taught Ellie and me before she died. And then I took over and taught Ellie until I had nothing left to teach."

"I can't imagine your running out of things to teach."

Victoria smiled. "By the time Ellie was ten, she was teaching *me* mathematics. She has always been—" She broke off, horrified by how comfortable she'd grown with him in these past few minutes. She stiffened and said, "It's no matter."

One corner of Robert's mouth lifted into a knowing smile, as if he knew exactly what she had been thinking. He looked back down at her notebook and turned a page. "You obviously take great pride in what you do," he said. "I thought you hated this position."

"I do. But that doesn't mean that I will do less than my best. That would be unfair to Neville."

"Neville is a brat."

"Yes, but he deserves a good education."

He stared at her, surprised by her convictions. She was a beautiful schemer whose only criterion for a husband was a fortune. And yet she worked herself to the bone to ensure that a detestable little boy received a good education.

He handed the notebook back to her. "I wish I'd had a governess like you."

"You were probably worse than Neville," she retorted. But she smiled as she said it.

His heart leapt, and he had to remind himself that he didn't like her, that he was out to seduce and ruin her. "I can't imagine that there is anything wrong with the boy that a bit of discipline can't mend."

"If it were only that easy. Lady Hollingwood has forbidden me to discipline him."

"Lady H. is a corkbrain, as my young cousin Harriet would say."

"Why did you come to her house party, then? She was quite beside herself that an earl would be in attendance."

"I don't know." He paused, then leaned forward. "But I'm glad I did."

She didn't move for a few seconds, couldn't have moved if her life depended on it. She could feel his breath on her cheek, and it was so achingly familiar. "Don't do this," she whispered.

"This?" He swayed forward, and his lips brushed her cheek in the most feather-light of caresses.

"Don't!" she said sharply, remembering her anguish at his desertion so many years before. She didn't need her heart broken again. It wasn't even completely mended from their last encounter. She jerked herself away and stood up, saying, "I have to tend to Neville. There is no telling what kind of trouble he will get himself into."

"Tend away," he murmured.

"Neville! Neville!"

The boy came galloping over. "Yes, Lyndon?" he said insolently.

Victoria clenched her teeth for a moment, trying to ignore his rudeness. She'd long since given up trying to get him to call her Miss Lyndon. "Neville, we—"

But she didn't get to finish, because in the space of a second, Robert was on his feet and looming over the boy. "What did you say?" he demanded. "How did you address your governess?"

Neville's mouth fell open. "I called her . . . I called her . . ."

"You called her Lyndon, didn't you?"

"Yes, sir, I did. I—"

"Do you realize how disrespectful that is?"

This time it was Victoria's mouth that fell open.

"No, sir, I did not. I—"

"Miss Lyndon works very hard to take care of you and give you an education, does she not?"

Neville tried to speak, but nothing came out.

"From now on you will address her as Miss Lyndon. Do you understand?"

By this point Neville was staring at Robert with an expression that hovered between awe and terror. He nodded furiously.

"Good," Robert said firmly. "Now shake my hand."

"Sh-shake your hand, sir?"

"Yes. By shaking my hand you officially promise to address Miss Lyndon properly, and a gentleman never reneges on his promises, does he?"

Neville thrust his tiny hand forward. "No, sir."

The two males shook hands, and then Robert gave the boy a little pat on the back. "Run along back to the nursery, Neville. Miss Lyndon will follow in a moment."

Neville practically sprinted back to the house,

leaving Victoria slackjawed and utterly limp. She turned to Robert, nearly dumbstruck. "What did you . . . How did you . . ."

Robert beamed. "Just offering you a bit of assistance. I hope you don't mind."

"No!" Victoria said with great emotion. "No, I don't mind. Thank you. Thank you."

"It was my pleasure, I assure you."

"I had better see to Neville." Victoria took several steps toward the house, then turned around, her expression still dazed. "Thank you!"

Robert leaned back against the tree trunk, utterly pleased with his progress. Victoria couldn't stop thanking him. It was a most satisfying state of affairs.

He should have disciplined the boy ages ago.

Chapter 6

A full day passed before Victoria saw him again. A full day of waiting, of wondering, of dreaming about him even when she knew that was absolutely the wrong thing to be doing.

Robert Kemble had broken her heart once, and she had no reason to believe that he wouldn't do it again.

Robert. She had to stop thinking of him that way. He was the earl of Macclesfield, and his title dictated his behavior in a way she could never hope to understand.

It was the reason he'd rejected her, the reason he'd never once seriously contemplated marrying a poor vicar's daughter. It was probably the reason he'd lied to her. During the past few years Victoria had learned that seducing young innocents was considered a kind of sport among noblemen. Robert had just been following the rules of his world.

His world. Not hers.

And yet he had solved her problems with Neville. He certainly didn't have to do that. The young boy was now treating her as if she were the queen. Victoria had never had such a peaceful day of governessing in her career.

Oh, she knew that heroes were supposed to slay dragons and quote verse and all that, but maybe, just maybe, all it really took to be a hero was getting the world's most difficult five-year-old to behave.

Victoria shook her head. She couldn't afford to place Robert on a pedestal. And if he tried to see her alone again, she would have to send him on his way. It didn't matter if her heart soared when she saw him, or if her pulse raced, or if her—

She forced herself to stop in mid-thought and turned her mind back to the matter at hand. She and Neville were taking their daily walk around the Hollingwood grounds. For the first time in memory, he hadn't stomped on her foot or poked at some poor insect with a stick. And he called her *Miss* Lyndon every chance he got. Victoria was pleased that he had finally learned a lesson in manners. Perhaps there might be hope for the boy after all.

Neville raced ahead, then whirled around and ran back to her side. "Miss Lyndon," he said with great gravity, "have we any special plans for today?"

"I am glad you asked, Neville," she replied. "We're going to play a new game today."

"A new game?" He looked at her with a bit of suspicion, as if he had already discovered all of Britain's worthwhile games.

"Yes," she said briskly, "we are. Today we are going to discuss colors."

"Colors?" he said with that particular brand of disgust only a boy of five years can convey. "I already know my colors." He began to list them. "Red, blue, green, yellow—"

"We are going to learn *new* colors," she cut in.

". . . purple, orange . . ." He was shouting now.

"Neville Hollingwood!" Victoria spoke in her sternest voice.

He quieted down, something he probably wouldn't have done before Robert's intervention.

"Do I have your attention now?" Victoria asked.

Neville nodded.

"Excellent. Now then, today we are going to study the color green. There are many different shades of green. For example, the leaf on that tree over there is not the exact same color as the grass we are standing on, is it?"

Neville's little head shot back and forth between the leaf and the grass. "No," he said, as if not quite believing what he was seeing. "It's not." He looked up excitedly. "And it's not quite the same color as the stripe on your dress!"

"Very good, Neville. I'm very proud of you."

He beamed.

"Let us see how many different shades of green we can find. And once we're done we shall find names for all these greens."

"There is moss on the rocks in the pond."

"Yes, indeed. We shall call that moss green."

"What is the green on your dress called?"

Victoria looked down and surveyed her drab dress. "I believe it is called forest green."

He narrowed his eyes suspiciously. "It's much darker than the forest."

"Not at night."

"I've never been outside in the forest at night."

Victoria smiled. "I have."

"You have?" He looked at her with new respect.

"Mmm-hmm. Now then, what other colors can you find?"

"What about the dress my mama was wearing this morning? It was an icky color, but it was green."

Victoria was inclined to agree with his assessment of Lady Hollingwood's dress, but she wasn't about to say so. "Your mother's dress was not 'icky,' Neville," she said diplomatically. "And we call that color—er, I suppose it would be called brackish green."

"Brackish." He let the word roll around in his mouth for a moment before pointing a stubby finger to Victoria's right. "What about his lordship's coat? That's green, too."

Victoria felt her stomach plummet to somewhere in the vicinity of her feet as she turned her head. She groaned. It would have to be Robert. There were at least a dozen "his lordships" on the property for the house party, but no, it would have to be Robert walking toward them.

Not that she thought this was any coincidence.

"Good morning, Miss Lyndon, Master Neville." Robert swept into a courtly bow.

Victoria nodded her head, trying to ignore the way her heart was soaring and her pulse was racing. She let out a snort, thoroughly disgusted with herself.

"*That* is certainly a nice greeting," Robert said, smiling at her reaction.

His gaze locked with hers, and Victoria felt the breath leave her body. She probably would have stood stock still all afternoon, staring into his eyes, if Neville had not interrupted them.

"My lord! My lord!" came the voice from below.

Reluctantly, both Victoria and Robert looked down.

"We're practicing colors," Neville said proudly.

"Is that so?" Robert crouched down to the boy's level. "Did you know that objects have their colors because of certain properties of light? One cannot see colors in the dark. Scientists call this concept the wave theory of light. It's a relatively new discovery."

Neville blinked.

"My lord," Victoria said, unable to suppress a smile. He'd always been so passionate about the sciences. "Perhaps that is a bit beyond the scope of a five-year-old."

He looked up at her sheepishly. "Oh yes, of course."

Neville coughed, clearly wanting to steer the conversation back to the matter at hand. "Today," he said firmly, "we are discussing green."

"Green, you say?" Robert lifted his arm and pretended to look at his sleeve with great interest. "I am wearing green."

Neville beamed at the attention he was receiving from Robert. "Yes, we were just talking about you."

Robert leveled a rather knowing look in Victoria's direction. "You were?"

"Yes." Neville turned to Victoria. "Miss Lyndon, weren't we talking about his lordship's coat?"

"*You* certainly were," Victoria retorted, not enjoying herself in the least.

The boy tugged at her sleeve. "What kind of green is it?"

Victoria regarded Robert's coat, an article of clothing so expertly tailored it might well be classified as a piece of art. "Bottle green, Neville. It is called bottle green."

"Bottle green," he repeated. "Thus far I have learned moss green, and bottle green, and brackish green, which I shall call icky green—"

"Neville!" Victoria reprimanded.

"Very well." He sighed. I shan't call it icky green. "But—" The boy looked up sharply at Robert. "Do you know what color the stripe on Miss Lyndon's dress is?"

Robert stood, letting his eyes rest on the stripe, which happened to be on her bodice. "No," said, not looking back down to Neville. "I don't know."

Victoria fought the urge to cover her breasts with her hands. It was absurd, she knew, because she was fully dressed. But she felt as if Robert could see straight to her skin.

"It's forest green," Neville proclaimed. "And Miss Lyndon should know, because she has been in the forest at night."

Robert arched a brow. "Has she?"

Victoria swallowed painfully, trying not to remember the magical evenings she'd sneaked out of her room and run through the forest in Kent with Robert. It was impossible, of course. Those memories played poignantly through her mind every day. "One can't see colors in the dark," she said peevishly. "The earl said so."

"But you said that forest green was as dark as the forest at night," Neville persisted.

"Perhaps if the moon was out," Robert mused. "One could see a bit of color, and it would be so very romantic."

Victoria glared at him before turning back to the boy. "Neville," she said, her voice sounding odd to her ears. "I'm sure the earl is not interested in our color games."

Robert smiled slowly. "I'm interested in everything you do."

Victoria tugged at Neville's hand. "We really should not keep his lordship. I am certain he has many important things to do. Things that *don't* involve us."

Neville didn't budge. He looked up at Robert and asked, "Are you married?"

Victoria coughed and managed to get out, "Neville, I'm sure that is none of our business."

"No, Neville, I'm not," Robert replied.

The boy cocked his head. "Maybe you should ask Miss Lyndon. Then you could come live here with us."

Robert looked as if he was trying very hard not to laugh. "I asked her once."

"Oh, God." Victoria groaned. Life didn't get very much worse than this.

"You did?" Neville said.

Robert shrugged his shoulders. "She wouldn't have me."

Neville whipped his head around to face Victoria. "You said *no?*" His voice rose to a horrified shriek on the last word.

"I-I-I—" Victoria was spluttering, quite unable to get a word out.

"Miss Lyndon?" Robert prodded, looking as if he hadn't enjoyed himself quite so heartily in many years.

"I didn't say— Oh, for God's sake." Victoria looked at Robert with a ferocious expression. "You should be ashamed of yourself, my lord."

"Ashamed?" He feigned innocence.

"Using a young boy like this to satisfy your . . . your . . ."

"My what?"

"Your need to hurt me. It is unconscionable."

"Why, Miss Lyndon, I'm insulted that you would think I would stoop to such levels."

"There is no need to stoop," she said icily. "You have always been lodged somewhere between the gutter and hell."

"Did you say *hell?*" Neville screeched.

Robert began to shake with silent laughter.

"Neville, we are going back to the house this instant," Victoria said firmly.

"But my colors! I want to finish with green."

She snatched his hand and started hauling him toward the house. "We shall have our tea in the green salon." Victoria didn't bother to look back. The last thing she wanted to see was Robert hunched over with laughter.

* * *

If Robert's intention was to torture her into insanity, Victoria thought wryly later that day, he was doing a rather good job of it.

She never dreamed that he would dare seek her out in her room again; she had made it abundantly clear that such behavior was unacceptable. But obviously he didn't care, because at one o'clock, while Neville was taking his riding lesson, he slipped into her room with nary a guilty look.

"Robert!" Victoria exclaimed.

"Are you busy?" he asked, his face a picture of innocence as he closed the door behind him.

"Busy!" she nearly screeched. "Get out!"

"If you didn't want company, you should have locked your door."

"You can be certain I will adopt that habit in the future." Victoria paused, trying to unclench her jaw. She wasn't successful. "What are you doing here?" she ground out.

He held up a plate. "Bringing you a piece of chocolate cake. I know how much you love it, and I didn't think Lady H. was the sort to share her sweets with the governess."

"Robert, you must leave."

He ignored her. "Although I cannot imagine that Lady H. is unaware that you are far more beautiful than she is, and I would not put it past her to purposefully try to make you fat."

"Have you lost your mind?"

"Really, Victoria, you are most unappreciative. Very bad manners. I'm surprised at you."

Victoria thought that she must be in the middle of a very strange dream. That could be the only explanation. Robert, lecturing her on propriety? "I must be insane," she muttered. "If you're not, then I must be."

"Nonsense. What could be wrong with two friends enjoying each other's company?"

"That is not our situation, and well you know it." Victoria planted her hands on her hips. "And I'm going to have to ask you not to play your silly games with me in front of Neville anymore. It isn't right."

He held up his hand as if making a solemn vow. "No more games in front of Neville."

"Thank you."

"Although I did convince him to call you *Miss* Lyndon, did I not?"

Victoria let out a sigh. She was beyond annoyed with him for that afternoon's antics, but her sense of fair play demanded that she thank him. "Yes, Robert, I do thank you for your intervention with Neville yesterday, but—"

He waved his hand. "It was nothing, I assure you."

"Nevertheless, I thank you. However—"

"The boy needed a firm hand."

"I agree with you, but—"

"It is really too bad that I had to be the one to do it, as that task ought to fall to his parents."

She planted her hands on her hips again. "Why do I get the idea that you are trying to stop me from speaking?"

"It may be"—he leaned casually against the doorjamb—"because I know you're trying to dismiss me."

"Exactly."

"Bad idea."

"I beg your pardon."

"I said it's a bad idea. Most inadvisable."

She blinked in aggravation. "It is quite possibly the most advisable idea I've had in a long time."

"But you wouldn't want to be deprived of my company," he returned.

"That is precisely the end I am trying to achieve."

"Yes, but you'll be miserable without me."

"I am quite certain I can judge my own emotions with greater clarity than you."

"Would you like to know what your problem is with Neville?"

"Would you like to tell me?" she asked, with no small amount of sarcasm.

"You don't know how to be stern."

"I beg your pardon. I am a governess. I make my living by being stern."

He shrugged. "You're not very good at it."

Her mouth opened in consternation. "I have spent the last seven years working as a governess. And in case you don't recall, just yesterday you said I was quite good at it."

"At the lesson plans and that sort of thing." He waved his hand nonchalantly in the air. "But discipline—Well, you'll never excel at that."

"That is not true."

"You've never known how to be properly stern." He chuckled and touched her cheek. "I remember it so clearly from before. You would try to scold me, but your eyes were always too warm. And your lips always turn up just a bit at the corners. I don't think you know how to make a serious frown."

Victoria eyed him suspiciously. What was he up to? He had been so furious with her yesterday morning when he stole into her room. But since then he'd been positively congenial. Utterly charming.

"Am I correct?" he asked, breaking into her thoughts.

She leveled a shrewd stare in his direction. "You're trying to seduce me again, aren't you?"

Robert wasn't eating or drinking anything, but he choked nonetheless, requiring Victoria to give him a hearty whack on the back. "I cannot believe you said that," he finally said.

"Is it true?"

"Of course not."

"So it *is* true."

"Victoria, are you listening to a word I am saying?"

Before she could reply, a knock sounded at the door. Victoria instantly panicked. She threw an agonized glance at Robert, who responded by putting his forefinger to his lips and grabbing the plate of cake as he tiptoed to her wardrobe and climbed in. Victoria blinked in disbelief as she watched him squeeze in. He looked most uncomfortable.

"Miss Lyndon! Open this door at once!" Lady Hollingwood sounded most displeased. "I know you're in there."

Victoria ran to the door, silently thanking her maker that Robert had been rude enough to lock the door behind him. "I'm so sorry, Lady Hollingwood," she said as she pulled the door open. "I was taking a nap. I often do while Neville is at the stables."

Lady Hollingwood's eyes narrowed. "I am certain I heard you speaking."

"It must have been in my sleep," Victoria said quickly. "My sister used to tell me that I kept her up half the night with my mumblings."

"How perfectly bizarre." This was said with disgust, not interest.

Victoria gritted her teeth into a smile. "Was there anything in particular you wanted, Lady Hollingwood? An update on Neville's lessons, perhaps?"

"I shall quiz you on his progress on Wednesday, as is our habit. I am here for a far graver reason."

Victoria's heart dropped. Lady Hollingwood was going to dismiss her. She had seen her with Robert. Perhaps she had even seen him enter her room not ten minutes earlier. Victoria opened her mouth to speak, but she couldn't think of any words in her defense. At least none that Lady Hollingwood would pay heed to.

"Miss Hypatia Vinton has taken ill," Lady Hollingwood announced.

Victoria blinked. That was all? "I trust it is not serious."

"Not at all. A putrid stomach, or something of the sort. It is my opinion that she will be well by morning, but she insists upon going home."

"I see," Victoria said, wondering what this had to do with her.

"We are now short a lady for my dinner party tomorrow evening. You will have to take her place."

"Me?" Victoria squeaked.

"It is the worst of possible situations, but I cannot think of any other course of action."

"What about this evening's dinner? Surely you'll need another lady."

Lady Hollingwood fixed a supercilious stare on Victoria's nose. "As it happens, one of my male guests has offered to escort Hypatia home, so we will be evenly matched. It is no use angling for another invitation, Miss Lyndon. I do not want you bothering my guests any more than necessary."

Victoria privately wondered why Lady Hollingwood had bothered to ask her if she was such an embarrassment. She murmured, "It was only a question, my lady."

Her employer frowned. "You do know how to comport yourself in polite society, do you not?"

Victoria said frigidly, "My mother was every inch a lady, Lady Hollingwood. As am I."

"If you disappoint me in this endeavor, I shall not hesitate to throw you out. Do you understand me?"

Victoria didn't see how she could do anything *but* understand her. Lady Hollingwood threatened to dismiss her every other day. "Yes, of course, Lady Hollingwood."

"Good. I don't suppose you've anything to wear."

"Nothing suitable for such an occasion, my lady."

"I shall have one of my old frocks sent up. It shall fit you well enough."

Victoria declined to mention that Lady Hollingwood was a good stone heavier than she. It just didn't seem in her best interest. Instead she opted for a noncommittal, "My lady."

"It will be a few years out of style," Lady Hollingwood mused, "but no one will comment on it. You are the governess, after all."

"Of course."

"Good. We will be serving drinks at eight, and dinner thirty minutes thereafter. Please come at twenty-five minutes past the hour. I do not want my guests to be forced to socialize with you for any longer than is necessary."

Victoria bit her tongue to keep herself from speaking.

"Good day, then." Lady Hollingwood stalked from the room.

Victoria had barely shut the door behind her when Robert bounded out of the wardrobe. "What a cow!" he exclaimed. "How can you bear her?"

"I haven't any other choice," she ground out.

Robert eyed her thoughtfully. "No, I don't suppose you do."

More than anything, Victoria wanted to slap him just then. It was one thing for her to be aware of her miserable lot in life. It was quite another for him to comment on it. "I think you had better leave," she said.

"Yes, of course," he concurred. "You have things to do, I'm sure. Governess things."

She crossed her arms. "Don't come here again."

"Why not? The wardrobe was not uncomfortable."

"Robert . . ." she warned.

"Very well. But first a small token of thanks

for the chocolate cake." He leaned down and kissed her hard and fast. "That should get me through the afternoon."

Victoria wiped her mouth with the back of her hand and bit out, "Contemptible swine."

Robert only chuckled. "I look forward to tomorrow evening, Miss Lyndon."

"Don't seek me out."

He raised a brow. "I don't see how you're going to be able to avoid me."

Chapter 7

⌢⌢◯◯⌢⌢

When that evening and the following morning passed without any contact from Robert, Victoria let herself be lulled into thinking that he might have decided to leave her alone.

She was wrong.

He found her a few hours before supper was due to begin. Victoria was walking briskly down a hall when Robert suddenly materialized before her. She jumped about a foot, startled out of her wits. "Robert!" she exclaimed, one of her hands pressing against her breastbone to calm her racing heart. She took a deep breath and looked both ways down the hall to be sure that no one else was about. "Please don't creep up on me like that again."

His lips formed a masculine smile. "I like to surprise you."

"I really wish you wouldn't," she muttered.

"I merely wanted to know how you are faring with your preparations for your grand debut."

"It isn't my grand debut," she snapped. "If you must know, I am dreading every moment of it. I have no love for the nobility, and the thought of spending several hours in your ranks makes my blood run cold."

"And what have the nobility ever done to you to warrant such distaste? Failed to marry you?" His eyes narrowed to slits. "'Tis a pity your plans went so awry. You toiled so tirelessly to achieve your goal."

"I have no idea what you're talking about," she said, utterly baffled.

"Don't you?" he mocked.

"I need to be going." She moved to her left to try to get around him, but he blocked her. "Robert!"

"I find myself loath to part with your company."

"Oh, please," she said disdainfully. That was a lie if ever she heard one. His eyes were clearly showing his disgust for her.

"Don't you believe me?" he asked.

"Your words and your eyes are not in agreement. Besides, I learned long ago not to trust a word out of your mouth."

Robert sparked with fury. "What the hell does that mean?"

"You know very well."

He advanced, forcing her to back up against the wall. "I was not the one who lied," he said in a low voice, jabbing his forefinger against her shoulder.

Victoria glared at him. "Get out of my way."

"And miss this extremely edifying conversation? I think not."

"Robert! If someone sees us . . ."

"Why the hell are you always so concerned about appearances?"

Victoria's anger grew to the point where she was shaking. "How dare you ask that?" she hissed.

"I dare a lot, darling."

Her hand itched. His cheek was very close, and it would look so good with a nice red welt on it. "I will ask you one last time—"

"Only one more time? Good. You're getting most tedious."

"I shall scream."

"And alert the masses whom you are so assiduously trying to avoid? I think not."

"Robert . . ."

"Oh, for God's sake." He whipped open a door, snatched her hand, and hauled her into a room, slamming the door behind him. "There. Now we're alone."

"Are you mad?" she screeched. She looked wildly about her surroundings, trying to figure out where she was.

"Do try to calm down," he said, standing in front of the door, looking very much like an implacable god. "This is my room. No one will walk in on us."

Victoria snorted. "This isn't the guest wing."

"Lady H. ran out of room," he said with a shrug. "She put me near the family quarters. Because I'm an earl, she said."

"I am well aware of your rank and all it entails," she said, her voice pure ice.

Robert let that barb pass. "As I said, we are

now alone, and we can finish this conversation without your incessant worrying that we will be discovered."

"Did it ever occur to you that perhaps I just don't like *you*? That perhaps *you* are the reason I do not want to be alone with you?"

"No."

"Robert, I have chores I must attend to. I can't be here."

"I don't see how you're going to leave," he said, leaning against the door.

"Stop jeopardizing my position. You may be able to return to your privileged life in London," she said in a furious, low voice, "but I do not have that option."

He stroked her cheek insolently. "It could be an option, if you should so choose."

"Don't!" She wrenched away from him, hating herself for loving his touch, hating him for touching her. She turned her back on him. "You insult me."

His hands came down lightly on her shoulders. "It was meant as the highest of compliments."

"A compliment!" she burst out, pulling away from him yet again. "You have a warped set of morals."

"That is certainly a bizarre statement, coming from you."

"I am not the one who spends all of my free time seducing innocents."

He countered with, "I am not the one who tried to sell my life and body for a fortune and a title."

"You're a fine one to talk. You, who have already sold your soul."

"Explain yourself," he bit out.

And then, just because his tone annoyed her so much, she said, "No."

"Do not defy me, Victoria."

"'Do not defy me,'" she mocked. "You are not in any position to give me orders. You might have been—" Her voice broke, and it took her a moment to regain her composure. "You might have been, but you gave up that right."

"Is that a fact?"

"It's no use talking with you. I don't know why I even try."

"Don't you?"

"Don't touch me," Victoria bit out. She could feel him drawing near. He radiated heat and a certain maleness that was his alone. Her skin began to tingle.

"You keep trying," he said softly, "because you know that matters between us have never been resolved."

Victoria knew it was true. Their relationship ended so abruptly. This was probably why seeing him after all these years was so difficult. But she didn't want to face him now. She wanted to sweep him under the rug and forget about him.

Most of all, she didn't want her heart broken anew, which she was fairly certain would happen if she let herself spend any time with him.

"Deny it," he whispered. "I dare you to."

She said nothing.

"You can't, can you?" He crossed the room

and put his arms around her, resting his chin on the top of her head. It was an embrace they'd shared a hundred times before, but never had it felt so bittersweet. Robert had no idea why he was holding her. He only knew that he couldn't *not* do it.

"Why are you doing this?" she whispered. "Why?"

"I don't know." And God help him, it was the truth. He'd told himself he wanted to ruin her. Part of him still wanted revenge. She'd cut his heart to ribbons. He'd hated her for years for that.

But holding her felt so right. There really wasn't another word for it. No other woman had ever fit quite so perfectly in his arms, and he'd spent the past seven years filling them with other women, trying desperately to blot this one from his memory.

Was it truly possible to love and hate at the same time? Robert had always scoffed at the notion, but he was no longer so certain. He let his lips trail along the warm skin of her temple. "Have you let other men hold you this way?" he whispered, dreading the answer. She had wanted only his fortune, but his heart still raced with jealousy at the thought of her with another man.

She made no reply for a moment, and Robert's entire body tensed. Then she shook her head.

"Why?" he asked, with just a touch of desperation. "Why?"

"I don't know."

"Was it the money?"

She stiffened. "What?"

He moved his lips to her neck, kissing her with a feral grace. "No one rich enough to keep you satisfied?"

"No!" she burst out. "I'm not like that. You know I'm not like that."

His only reply was a chuckle, and Victoria felt his laugh directly on her skin.

"Oh, my God," she breathed, wrenching herself out of his grasp. "You thought . . . You thought . . ."

He crossed his arms and looked down at her, the very picture of urbane elegance. "What did I think, Victoria? You tell me."

"You thought I wanted your money. That I was an adventuress."

He made no movement except for an arching of his right brow.

"You . . . You . . ." Seven years of anger exploded within Victoria, and she launched herself at him, pummeling his chest with her fists. "How dare you think that? You monster! I hate you. I hate you."

Robert raised his arms to fend off her unexpected attack, then neatly caught both her wrists in one hand. "It's a bit late to feign outrage, don't you think?"

"I never wanted your money," she said hotly. "It never mattered to me."

"Oh, come now, Victoria. Do you think I don't remember how you begged me to settle my differences with my father? You even said you wouldn't marry me unless I tried to mend the rift."

"That was because—Oh, why am I even trying to explain myself to you?"

He moved his face very close to hers. "You are trying to explain yourself because you want to snare what you missed seven years ago. Me."

"I am beginning to realize that you were never such a spectacular catch to begin with," she ground out.

He laughed harshly. "Perhaps not. Which would explain your failure to show up for our elopement. But my money and title never lacked appeal."

Victoria yanked her wrists from his grasp, surprised when he yielded so easily. She sat down on the bed, burying her face in her hands. The fragments of her life were beginning to fall into place. When she hadn't kept their assignation, he had assumed she had backed out of the marriage because his father had disinherited him. He had thought— Oh, God, *how* could he have thought that of her?

"You never knew me," she whispered, as if only just realizing it. "You never really knew me."

"I wanted to," he said harshly. "Lord, how I wanted to. And God help me, I still do."

There was no point in trying to explain the truth to him, she realized. The truth no longer mattered. He hadn't had any faith in her, and nothing could mend that breach. She wondered if he had ever trusted any woman.

"Contemplating your sins?" he drawled from across the room.

She lifted her head to face him, her eyes

glinting oddly. "You're a cold man, Robert. And a lonely one, too, I'd wager."

He stiffened. Her words cut to the quick, and they were startling in their accuracy. With blinding speed he moved to her side, his hands grasping at her shoulders. "I am what I am because of you."

"No," she said, shaking her head sadly. "You did this to yourself. If you had trusted me—"

"You never gave me a damn reason to," he exploded.

She was trembling. "I gave you every reason," she replied. "You just chose to ignore them."

Disgusted, Robert pushed himself away from her. She was comporting herself like some kind of noble victim, and he didn't have patience with such hypocrisy. Especially when every fiber of his being was screaming with desire for her.

That was what appalled him the most. He was every bit as big a hypocrite. Wanting her so badly. Wanting Victoria, of all people, the one woman he should have had enough sense to avoid like the plague.

But he was learning that this need was something he just couldn't control. And hell, why should he have to? She wanted him every bit as much as he wanted her. It was right there in her eyes every time she looked at him. He said her name, his voice husky with promise and desire.

Victoria stood up and walked to the window. She leaned her face against the glass, not trusting herself to look at him. Somehow, the knowledge that he had never trusted her hurt more than when she thought he was only out to seduce her.

He said her name again, and this time she could tell he was very close. Close enough for her to feel his breath on her neck.

He turned her around so she was facing him. His eyes burned blue flame to the very depths of her soul, and Victoria was mesmerized.

"I'm going to kiss you now," he said slowly, his words punctuated by ragged breathing. "I'm going to kiss you, and I'm not going to stop. Do you understand?"

She didn't move.

"Once my lips touch yours . . ."

His words sounded vaguely like a warning, but Victoria could not make herself heed it. She felt warm—hot, really, and yet she shivered. Her thoughts were racing at lightning speed, but her mind was somehow a total blank. Everything about her was in contradiction, and that was probably why she suddenly thought that kissing him might actually not be such a terrible idea.

A taste of yesterday—that was all she wanted. Just a taste of what might have been. What could have been. What *should* have been.

She swayed forward, and that was all the invitation he needed. He crushed her to him in a stunning embrace, his lips devouring hers. She could feel his arousal pressing against her, and it was utterly thrilling. He might be a rake and a philanderer, but she couldn't believe he had ever wanted a woman the way he wanted her this very minute.

Victoria felt like the most powerful woman on earth. It was a heady sensation, and she arched herself against him, shuddering as her breasts flattened against his chest.

"I need more." He moaned, his hands grasping frantically at her backside. "I need it all."

Victoria couldn't have said no if God himself had come down and told her to. And she had no doubt that she would have surrendered herself completely to Robert if a voice hadn't suddenly sounded in the room.

"Excuse me."

Robert and Victoria flew apart, both whirling to face the door. An extremely well-dressed gentleman stood there. Victoria had never seen him before, although she had no doubt that he was a member of the house party. She looked away, utterly mortified at having been caught in such a compromising position.

"Eversleigh," Robert said, his voice cold.

"I beg your pardon, Macclesfield," the gentleman said. "But I thought this was my room."

Victoria's eyes flew to Robert's face. The lying bastard! He'd probably had no idea whose room they were in all along. He'd only wanted to get her alone. He hadn't given a thought to her reputation. Or the threat to her position as governess.

Robert grabbed Victoria's hand and pulled her toward the door. "We'll be on our way, Eversleigh."

Victoria could tell that Robert didn't like this Lord Eversleigh, but she was too furious with him at that moment to ponder the ramifications.

"The governess, eh?" Eversleigh said, assessing Victoria rudely. "It would be very difficult for you should the Hollingwoods learn of this little indiscretion."

Robert halted in his tracks and turned on

Eversleigh with a thunderous expression. "If you mention this to anyone, even your damned *dog,* I will rip your throat out."

Eversleigh clucked. "You really ought to conduct your affairs in your own room."

Robert hauled Victoria back into the hall and slammed the door shut. She immediately wrenched her arm free and turned on him. *"Your* room?" she practically yelled. *"Your* room? You bloody liar."

"You were the one who was so anxious about being in the hall. And you'd do well to keep your voice down now if you truly do not wish to attract attention."

"Don't you dare try to lecture me." Victoria took a deep breath, trying to calm her shaking body. "I don't even know who you are anymore. You are certainly not the boy I met seven years ago. You are ruthless, and worthless, and amoral, and—"

"I believe I understand your general idea."

Robert's civilized blandness only served to make her angrier. "Don't you ever approach me again," she said in a shaking, low voice. "Ever."

She stalked off, wishing she had a door to slam in his face.

Chapter 8

Victoria had no idea how she was going to make it through that evening. Spending several hours in Robert's company was bad enough, but now she would also have to face Lord Eversleigh, who surely thought her a fallen woman.

She briefly considered inventing a case of the putrid stomach herself. She would say that she had crossed paths with Miss Hypatia Vinton the day before; it was not impossible for her to have contracted the same affliction. Surely Lady Hollingwood would not force her to attend a dinner party while ill. But then again Lady H. was the sort to assume that Victoria had developed nausea just to spite her. It would be grounds for dismissal. With Lady Hollingwood, anything was grounds for dismissal.

With a sigh Victoria regarded the dress laying on her bed. It wasn't quite as ugly as she'd feared, but it was too large and would hang on her body like a sack. Furthermore it was yellow, a color that had always made her look sallow. Feminine vanity aside, however, she decided not to let it upset her—she didn't want to attract attention, anyway. Victoria was more than happy to play the wallflower at this particular soiree. That such meek behavior would probably impress her employer was an added boon.

Victoria checked the clock in her room. It was a quarter of an hour before eight—time to start getting ready if she was to arrive downstairs at twenty-five minutes past the hour. *Precisely* twenty-five minutes past the hour, she thought with a grimace. Not a second sooner and not a second later. Victoria didn't doubt that her job depended on it.

She dressed her hair as best as she could. It wouldn't be as elegant as the other ladies', but she had no maid to fashion fancy ringlets or curl a fringe. A simple yet elegant chignon was the best she could do.

A look at the clock told her that it was time to head downstairs, and so she slipped out of her room, shutting and locking the door behind her. When she arrived in the drawing room, the Hollingwoods' guests were all present, sipping their drinks and chatting amiably. Lord Eversleigh was in a corner with his back mercifully toward her as he flirted with a young blond woman. Victoria breathed a sigh of relief; she was still mortified about that afternoon's incident.

Robert was leaning against a wall, his expression foreboding enough to scare off all but the most foolish socialites. His eyes were intent and they had been focused on the door when she entered. He had obviously been watching for her.

Victoria looked around. No one seemed inclined to approach him. Tonight's batch of socialites must have been considerably less foolish than average.

Robert took a step in her direction, but was cut off by Lady Hollingwood, who made her way immediately to Victoria's side. "Thank you for being prompt," she said. "Mr. Percival Hornsby will be escorting you in to dinner. I will introduce you to him presently."

Victoria followed her employer, barely able to believe the woman had actually uttered the words "thank" and "you" in the same sentence. Then, just when she and Lady Hollingwood had nearly crossed the room, she heard Robert's voice.

"Miss Lyndon? Victoria?"

Victoria turned around, dread filling her stomach.

"My word, it *is* you!" Robert's face was a picture of incredulity as he closed the distance between them in easy strides.

Victoria narrowed her eyes. What the devil was he up to?

"Lord Macclesfield!" Lady Hollingwood said, just a touch breathlessly. "Do not tell me that you are acquainted with Miss Lyndon."

"I am well acquainted with Miss Lyndon."

Victoria wondered if anyone else could hear the double meaning in his voice. She itched to let her temper loose and tell him exactly what she thought of his games.

Lady Hollingwood turned to Victoria with an accusing expression. "Miss Lyndon, you did not

tell me you were acquainted with Lord Macclesfield."

"I did not know he was a guest, my lady." If
he could lie, confound him, so could she.

"We grew up together," Robert added. "In
Kent."

Well, Victoria conceded to herself, that much
was not entirely untrue. She may have moved to
Kent at the age of seventeen, but she had certainly done some growing up while there. De-
ception and betrayal had a way of doing that to a
person.

"Is that so?" Lady Hollingwood asked, looking terribly interested and just a little bit baffled
that her governess might have once moved in the
same circles as an earl.

"Yes, our families are great friends."

Victoria coughed so hard that she had to
excuse herself to get something to drink.

"Oh, no, allow *me*," Robert said grandly. "I
can think of nothing I'd rather do."

"I can think of many things I'd rather do,"
Victoria muttered under her breath. Stomping
on his foot would be nice, as would dumping a
glass of wine over his head. She'd already done
that once with a basin of water, and it had
proved most enjoyable. Wine had the added
bonus of being red.

While Robert was off procuring Victoria a
glass of lemonade, Lady Hollingwood turned on
her. "You know Macclesfield?" she hissed.
"Why didn't you tell me?"

"I told you, I didn't know he was a guest."

"Whether or not he is a guest is irrelevant. He
is beyond influential. When I hired you, you

should have informed me you were— Oh, hello, Lord Macclesfield."

Robert nodded as he held up two glasses. "Lady Hollingwood, I took the liberty of obtaining lemonade for both of you."

Lady Hollingwood simpered her thanks. Victoria said nothing, well aware that if she opened her mouth, she'd say something unfit for polite company. Just then, Lord Hollingwood came by, asking his wife if it was time to go in to dinner. "Ah, yes," Lady Hollingwood said. "I merely need to introduce Miss Lyndon to Mr. Hornsby."

"Perhaps I might escort Miss Lyndon to dinner," Robert said.

Victoria's mouth fell open. Surely he realized what a dreadful insult that was to Lady Hollingwood. As the highest ranking gentleman in the party, it was his duty to escort the hostess.

Victoria snapped her mouth closed just as Lady Hollingwood opened hers in consternation. "But . . . but . . ."

Robert offered her a warm smile. "It has been so long, and I'm certain Miss Lyndon and I have much catching up to do. Why, I haven't even the slightest knowledge of how her sister fares." He turned to Victoria with an expression that was *so* concerned. "And how is dear Eleanor?"

"Ellie is fine," Victoria ground out.

"Is she still as impertinent as ever?"

"Not as impertinent as you," Victoria retorted. Then she bit her tongue.

"Miss Lyndon!" cried Lady Hollingwood. "How dare you speak to Lord Macclesfield in such a tone. Remember your place."

But Robert was only chuckling. "Miss Lyndon and I have always spoken frankly to each other. It is one of the reasons we so enjoy each other's company."

Victoria was still kicking herself for letting him goad her into her previous retort, so she held her tongue, even though she really wanted to declare that she did not enjoy his company in the least.

Obviously at a loss, Lady Hollingwood looked as if she didn't know how to handle this irregular situation. She certainly did not appear to be even remotely pleased at the thought of her governess claiming the highest ranking guest as her dinner partner.

Victoria, who had quickly realized that this slight might escalate into a dismissable offense, interceded. "I am certain it is not necessary that the earl and I sit with each other. We may—"

"Oh, but it *is* necessary," Robert interrupted, flashing the ladies a debonair smile. "It has been an age."

"But Lady Hollingwood's seating arrangements—"

"We are not such an inflexible group. Mr. Hornsby will be happy to take my place near the head of the table, I am sure."

Lady Hollingwood turned quite green. Mr. Hornsby was not and never would be a person of importance. But before she could object Robert had called over the gentleman in question.

"Percy," he said in his most amiable tone, "you wouldn't mind leading Lady Hollingwood in to dinner? I would be much indebted to you if you would agree to take my place at the table."

Percy blinked. "B-b-but I am m-merely—"

Robert gave him a hearty whack on the back as an interruption, sparing him future stutters. "You'll have a smashing time. Lady Hollingwood is an astonishing conversationalist."

Percy shrugged and offered Lady Hollingwood his arm. She accepted it—indeed, there was nothing else she could do without insulting an earl—but not before she threw a furious glance over her shoulder at Victoria.

Victoria closed her eyes in agony. There was no way Lady Hollingwood was going to believe that this disaster was not her doing. It didn't matter that Robert had done all of the talking, that he was the one who'd been so insistent. Lady H. would find a way to pin this on the governess.

Robert leaned down and smiled. "That wasn't so difficult, now was it?"

She glowered at him. "If I had a pitchfork, I swear unto God I would run you through."

He only chuckled. "A pitchfork? It must be your country upbringing. Most women of my acquaintance would have chosen a dagger. Or perhaps a letter opener."

"She is going to have my head," Victoria hissed, watching as the other couples promenaded into the dining room in order of rank. Since Robert had swapped places with Mr. Hornsby, he would be the last to enter the dining room and would sit at the lower end of the table.

"A disrupted seating arrangement is not the end of the world," Robert said.

"To Lady Hollingwood it is," Victoria retorted. "I may know you for the cretin you are, but all she sees is a lofty earl."

"It does come in handy on occasion," he murmured.

That earned him yet another furious glare. "She has been boasting about your presence at the house party for the past two days," Victoria added. "She will not be happy that you will be sitting with the governess."

Robert shrugged. "I sat with her last night. What more could she want?"

"I didn't even want to sit with you in the first place! I would have been perfectly happy with Mr. Hornsby. I would have been even happier with a tray in my room. I find the lot of you despicable."

"Yes, you have said as much."

"I will be lucky if she only dismisses me. I am sure she is fantasizing about some other more painful form of torture even as we speak."

"Chin up, Torie. It's our turn." Robert took her arm and led her into the dining room, where they took their places. The other guests looked startled to see Robert at the end of the table. He smiled blandly and said, "Lady Hollingwood granted me a boon. Miss Lyndon is an old childhood friend, and I wanted to sit with her."

The other guests nodded furiously, clearly relieved to be provided with an explanation for this egregious breach of etiquette.

"Miss Lyndon," barked a portly middle-aged man. "I do not believe we have met. Who are your people?"

"My father is the vicar in Bellfield, in Kent."

"Very close to Castleford," Robert added. "We were children together."

Victoria barely suppressed a snort. Children, indeed. They had done things no child should do.

While she was sitting there fuming, Robert introduced her to the people at their end of the table. The man on Victoria's left was Captain Charles Pays, of His Majesty's navy. Victoria thought he was rather handsome in a non-Robert sort of way. The portly man was Mr. Thomas Whistledown, and the lady to his right was Miss Lucinda Mayford, who, Victoria was quickly informed by Captain Pays, was a great heiress looking to snag a title. And finally, across from Robert was Mrs. William Happerton, a widow who had wasted no time in instructing Robert to call her Celia.

Victoria rather thought that Mrs. Happerton was looking at Robert just a trifle too intently, which seemed reason enough for Victoria to turn her attention to Captain Pays. Not, she reasoned, that she was the least bit jealous. Still, there seemed some justice in it, and it required that she turn her back on Robert, which was appealing in and of itself.

"Tell me, Captain Pays," she said with a smile, "have you been in the navy very long?"

"Four years, Miss Lyndon. It is a dangerous life, but I enjoy it."

"If you enjoy it so much," Robert cut in, "why the devil aren't you on the continent doing your job?"

Seething, Victoria turned to Robert and said, "Captain Pays is in the navy, which implies that he serves on a boat. It would be quite difficult to steer a boat *on* the continent, my lord. Boats tend to require water." And then, while everyone was gaping at her for speaking to an earl as if he were a lackwit, she added, "Besides, I wasn't aware that you were included in our conversation."

Miss Mayford choked so hard on her soup that Mr. Whistledown was moved to whack her on the back. He looked as if he enjoyed the endeavor.

Victoria turned back to Captain Pays. "You were saying . . ."

He blinked, clearly uncomfortable with the way Robert was glowering at him over Victoria's head. "I was?"

"Yes," she said, trying to sound like a sweet, gentle lady. She soon discovered, however, that it was difficult to sound sweet and gentle through clenched teeth. "I would love to hear more about what you do."

Robert was having similar problems with his temper. He was not finding Victoria's flirtations with the handsome captain amusing. It didn't matter that he knew she was doing it to rile him—her plan was working like a dream. It left him unpleasantly jealous, and what he really wanted to do was fling a forkful of peas at Captain Pays.

He probably would have done it, too, if they weren't still on the soup course. Instead he stabbed at the soup with his spoon, but it didn't offer much resistance and thus did nothing to reduce his tension.

He looked over at Victoria again. Her back was resolutely turned to him. He cleared his throat.

She didn't move.

He cleared his throat again.

If anything, she leaned even closer to Pays.

Robert looked down and watched his knuckles grow white from gripping his spoon too hard. He didn't want Victoria, but he damn well didn't want anyone else to have her.

Well, that was not entirely true. He wanted her. Badly. He just didn't want to want her. He forced himself to remember every humiliating and pathetic moment of her betrayal. She was the worst sort of adventuress.

And still he wanted her.

He groaned.

"Is aught amiss?" inquired the merry widow from across the table.

Robert swung his head around to face Mrs. Happerton. She had been making eyes at him all night, and he had half a mind to take her up on her unspoken offer. She was certainly attractive enough, although she'd probably be more appealing if her hair were darker. Black, to be precise. Like Victoria's.

It wasn't until he looked down that he realized he'd torn his napkin in two. His *cloth* napkin.

"My lord?"

He looked back up. "Mrs. Happerton. I must apologize. I have not been appropriately sociable." He smiled devilishly. "You should give me a scolding."

He heard Victoria mutter something under her breath. He stole a glance in her direction. Her attention was not as single-mindedly focused on Captain Pays as she would like him to believe.

A footman appeared on Robert's right, holding out a plate of—could it be?—peas. Victoria helped herself to a spoonful, exclaiming, "I adore peas." She turned to Robert. "If I recall, you detest them. Pity we weren't served pea soup."

Miss Mayford coughed again, then lurched to her left to avoid Mr. Whistledown's blows to her back.

"Actually," Robert said, beaming, "I have developed a sudden fondness for peas. Just this evening, as a matter of fact."

Victoria harrumphed and returned her attention to Captain Pays. Robert slid some peas onto his fork, made certain that no one was looking, took aim, and let fly.

And missed. The peas went flying in every direction, but none of them managed to connect with either Victoria or Pays. Robert grunted in disappointment. That was the sort of evening he was having. And it had started so nicely, too. Torturing Victoria and Lady H. in the drawing room had been such great fun.

The meal wore on. No one enjoyed themselves, with the possible exception of Mr. Whistledown, who seemed oblivious to the barbs being hurled back and forth. Indeed, once the food was served, he seemed oblivious to everything.

By the time dessert was cleared away, five of the six guests seated at the end of the table looked exhausted. The sixth, Mr. Whistledown, just looked full.

Victoria had never been so thankful for anything when Lady Hollingwood suggested that the ladies retire to the drawing room. She had no desire for close contact with her employer, who was surely already deciding the best way to dismiss her. But even Lady H. was preferable to Robert, whose last contribution to the general conversation was, "It is indeed difficult to find good help. Governesses especially."

In the drawing room the ladies gossiped about this and that. Victoria, as a governess, had not been privy to "this" or "that," so she remained silent. The frequent glares sent her way by Lady Hollingwood further convinced her to hold her tongue.

After about half an hour, the gentlemen rejoined them for more conversation. Victoria noticed that Robert was not present and breathed a sigh of relief. She simply did not feel up to sparring with him any longer. As soon as she could politely excuse herself and retire to her room, she would.

An opportunity presented itself a few minutes later. Everyone except Victoria had settled into little conversational groups. She edged toward the door, but when she was but three steps away, a male voice brought her to a halt.

"It is my pleasure to meet you again, Miss Lyndon."

Victoria turned around, her face burning a dull red. "Lord Eversleigh."

"I did not know you would be gracing us with your presence this evening."

"I was a last minute replacement."

"Ah, yes, Miss Vinton's putrid stomach."

Victoria smiled tightly and said, "If you will excuse me, I must be getting back to my chamber." With the briefest of nods she slipped out of the drawing room.

From across the room, Robert narrowed his eyes as he watched Lord Eversleigh sweep his body into a vaguely mocking bow. Robert had been late returning to the drawing room, having stopped in a bath chamber to relieve himself along the way. When he arrived he had found Eversleigh cornering Victoria.

And the way he was looking at her made Robert's blood boil. Captain Pays, for all his dashing good looks, was relatively harmless. Eversleigh was completely without morals or scruples.

Robert started to cross the room, wanting to rip Eversleigh's head from his shoulders, but deciding to try a word or two of warning instead. But before he could reach him, Lady Hollingwood stood and announced the evening's entertainment. Singing and playing in the music room and cards for the gentlemen should they desire to gamble.

Robert tried to pin down Eversleigh as the crowd dispersed, but Lady Hollingwood descended on him with an expression that could only be called purposeful, and he found himself trapped in conversation for the better part of an hour.

Chapter 9

~~~

Robert stood on the fringes of the music room, trying not to listen to the way Miss Mayford was mauling Scarlatti at the harpsichord. But her musical endeavors were not responsible for the sick feeling in his stomach.

Funny how one's conscience surfaced at the damnedest of times.

He'd spent the last few days dreaming about ruining Victoria. He hadn't been sure which he would enjoy more—the actual ruination, which promised to be a most heady affair indeed, or the simple knowledge that he had brought her low.

But that evening something had shifted in Robert's heart. He didn't want anyone *ever* looking at Victoria with the kind of lecherous derision he'd seen in Eversleigh's eyes. And he wasn't particularly enamored with the polite interest he'd noticed in the good captain's expression, either.

And he knew that he wanted her with him. If the last seven years were any indication, he didn't do very well without her. He might not trust her entirely, but he still wanted her in his life.

But first there were other matters to attend to. Eversleigh. The fact that the other man had sought her out in the drawing room was a bad sign, indeed. Robert had to make certain that Eversleigh understood he was very serious about protecting Victoria from vicious rumors. The two men had known each other for years, ever since they'd attended Eton together as young boys. Eversleigh had been a bully then, and he was a bully now.

Robert glanced around the room. Lady Hollingwood's incessant chatter had made him late to the impromptu recital, and now Eversleigh was nowhere to be seen. Robert pushed himself away from the wall and headed into the great hall. He'd find the bastard himself and make sure he kept quiet.

Victoria tried to work on her lesson plans, but she couldn't concentrate. *Damn* him. She now believed that Robert had been serious in his courtship of her seven years ago, but his actions of late were deplorable at best.

He'd tried to seduce her. Worse, he'd done it in a stranger's room, aware that they could be discovered at any moment. Then he'd had the audacity to bait her in front of her employer and her employer's guests. And then finally he had put her in an impossible position, forcing her to accept him as a dinner partner. Lady Hollingwood would never forgive her for that. Victoria might as well begin packing her bags that night.

But the worst part of all was that he'd made

her desire him again. With an intensity that startled her.

Victoria shook her head, trying to change the direction of her thoughts. She turned back to her lesson plans, determined to get at least a bit of work done that evening. Neville had enjoyed their color exercise the previous afternoon. Perhaps she would continue with blue for tomorrow. They could have tea in the blue salon. They could discuss azure and cobalt and midnight and sky. Perhaps she would bring a mirror so they could compare the colors of their eyes. Victoria's were dark blue, while Neville's were light, rather like Robert's.

She sighed, wondering if the man would ever be far from her thoughts.

She lifted her notebook again, preparing to read over the previous days' entries. She spent ten minutes looking at the words without actually reading a thing, and then a knock sounded at the door.

Robert. It had to be.

She had half a mind to ignore the summons, but she knew that he wouldn't go away. Wrenching open the door, she said, "I'm all aquiver to hear your excuse for your behavior, my lord."

Lord Eversleigh stood on the threshold, his eyes mocking but his mouth amused. "I see you were expecting someone else. Lord Macclesfield, perhaps?"

Victoria flushed red, mortified. "No, I am not expecting him. But I—"

He pushed his way past her, leaving her standing by the door.

"Close it," he ordered in a low voice.

"I beg your pardon, my lord."

"The door."

She did nothing but blink, slowly becoming aware that she was in a very bad position. She took a tentative step toward the hall, not certain where she could run to escape him but willing to give it a try.

He moved like a cat, though, and before she knew it, he'd slammed the door closed and was leaning insolently against it. "You're a very beautiful woman," he said.

"I think you have the wrong idea, my lord," she said quickly.

He moved forward, stalking her. "I pride myself on always having the right idea."

"No, what I mean is . . . Lord Macclesfield . . . He and I . . . We . . ."

He touched her cheek. "Does Macclesfield find such protestations of innocence endearing? I assure you there is no need to playact on my behalf. I am quite pleased with you the way you are. Spoiled goods can be so very tasty."

Victoria shuddered with revulsion. "My lord," she said, attempting to reason with him. "I beg of you—"

He chuckled. "I do like to hear a woman beg. I believe I'm going to enjoy you, Miss Lyndon." He reached out and pulled her harshly against him. "Just a taste of what you've already given so freely. I promise you won't regret it. I'm a most generous man."

"I don't want your money," she ground out, twisting her head to the side. "I just want you to leave."

"We can do this two ways," he said, his eyes

growing menacingly dark. "You can stop your pretending and have a bit of fun, or you can fight me all the way. I don't particularly care which you choose. Either way, I am assured a good time."

She slapped him across the face.

"That," he bit out, "was a mistake." He threw her onto the bed and then pinned her there with the weight of his body.

Victoria began to fight. And then she began to scream.

Robert tried Eversleigh's room first, but he wasn't terribly surprised when he didn't find him. He then searched the guest wing, thinking that Eversleigh might be entertaining himself with a female guest. No luck, although he did discover that Lord Winwood's wife happened to be having an affair with the husband of Lord Winwood's mistress.

Robert didn't even bat an eyelash. Such behavior was common enough among his set, much as it was beginning to sicken him.

He then tried the card room, knowing that Eversleigh had a fondness for gambling.

"Eversleigh?" one of the players said. "He was here earlier."

"Was he?" Robert asked, trying to ignore the speculative glances from his friends. It was common knowledge that the two men were not friendly. "Do you know where he went?"

"I saw him heading upstairs," someone said.

Robert stifled a groan. He would have to search the entire guest wing again.

"Most odd," someone else added. "He used the servants' stairs."

The sick feeling that had been rolling around in Robert's stomach all evening exploded with blinding terror. He ran from the room, taking the steps on the servants' stairs three at a time.

And then he heard the screams.

Victoria. If he failed her now . . .

Robert couldn't even complete the thought.

Victoria refused to resign herself to her fate. She fought like a madwoman, clawed like a cat. She knew that her actions only made Eversleigh angrier, but she could not allow herself to be raped with nary a protest.

But he was strong. Much stronger than she was, and it wasn't difficult for him to hold her down while he tore at her clothing. He lifted his hand from her mouth to yank at the neckline of her gown, and she seized the opportunity to scream. Loud.

"Shut up, you bitch," he hissed, twisting her head sideways and forcing her cheek into the pillow. Victoria bit his hand.

"Goddamn, you little whore!" he yelled. He grabbed another pillow and jammed it over her face.

Suddenly Victoria couldn't breathe. Good Lord, did he mean to kill her? Her terror increased until she thought she might go mad. She kicked and scraped, but she couldn't see a thing, and she was growing weaker.

And then, just when the world began to turn black around the edges, she heard a splintering crash, followed by a cry of rage unlike anything in her comprehension.

Eversleigh was abruptly lifted from her, and Victoria immediately threw the pillow aside and scrambled off the bed. She ran to a corner, her lungs burning with every breath and movement, but she had to get off that bed. She had to.

The room filled with noise. Something crashed, someone yelled. There was a sickening sound that could only be flesh against bone. But Victoria didn't look up. She couldn't even open her eyes. All she wanted to do was block out the terror.

Finally, however, she forced herself to face her demons, and when she did she saw Robert. He had knocked Eversleigh to the ground and was straddling him, beating his fist mercilessly into Eversleigh's face.

"Robert," she said, her voice barely a whisper. "Thank God."

Robert made no indication he'd heard her. He just kept pummeling Eversleigh.

"Robert," she said, louder this time. She was still in a daze, and she couldn't stop shaking, and she needed him.

But Robert was beyond communication. He said nothing, just grunted and yelled, and when he finally looked up at Victoria, there was something wild and primitive in his eyes. Finally, still straddling the now unconscious Eversleigh, he paused for a moment to catch his breath and said, "Did he hurt you?"

Her mouth opened a fraction of an inch, but she couldn't say anything.

"Did he *hurt* you?" Robert's eyes burned with

rage, and Victoria realized in that instant that if she said yes, he would kill Eversleigh. She shook her head frantically. It wasn't a lie. Not really. Eversleigh hadn't hurt her. Not in the way Robert meant.

Robert dropped the unconscious man and rushed to her side. He crouched down beside her and touched her cheek. His hand was shaking. "Are you all right?"

She shook her head again.

"Victoria, I—"

He was interrupted by a groan coming from the middle of the room. Robert cursed under his breath and then muttered a quick "Excuse me." He stalked back to Eversleigh, picked him up by his collar and the seat of his pants, and tossed him into the hall, where he landed in a crumpled heap. Robert closed the door gently and made his way back to Victoria's side.

She was shaking violently, the tremors rocking her entire body. Tears rolled down her cheeks, but she didn't make a sound. Robert felt panic rise up within him anew. What had that bastard done to her?

"Shhhh," he crooned, having no idea what he would say that could make her feel better. "Shhhh."

"Robert," she gasped. "Robert."

"I'm here, my love." He reached down and picked her up. Her arms wrapped around his neck with surprising swiftness. She was grasping him frantically, as if letting go would mean the very difference between life and death.

He moved to the bed, intending to sit down and hold her until her shaking subsided, but she suddenly bucked in his arms. "Not the bed!" she said desperately. "Not there."

Robert looked down at the tangled sheets and was sickened. When he'd burst into the room, Eversleigh had had a pillow over Victoria's face. She could have been killed.

The thought was like a punch in the gut.

Robert looked around the room. It was sparsely furnished, so he sat down on the floor, leaning against the side of the bed. He held Victoria silently for several minutes.

Finally she looked up, her eyes entreating. "I tried to fight him," she said. "I did."

"I know you did, Torie."

"He was too strong." She looked as if she was trying to convince him of something that was very important to her. "He was stronger than me."

"You were wonderful," he said, trying to ignore the tears that were pricking at his eyes.

"But he put a pillow over me. And then I couldn't breathe. And I couldn't fight." She began to shake anew. "I didn't want to let him . . . I didn't want it. I swear I didn't want it."

He gripped her shoulders and turned her until they were nose to nose. "This was *not* your fault, Torie," he said fiercely. "Do not blame yourself."

"If you hadn't come—"

"But I did." Robert settled her back into his arms and held her tightly. It would be a long time before she stopped shaking, a long time until Eversleigh's face was no longer imprinted on her brain.

It would be a long time for him, too, he realized. He was not unaware that this incident was at least partly his fault. If he hadn't been so damned angry at her this afternoon and so damned eager to get her alone, he wouldn't have hauled her from the hall into the nearest room. A room that happened to belong to Eversleigh. And that evening—flaunting convention by insisting that he lead Victoria into dinner. Most of the guests would believe his story that they were childhood friends, but Eversleigh knew there was more.

Of course the bastard would think that Victoria was a loose woman. Eversleigh had always been the sort to believe that any female without the protection of a powerful family was his for the plucking. Robert should have realized that from the first, and taken measures to protect her.

He didn't know how long he sat there on the ground, cradling Victoria in his arms. It could have been an hour; it could have been just ten minutes. But eventually her breathing evened out, and he knew she had fallen asleep. He didn't want to speculate on what her dreams might be that night; he prayed she didn't dream at all.

Gently he set her down on her bed. He knew she had an aversion to the spot after Eversleigh's attempted rape, but he didn't know where else to put her. He couldn't bring her to his room. Such an action could only bring about her ruin, and Robert had realized that, regardless of her actions seven years earlier, he couldn't bring himself to destroy her life so completely. The irony of it nearly unmanned him. All these years he'd dreamed about her, fantasized about the revenge he might enact if he saw her again.

But now, with vengeance within his sights, he just couldn't do it. Something within her still spoke to his heart, and he knew he could never live with himself if he purposefully caused her pain.

Robert leaned down and dropped a soft kiss on her forehead. "Until tomorrow, Torie," he whispered. "We'll talk tomorrow. I'm not going to let you leave me again."

When he left the room he noticed that Eversleigh was gone. With grim determination, he set out to find him. He had to make certain that the bastard understood one simple fact: if Eversleigh even so much as breathed a syllable of Victoria's name ever again, the next beating Robert gave him wouldn't stop within an inch of his life.

Victoria woke up the next morning and tried to go about her daily routine as if nothing had happened. She washed her face, pulled on her dress, ate breakfast with Neville.

But every now and then she'd notice little tremors in her hands. And she found herself trying not to blink, for every time she closed her eyes she saw Eversleigh's face as he descended upon her.

She conducted her morning lesson with Neville, then accompanied the boy down to the stables for his riding lesson. Normally she welcomed these brief respites from the demands of her job, but today she was loath to part with the little boy's company.

The last thing she wanted was to be alone with her thoughts.

Robert saw her from across the lawn, and he dashed out to intercept her before she reentered the house. "Victoria!" he called out, his voice a touch breathless from running.

She looked at him, her eyes flashing with a moment of terror before filling with relief.

"I'm sorry," he said immediately. "I didn't mean to startle you."

"You didn't. Well, actually you did, but I'm rather glad it's only you."

Robert forced down the fresh wave of fury rising within him. He hated to see her so fearful. "Don't worry about Eversleigh. He left for London early this morning. I saw to it."

Her entire body sagged, as if all the tension she was carrying drained right out of her. "Thank God," she breathed. "Thank you."

"Victoria, we must talk."

She swallowed. "Yes, of course. I must thank you properly. If you hadn't—"

"*Stop* thanking me!" he exploded.

She blinked, confused.

"What happened last night was as much my fault as anyone else's," he said bitterly.

"No!" she cried out. "No, don't say that. You saved me."

Part of Robert wanted nothing more than to let her go on thinking him a hero. She had always made him feel big and strong and noble, and he had missed that after their separation. But his conscience wouldn't allow him to accept gratitude where none was due.

He let out a shaky breath. "We will discuss that later. Right now there are more pressing matters."

She nodded and let him lead her away from the house. She looked up with questioning eyes when she realized they were heading for the hedgerow maze.

"We'll need privacy," he explained.

She allowed herself a small smile, the first she'd felt all day. "Just so long as I know the way out."

He chuckled and wended his way through the maze until they reached a stone bench. "Two lefts, a right, and two more lefts," he whispered.

She smiled again as she smoothed her skirts down and sat. "It is engraved on my brain."

Robert sat beside her, his expression suddenly growing a touch hesitant. "Victoria— Torie."

Victoria's heart fluttered at the way he switched to the use of her nickname.

Robert's face moved expressively, as if he was seeking out the best words. Finally he said, "You cannot stay here."

She blinked. "But I thought you said that Eversleigh has left for London."

"He has. But that doesn't matter."

"It matters a great deal to me," she said.

"Torie, I can't leave you here."

"What are you saying?"

He raked a hand through his hair. "I cannot leave knowing that you are unprotected. What happened last night could easily happen again."

Victoria looked at him steadily. "Robert, last night was not the first time I have been subjected to unwanted attentions from a gentleman."

His entire body tensed. "Was that supposed to set my mind at ease?"

"I have never before been attacked with such force," she continued. "I am merely trying to say that I have become quite adept at fending off advances."

He gripped her shoulders. "If I hadn't intervened last night, he would have raped you. Possibly even killed you."

She shuddered and looked away. "I can't imagine that anything like . . . like . . . *that* will ever come to pass again. And I can protect myself against the odd pinch and lewd word."

"That is unacceptable!" he exploded. "How can you let yourself be demeaned that way?"

"No one can demean me but myself," she said in a very low voice. "Don't forget that."

He let his hands drop away from her shoulders and stood. "I know that, Torie. But you shouldn't have to remain in this intolerable situation."

"Oh, really?" She let out a hollow laugh. "And how am I supposed to extricate myself from this situation, as you so delicately put it? I have to eat, my lord."

"Torie, don't be sarcastic."

"I'm not being sarcastic! I have never been more thoroughly serious in my life. If I do not work as a governess, I will starve. I don't have any other choice."

"Yes, you do," he whispered urgently, dropping to his knees before her. "You can come with me."

She stared at him in shock. "With you?"

He nodded. "To London. We can leave today."

Victoria swallowed nervously, trying to suppress the urge to throw herself into his arms. Something burst to life within her, and she suddenly remembered exactly how she'd felt so many years ago when he had first said he wanted to marry her. But heartbreak had made her wary, and she measured her words carefully before asking, "What exactly are you proposing, my lord?"

"I'll buy you a house. And hire a staff."

Victoria felt every last hope for the future drain away. Robert wasn't proposing marriage. And he never would. Not if he made her his mistress first. Men didn't marry their mistresses.

"You'll never want for anything," he added.

Except love, Victoria thought miserably. And respectability. "What would I have to do in return?" she asked, not because she had any intention of accepting his insulting offer. She just wanted to hear him say it.

But he looked dumbfounded, startled that she'd voiced the question. "You . . . Ah . . ."

"What, Robert?" she asked sharply.

"I just want to be with you," he said, clasping her hands. His eyes slid away from hers, as if he realized just how lame his words were.

"But you won't marry me," she said, her voice dull. How silly of her to have thought, even for a moment, that they could be happy again.

He stood. "Surely you didn't think . . ."

"Obviously not. How could I possibly think that you, the Earl of Macclesfield, would deign to marry a vicar's daughter?" Her voice grew shrill. "Goodness, I've probably been plotting to fleece you out of your fortune for seven years."

Robert winced at her unexpected attack. Her words poked at something unpleasant in his heart—something that felt a bit like guilt. The image of Victoria as a greedy adventuress had never rung completely true, but what else was there for him to think? He'd seen her himself, lying in bed, sleeping soundly on the night they were supposed to elope. He felt the protective armor around his heart lock back into place and said, "Sarcasm doesn't become you, Victoria."

"Fine." She waved her arm at him. "Then our discussion is concluded."

His hand shot out like a bullet and wrapped around her wrist. "Not quite."

"Release me," she said in a low voice.

Robert took a deep breath, trying to use the time to get over the incredibly strong urge to shake her. He couldn't believe the little nitwit would rather stay here at a job she detested than come with him to London. "I am going to say this one more time," he said, his hard stare drumming into her. "I am not going to leave you here to be pawed at by every unscrupulous male who happens along."

She laughed, which really infuriated him. "Are you saying," she asked, "that the only unscrupulous male with whom I may consort is *you*?"

"Yes. No! For the love of God, woman, you can't stay here."

She lifted her chin proudly. "I don't see any other option."

Robert ground his teeth together. "I just got through telling you—"

"I said," she stated pointedly, "that I don't see

any other option. I will be no man's mistress."
She wrenched herself free of him and walked
out of the maze.

And, he realized in a daze, out of his life.

Chapter 10

Robert returned to London and attempted to immerse himself in his regular routine. He was miserable, though, so miserable that he didn't even bother to try to convince himself that he didn't care about Victoria's rejection.

He couldn't eat, he couldn't sleep. He felt like a character in a very bad, melodramatic poem. He saw Victoria everywhere—in the clouds, in the crowds, even in his damned *soup*.

If he hadn't been so wretchedly pathetic, Robert later reflected, he probably wouldn't have bothered to answer his father's summons.

Every few months, the marquess sent Robert a letter requesting his presence at Castleford Manor. At first the notes were terse orders, but lately they'd taken on a more conciliatory, almost imploring tone. The marquess wanted Robert to take a greater interest in his lands; he wanted his son to show pride in the marquessate that would one day be his. Most of all he wanted him to marry and produce an heir to carry on the Kemble name.

All of this was spelled out quite clearly—and

with increasing graciousness—in his letters to his son, but Robert merely scanned the notes and then tossed them into the fireplace. He hadn't been back to Castleford Manor in more than seven years, not since that awful day when his every dream had been shattered, and his father, instead of patting him on the back and offering him comfort, had shouted with glee and danced a jig right on his priceless mahogany desk.

The memory still made Robert's jaw clench with fury. When he had children he'd offer them support and understanding. He certainly wouldn't laugh at their defeats.

Children. Now there was an amusing concept. He wasn't very likely to leave his mark on the world in the form of little heirs. He couldn't bring himself to marry Victoria, and he was coming to realize that he couldn't imagine himself married to anyone else.

What a muck.

And so, when the latest note from his father arrived, saying that he was on his deathbed, Robert decided to humor the old man. This was the third such note he'd received in the past year; none of them had proved to be even remotely truthful. But Robert packed his bags and left for Kent anyway. Anything to get his mind off *her*.

When he arrived at his childhood home, he was not surprised to find that his father was not ill, although he did look quite a bit older than he'd remembered.

"It's good to have you home, son," the marquess said, looking rather surprised that Robert had actually answered his summons and come down from London.

"You look well," Robert said, emphasizing the last word.

The marquess coughed.

"A chest cold, perhaps?" Robert asked, raising a brow in an insolent manner.

His father shot him an annoyed glance. "I was just clearing my throat, and you well know it."

"Ah, yes, healthy as horses, we Kembles are. Healthy as mules, and just as stubborn, too."

The marquess let his nearly empty glass of whiskey clunk down on the table. "What has happened to you, Robert?"

"I beg your pardon?" This was said as Robert sprawled out on the sofa and put his feet on the table.

"You are a miserable excuse for a son. And get your feet off the table!"

His father's tone was just as it had always been when Robert was a young boy and had committed some awful transgression. Without thinking, Robert obeyed and set his feet on the floor.

"Look at you," Castleford said with distaste. "Lazing your days away in London. Drinking, whoring, gambling away your fortune."

Robert smiled humorlessly. "I'm an appallingly good card player. I've doubled my portion."

His father turned slowly around. "You don't care about anything, do you?"

"I once did," Robert whispered, suddenly feeling very hollow.

The marquess poured himself another glass of whiskey and downed it. And then, as if making a last-ditch effort, he said, "Your mother would be ashamed of you."

Robert looked up sharply and his mouth went dry. His father rarely mentioned his mother. It was several moments before he was able to say, "You don't know how she would have felt. You never really knew her. You don't know what love is."

"I loved her!" the marquess roared. "I loved your mother in ways you will never know. And by God, I knew her dreams. She wanted her son to be strong and honest and noble."

"Don't forget my responsibilities to the title," Robert said acidly.

His father turned away. "She didn't care about that," he said. "She just wanted you to be happy."

Robert closed his eyes in agony, wondering how his life would have been different if his mother had been alive when he'd courted Victoria. "I see that you have made it a priority to see her dreams fulfilled." He laughed bitterly. "Clearly, I am a happy man."

"I never meant for you to be like this," Castleford said, his face showing every one of his sixty-five years and a good ten more. He shook his head and sank down onto a chair. "I never wanted this. My God, what have I done?"

A very queer feeling began to spread in Robert's stomach. "What do you mean?" he asked.

"She came here, you know."

"*Who* came here?

"Her. The vicar's daughter."

Robert's fingers tightened around the arm of the sofa until his knuckles grew white. "Victoria?"

His father gave a curt nod.

A thousand questions raced through Robert's mind. Had the Hollingwoods turned her out? Was she ill? She must be ill, he decided. Something must be dreadfully wrong if she'd actually sought out his father. "When was she here?"

"Right after you left for London."

"Right after I—What the devil are you talking about?"

"Seven years ago."

Robert sprang to his feet. "Victoria was here seven years ago and you never told me?" He began to advance on his father. "You never said a word?"

"I didn't want to see you throw your life away." Castleford let out a bitter laugh. "But you did that anyway."

Robert clenched his fists at his sides, knowing that if he didn't he was liable to go for his father's throat. "What did she say?"

His father didn't answer quickly enough. "What did she *say*?" Robert bellowed.

"I don't remember precisely, but . . ." Castleford took a deep breath. "But she was quite put out that you had left for London. I think she really meant to keep her assignation with you."

A muscle worked violently in Robert's throat, and he doubted he was capable of forming words.

"I don't think she was after your fortune," the marquess said softly. "I still don't think a woman of her background could ever make a proper countess, but I will admit—" He cleared his throat. He was not a man who liked to show weakness. "I will admit that I might have been mistaken about her. She probably did love you."

Robert was frighteningly still for a moment, and then he suddenly whirled around and slammed his fist against the wall. The marquess stepped back nervously, aware that his son very likely had wanted to plant that fist squarely in his face.

"God*damn* you!" Robert exploded. "How could you have done this to me?"

"At the time I thought it was best. I see now that I was wrong."

Robert closed his eyes, his face agonized. "What did you say to her?"

The marquess turned away, unable to face his son.

"What did you say to her?"

"I told her you'd never intended to marry her." Castleford swallowed uncomfortably. "I told her you were just dallying with her."

"And she thought . . . Oh, God, she thought . . ." Robert sank down on his haunches. When she'd discovered he'd left for London, Victoria must have thought that he'd been lying to her all along, that he'd never loved her.

And then he'd insulted her by asking her to become his mistress. Shame washed over him, and he wondered if he would ever be able to look her in the eye again. He wondered if she would even allow him enough time in her presence to apologize.

"Robert," his father said. "I'm sorry."

Robert rose slowly, barely aware of his motions. "I will never forgive you for this," he said, his voice flat.

"Robert!" the marquess yelled.

But his son had already left the room.

Robert didn't realize where he was going until the vicar's cottage came into view. *Why* had Victoria been in bed that night? Why hadn't she met him as she'd promised?

He stood in front of the house for five long minutes, doing nothing but staring at the brass knocker on the front door. His thoughts were running in every direction, and his eyes were so unfocused that he didn't see the ruffle of the curtains in the drawing room window.

The door suddenly opened, and Eleanor Lyndon appeared. "My lord?" she said, obviously surprised to see him.

Robert blinked until he was able to focus on her. She looked much the same, except that her strawberry blond hair, which had always been such a cloud around her face, was now pulled back into a neat bun. "Ellie," he said hoarsely.

"What are you doing here?"

"I-I don't know."

"You don't look well. Would you—" She swallowed. "Would you like to come in?"

Robert nodded unsteadily and followed her into the drawing room.

"My father isn't here," she said. "He's at the church."

Robert just stared at her.

"Are you certain you're not ill? You look rather queer."

He let out a funny little breath, one that would have been a laugh if he hadn't been so dazed. Ellie had always been refreshingly forthright.

"My lord? Robert?"

He remained silent for a few moments more, and then he suddenly asked, "What happened?"

She blinked. "I beg your pardon?"

"What happened that night?" he repeated, his voice taking on a desperate urgency.

Comprehension dawned on Ellie's face and she looked away. "You don't know?"

"I thought I did, but now I . . . I don't know anything anymore."

"He tied her up."

Robert felt as if he'd been punched in the stomach. "What?"

"My father," Ellie said with a nervous swallow. "He woke up and found Victoria packing her bags. Then he tied her up. He said you would ruin her."

"Oh, my God." Robert couldn't breathe.

"It was awful. Papa was in such a rage. I've never seen him like that. I wanted to help her. I really did. I covered her up with her blankets so she wouldn't catch a chill."

Robert thought of her lying in bed. He'd been so furious with her, and all the time she'd been bound hand and foot. He suddenly felt intensely ill.

Ellie continued her story. "But he tied me up, too. I think he knew that I would have freed her so she could go to you. As it was, she sneaked out of the house and ran to Castleford Manor just as soon as she was free. When she returned, her skin was all scratched from running through the woods."

Robert looked away, his mouth moving but unable to form words.

"She never forgave him, you know," Ellie said. Her shoulders lifted into a sad shrug. "I have made my peace with my father. I don't think what he did was right, but we have reached an understanding of sorts. But Victoria . . ."

"Tell me, Ellie," Robert urged.

"She never returned home. We haven't seen her in seven years."

He turned to her, his blue eyes intense. "I didn't know, Ellie. I swear it."

"We were very surprised when we learned you'd left the district," she said flatly. "I thought Victoria might perish of a broken heart."

"I didn't know," he repeated.

"She thought you'd been planning to ravish her, and that when you didn't succeed you grew bored and left." Ellie's gaze dropped to the floor. "We didn't know what else to think. It was what my father had predicted all along."

"No," Robert whispered. "No. I loved her."

"Why did you leave, then?"

"My father had threatened to cut me off. When she didn't meet me that night, I assumed she'd decided I wasn't worth it anymore." He felt ashamed just saying the words. As if Victoria would have ever cared about such a thing. He stood suddenly, feeling so off balance that he had to hold on to the end of a table for a moment to steady himself.

"Would you like a spot of tea?" Ellie asked as she rose. "You really don't look at all well."

"Ellie," he said, his voice growing resolute for the first time during their conversation, "I haven't been well for seven years. If you'll excuse me."

He left without another word, and in a great hurry.

Ellie had no doubt where he was going.

"What do you mean you turned her out?"

"Without a reference," Lady Hollingwood said proudly.

Robert took a deep breath, aware that for the first time in his life he was sorely tempted to punch a woman in the face. "You let—" He stopped and cleared his throat, needing the time to get his temper under control. "You dismissed a gently bred woman without a character? Where do you expect her to go?"

"I can assure you that is none of my concern. I certainly did not want that trollop near my son, and it would have been unconscionable of me to give her a reference so that she might corrupt other young children with her unsavory influence."

"It would behoove you not to call my future countess a trollop, Lady Hollingwood," Robert said tightly.

"Your future countess?" Lady Hollingwood's words came out in a panicked rush. "Miss Lyndon?"

"Indeed." Robert had long ago perfected the art of the glacial stare, and he speared Lady Hollingwood with one of his best.

"But-but you cannot marry her!"

"Is that so?"

"Eversleigh told me that she all but threw herself at him."

"Eversleigh is an ass."

Lady Hollingwood stiffened at his foul language. "Lord Macclesfield, I must ask you—"

He cut her off. "Where is she?"

"I certainly do not know."

Robert advanced on her, his eyes cold and hard. "You have no idea? Not a single thought in your head?"

"She, ah, she might have contacted the employment agency she used when I hired her."

"Ah, now we're getting somewhere. I knew you were not completely useless."

Lady Hollingwood swallowed uncomfortably. "I have the information right here. Let me copy it down for you."

Robert nodded curtly and crossed his arms. He'd learned to use his size to intimidate, and right then he wanted nothing more than to intimidate the hell out of Lady Hollingwood. She scurried across the room and fished a sheet of paper from a desk. With shaking hands she copied an address down for him.

"Here you are," she said, holding out the slip. "I do hope this little misunderstanding will not affect our future friendship."

"My dear lady, I cannot conceive of a single thing you could do that would ever make me want to lay eyes on you again."

Lady Hollingwood paled, watching all her social aspirations go up in flames.

Robert looked at the London address on the paper in his hand, then left the room without even so much as a nod toward his hostess.

Victoria had come looking for a job, the woman at the employment agency told him with an unsympathetic shrug, but she'd sent her away. It was impossible to place a governess without a character reference.

Robert's hands began to shake. Never had he felt so damned impotent. Where the hell was she?

Several weeks later Victoria hummed cheerfully as she carried her load of sewing to work. She couldn't remember the last time she'd felt so happy. Oh, there was still the lingering heartache over Robert, but she'd come to accept that it would always be a part of her.

But she was content. There had been a moment of wrenching panic when the lady at the employment agency had declared her unemployable, but then Victoria had remembered the sewing she had done while growing up. If there was one thing she could do, it was stitch a perfect seam, and she soon found employment in a dressmaker's shop.

She was paid by the piece, and she found the work immensely satisfying. If she did a good job, she did a good job, and no one could say otherwise. There were no Lady Hollingwoods leaning over her shoulder complaining that their children couldn't recite the alphabet fast enough and then blaming Victoria when they stumbled over M, N, and O. Victoria rather liked the non-subjective aspect of her new job. If she sewed a seam straight, no one could say it was crooked.

So unlike being a governess. Victoria couldn't have been more pleased.

It had been a dreadful blow when Lady Hollingwood dismissed her. That rat Eversleigh had grown spiteful and spread tales, and of course Lady H. would never take the word of a governess over that of a peer of the realm.

And Robert was gone, so he couldn't defend her. Not that she wanted him to, or expected him to. She expected nothing from him after he'd insulted her so terribly by asking her to be his mistress.

Victoria shook her head. She tried not to think about that awful encounter. Her hopes had been raised so high and then dashed so low. She would never, ever forgive him for that.

Ha! As if he would ever beg her forgiveness, the lout.

Victoria found it made her feel much better to think of him as Robert-the-lout. She wished she'd thought of it seven years earlier.

Victoria balanced her load of sewing on her hip as she pushed open the rear door to Madame Lambert's Dress Shop. "Good day, Katie!" she called out, greeting the other seamstress.

The blond girl looked up with relief in her eyes. "Victoria, I'm so glad you're finally 'ere."

Victoria set her bundle down. "Is something amiss?"

"Madame is . . ." Katie paused, looked over her shoulder, and then continued in a whisper, "Madame is frantic. Four customers in the front, and she—"

"Is Victoria here?" Madame Lambert burst into the back room, not bothering to adopt the French accent she used with customers. She spied Victoria, who was sorting through the sewing she'd brought home with her the previous night. "Thank the heavens. I need you in front."

Victoria quickly put down the sleeve she was holding and hurried out. Madame Lambert liked to use Victoria in the front of the shop because she spoke with a cultured accent.

Madame led Victoria over to a girl of about sixteen years who was doing her best to ignore the stout woman—most probably her mother—standing next her.

"Veectoria," Madame said, suddenly French, "zees eez Miss Harriet Brightbill. Her mother"—she motioned to the other lady—would like some assistance een outfitting zee young lady."

"I know exactly what I want," Mrs. Brightbill said.

"And I know exactly what I want," Harriet added, hands planted firmly on hips.

Victoria bit back a smile. "Perhaps we might be able to find something that you both admire."

Mrs. Brightbill let out a loud harrumph, which caused Harriet to turn to her with a beleaguered expression and say, "Mother!"

For the next hour, Victoria displayed bolt upon

bolt of fabric. Silks, satins, and muslins—they were all brought out for inspection. It was soon apparent that Harriet had much better taste than her mother, and Victoria found herself spending a great deal of time convincing Mrs. Brightbill that flounces were not necessary for social success.

Finally Mrs. Brightbill, who really did love her daughter and was obviously just trying to do what she thought was best, excused herself and went off to the retiring room. Harriet sank into a nearby chair with a huge sigh. "She's exhausting, isn't she?" she asked Victoria.

Victoria just smiled.

"Thank goodness my cousin has offered to take us out for cakes. I shouldn't be able to bear another bout of shopping just now. We still must attend to the milliner and the glove maker."

"I'm certain you will have a lovely time," Victoria said diplomatically.

"The only lovely time I shall have is when all the packages arrive home and I may open them— Oh look! There is my cousin walking by the window. Robert! Robert!"

Victoria didn't even stop to react. The name Robert did strange things to her, and she immediately darted behind a potted plant. The bell on the door jingled, and she peeked out between the leaves.

Robert. *Her* Robert.

She nearly groaned. Her life only needed this. Just when she had begun to carve out a bit of contentment, he had to come along and turn everything topsy-turvy. She wasn't entirely sure what she felt about him anymore, but one thing she was sure of—she didn't want a confrontation with him here.

She began to inch toward the door to the rear room.

"Cousin Robert," she heard Harriet say as she crouched behind a chair, "thank goodness you are here. I declare that Mother is going to drive me mad."

He chuckled—a rich, warm sound that made Victoria's heart ache. "If she hasn't driven you batty as of yet, I'd say you're immune, dear Harriet."

Harriet let out a world-weary sigh, the sort that only a sixteen-year-old who hasn't seen the world can do. "If it hadn't been for the lovely saleslady here—" There was a dreadful pause, and Victoria scurried on her hands and knees along the back of the sofa.

Harriet planted her hands on her hips. "I say, what happened to Victoria?"

"Victoria?"

Victoria gulped. She didn't like the tone of his voice. Only five more feet to the back door. She could make it. She slowly rose to her feet behind a dressmaker's dummy wearing a gown of forest green satin, and, scrupulously keeping her back to the room, sidestepped the last few feet to the back room.

She could make it. She knew she could.

Her hand reached for the knob. She twisted. She was in. It was almost too easy.

She'd made it! She breathed an enormous sigh of relief and sagged against the wall. Thank the

Lord. Dealing with Robert would have been beyond dreadful.

"Victoria?" Katie said, looking up at her questioningly. "I thought you were 'elping—"

The door burst open with a thundering crash. Katie shrieked. Victoria groaned.

"Victoria?" Robert yelled. "Thank God, Victoria!"

He leapt over a pile of fabric bolts and knocked down a dressmaker's dummy. He stopped when he was barely a foot away from her. Victoria stared at him, bewildered. He was breathing hard, his face was haggard, and he appeared to be completely unaware that a length of Spanish lace was draped over his right shoulder.

And then, either unmindful of his audience, or simply unaware that Katie, Madame Lambert, Harriet, Mrs. Brightbill, and three other customers were watching, he reached out like a starving man and yanked her against him.

Then he began to kiss her. Everywhere.

Chapter 11

Robert ran his hands up her arms, across her shoulders, down her back—all just to assure himself that she was really there. He paused for just a moment to stare into her eyes, and then took her face in his hands and kissed her.

He kissed her with all the passion he'd kept bottled up for seven years.

He kissed her with all the agony he'd experienced these last few weeks, not knowing if she was dead or alive.

He kissed her with everything he was and everything he wanted to be. And he would have kept kissing her if a hand hadn't closed around his left ear and yanked him away.

"Robert Kemble!" his aunt yelled. "You should be ashamed of yourself."

Robert shot a beseeching glance at Victoria, who looked quite dazed and mortified. "I need to talk to you," he said firmly, pointing his finger at her.

"What is the meaning of this?" Madame Lambert demanded, with nary a trace of a French accent.

"This woman," Robert said, "is my future wife."

"What?" Victoria screeched.

"Heavens above," Mrs. Brightbill breathed.

"Oh, Victoria!" Katie said excitedly.

"Robert, why didn't you tell us?" Harriet exclaimed.

"Who the devil are you?" Madame Lambert asked, and no one was quite sure if the question was directed at Robert or Victoria.

All of the above was uttered at much the same time, leading to such confusion that Victoria finally yelled, "Stop! All of you!"

Every head swiveled in Victoria's direction. She blinked, not quite certain what to do now that she had everyone's attention. Finally she cleared her throat and lifted her chin. "If you'll all excuse me," she said with what she knew was a pathetic display of pride, "I'm not feeling at all the thing. I believe I'll go home a touch early today."

All hell broke loose again. Everyone had a firm and vocal opinion about the uncommon situation. In the melee Victoria tried to slip out the back door, but Robert was too fast. His hand wrapped around her wrist, and she felt herself being hauled back into the center of the room.

"You're not going anywhere," he said, his voice somehow fierce and tender at the same time. "Not until I talk to you."

Harriet scooted under her mother's frantically waving arms and darted to Victoria's side. "Are you really going to marry my cousin?" she asked, her face a picture of romantic delight.

"No," Victoria said, shaking her head weakly.

"Yes," Robert barked. "She is."

"But you don't want to marry me."

"Obviously I do, or I wouldn't have declared it in front of the biggest gossip in London."

"He means my mother," Harriet said helpfully.

Victoria sat down on a bolt of green satin and let her face fall into her hands.

Madame Lambert marched over to her side. "I don't know who you are," she said, jabbing her finger into Robert's shoulder, "but I cannot have you assaulting my shopgirls."

"I am the Earl of Macclesfield."

"The Earl of—" Her eyes bugged out. "An *earl?*"

Victoria moaned, wanting to be anyplace but where she was.

Madame crouched down beside her. "Really, my girl, he's an earl. And did he say he wanted to marry you?"

Victoria just shook her head, her face still in her hands.

"For the love of God!" an imperious voice demanded. "Can none of you see that the poor girl is distressed?"

An older lady dressed all in purple made her way to Victoria's side and cast a maternal arm around her shoulders.

Victoria looked up and blinked. "Who are you?" she asked.

"I am the dowager Duchess of Beechwood."

Victoria looked over at Robert. "Another relation of yours?"

The dowager answered in his stead. "I can assure you that scoundrel is no relation of mine. I was minding my own business, shopping for a new gown for my granddaughter's first ball, and—"

"Oh, God," Victoria moaned, letting her head fall back into her hands. This brought new meaning to the word "mortification." When total strangers felt the need to pity her . . .

The dowager fixed a sharp stare at Madame Lambert. "Can't you see that the poor dear needs a cup of tea?"

Madame Lambert hesitated, clearly not wanting to miss a minute of the action, then nudged Katie in the ribs. The shopgirl ran off to prepare some tea.

"Victoria," Robert said, trying to sound calm and patient—a difficult endeavor considering his audience. "I need to talk with you."

She lifted her head and wiped her damp eyes, feeling a bit emboldened by all of the feminine sympathy and outrage surrounding her. "I don't want to have anything to do with you," she said with a slight sniffle. "Not a thing."

Her performance caused Robert's aunt to move to the side of Victoria not occupied by the dowager Duchess of Beechwood and drape her with yet another maternal arm.

"Aunt Brightbill," Robert said in an exasperated voice.

"*What* did you do to the poor girl?" his aunt demanded.

Robert's mouth fell open in disbelief. It was

now quite obvious that every female in Britain—with the possible exception of the odious Lady Hollingwood—was aligned against him. "I am trying to ask her to marry me," he bit out. "Surely that counts for something."

Mrs. Brightbill turned to Victoria with an expression that flickered between concern and practicality. "He *is* offering for you, poor dear." Her voice dropped an octave. "Is there a reason why it would be imperative you accept?"

Harriet's mouth fell open. Even she knew what that meant.

"Absolutely not!" Victoria said loudly. And then, just because she knew it would get him into such big trouble with their conventional female audience, and, of course, because she was still rather furious with him, she added, "He tried to compromise me, but I didn't let him."

Mrs. Brightbill jumped to her feet with surprising speed considering her girth and swatted her nephew with her reticule. "How dare you!" she yelled. "The poor dear is clearly gently bred, even if circumstances have brought her low." She paused in mid-thought, clearly just realizing that her nephew—an *earl*, for goodness' sake—was offering for a shopgirl, and turned back to Victoria. "I say, you are gently bred, aren't you? I mean to say, you do sound gently bred."

"Victoria is all that is gentle and kind," Robert said.

The woman of whom he spoke merely sniffed and ignored his compliment.

"Her father is the vicar at Bellfield," he added, and then gave a very brief recounting of their history.

"Oh, how romantic." Harriet sighed.

"It was not in the least bit romantic," Victoria snapped. Then she added a bit more gently, "Just so you don't get any foolish notions of elopement in your head."

Harriet's mother patted Victoria approvingly on the shoulder. "Robert," she announced to the room at large, "you will be a lucky gentleman indeed if you can persuade this exceedingly lovely and practical young woman to accept your suit."

He opened his mouth to say something, but was interrupted by the howl of the teakettle. He was then roundly ignored while the women saw to the tea. Victoria sipped from her cup while she received more approving pats and several concerned "poor dears."

Robert wasn't sure when it had happened, but the balance of power had definitely shifted against him. He was only one man against—his eyes swept the room—eight women.

Eight? Bloody hell. The room started to feel very tight. He tugged at his cravat.

Finally, when some woman in a pink dress—he had no idea who she was and could only deduce that she was another innocent by-stander—moved to allow him a view of Victoria's face, he said for what seemed like the hundredth time, "Victoria, I need to talk with you."

She took another sip of her tea, received another maternal pat from the dowager Duchess of Beechwood, and said, "No."

He took a step forward and his tone grew vaguely menacing. "Victoria . . ."

He would have taken another step forward, but eight women simultaneously speared him with disdainful glares. Even he was not man enough to withstand that. He threw up his arms and muttered, "Too many hens."

Victoria just sat there amidst her new band of admirers, looking disgustingly serene.

Robert took a deep breath and jabbed his finger in the air. "This is not the end of this, Victoria. I *will* speak with you."

And then, with another incomprehensible comment about roosters and hens, he stalked from the dress shop.

"Is he still there?"

At Victoria's request, Katie once again peered through the storefront window. "'Is carriage 'asn't moved."

"Damn and blast," Victoria muttered, which caused Mrs. Brightbill to say, "I thought you said your father was a vicar."

Victoria glanced at the clock. Robert's carriage had been parked in front of the dress shop for two hours now, and he showed no signs of leaving. Neither did any of the ladies who had witnessed their bizarre reunion. Madame Lambert had had to boil four more pots of tea to accommodate everyone.

"He cannot remain in the street all day," Harriet said. "Can he?"

"He's an earl," her mother replied in a matter-of-fact voice. "He can do anything he pleases."

"And that," Victoria declared, "is just the problem." How dare he come waltzing back into her life, assuming that she would throw herself prostrate at his feet, and just because he suddenly had it in his head that he once more wanted to marry her.

He wanted to *marry* her. Victoria shook her head, quite unable to believe it. Once it had been her deepest dream; now it seemed more like a cruel mockery of fate.

He wanted to marry her? Ha! It was too damned late for that.

"Did you just curse again?" Harriet whispered, darting a furtive glance at her mother.

Victoria looked up, surprised. She hadn't realized she'd spoken her thoughts. "*He* does that to me," she growled.

"Cousin Robert?"

Victoria nodded. "He thinks he can manage my life."

Harriet shrugged. "He tries to manage everyone's life. He usually does a bang-up job of it, actually. We've never been in such good funds as since he started managing our money for us."

Victoria looked at her oddly. "Isn't it considered bad *ton* to discuss money?"

"Yes, but you're family." This was said with an expansive wave of Harriet's arm.

"I am not family," Victoria ground out.

"You will be," Harriet replied, "if Cousin Robert has anything to do with it. And he usually gets what he wants."

Victoria planted her hands on her hips and glared out the window at his carriage. "Not this time."

"Er, Victoria," Harriet said, looking a touch anxious, "I haven't known you for very long, so it would be quite beyond me to know the intricacies of your facial expressions, but I must say I don't like the look in your eye."

Victoria turned slowly around, baffled. "What the devil are you talking about?"

"Whatever it is you're thinking of doing, I must caution you against it."

"I'm going to talk with him," Victoria said resolutely, and then, before anyone could stop her, she marched out of the dress shop.

Robert jumped down from his carriage in an instant. He opened his mouth as if to say something, but Victoria cut him off. "You wanted to speak with me?" she said, her voice sharp.

"Yes, I—"

"Good. I want to talk with you, too."

"Torie, I—"

"Don't think, even for a second, that you may manage my life. I don't know what has prompted your remarkable change of heart, but I am not a puppet who may be maneuvered at your will."

"Of course not, but—"

"You cannot insult me the way you did and expect me to forget about it."

"I realize that, but—"

"Furthermore, I am quite content without you. You are high-handed, arrogant, insufferable—"

"—and you love me," Robert interrupted, looking quite pleased to have finally gotten a word in edgewise.

"I most certainly do not!"

"Victoria," he said in an irritatingly pacifying tone, "you will always love me."

Her mouth fell open. "You are mad."

He swept into a courtly bow and raised her limp hand to his lips. "I have never been saner than I am at this very moment."

Victoria's breath caught in her throat. Fragments of memory flashed through her mind, and she was seventeen again. Seventeen, utterly in love, and desperate to be kissed. "No," she said, choking on her words. "No. You are not going to do this to me again."

His eyes burned into hers. "Victoria, I love you."

She wrenched her hand away. "I can't listen to this." And then she ran back into the shop.

Robert watched her retreating form and sighed, wondering why he was so surprised that she hadn't fallen into his arms and passionately declared her undying love for him. Of course she was going to be angry with him. Furious. He had been so insane with worry and so racked with guilt that he hadn't for a moment stopped to think how she might react to his sudden reappearance in her life.

He didn't have time to ponder this any further, however, because his aunt came storming out of the dress shop.

"What," she screeched, "did you say to that poor girl? Don't you think you've done enough to her for one day?"

Robert impaled his aunt with a glare. Really, all of this interference was getting to be most annoying. "I told her that I love her."

That seemed to take some of the air out of her sails. "You did?"

Robert didn't even bother to nod.

"Well, whatever you said, don't say it again."

"You want me to tell her that I *don't* love her?"

His aunt planted her hands on her ample hips. "She is very upset."

Robert had had just about enough of female meddling. "Damn it, so am I."

Mrs. Brightbill drew back and placed an affronted hand on her chest. "Robert Kemble, did you just curse in my presence?"

"I have spent the last seven years utterly miserable because of a stupid misunderstanding propagated by a pair of goddamn interfering fathers. Frankly, Aunt Brightbill, your offended sensibilities are not high on my list of priorities just now."

"Robert Kemble, I have never been more insulted—"

"—in your entire life." He sighed, rolling his eyes.

"—in my entire life. And I don't care if you *are* an earl. I'm going to advise that poor, poor, dear of a girl not to marry you." With a loud harrumph, Mrs. Brightbill turned on her heel and stomped back into the dress shop.

"Hens!" Robert yelled at the door. "All of you! You're nothing but a bunch of hens!"

"Begging your pardon, milord," said the groom who'd been leaning against the side of the carriage, "but I don't think it's such a bonny time to be a rooster."

Robert turned a withering glare on the man. "MacDougal, if you weren't so bloody good with the horses—"

"I know, I know, you'd have thrown me out years ago."

"There is always today," Robert growled.

MacDougal smiled with the confidence of a man who has become more friend than servant. "Did you notice how quickly she said she didna love you?"

"I noticed," Robert growled.

"Just wanted to let you know. In case you didna notice."

Robert whipped his head around. "You do realize that you're rather impertinent for a servant."

"It's why you keep me on, my lord."

Robert knew it was true, but he didn't much feel like admitting it just then, so he turned his attention back to the storefront. "You can barricade yourselves all you want," he yelled, waving his fist in the air. "I'm not leaving!"

"What did he say?" Mrs. Brightbill asked, nursing her bruised feelings with her seventh cup of tea.

"He said he's not leaving," Harriet replied.

"I could have told you that," Victoria muttered. -

"More tea, please!" Mrs. Brightbill said, waving her now empty cup in the air. Katie hurried over with more of the steaming beverage. The older lady drained the cup and then stood, smoothing her skirts with her hands. "If you'll all excuse me," she announced to the room at large. Then she toddled off to the retiring room.

"Madame's going to have to buy another chamber pot," Katie muttered.

Victoria shot her a disapproving look. She'd been trying to educate the girl in manners and deportment for several weeks now. Still, it was a sign of her jangled nerves that she replied, "No more tea. Not another drop for any of you."

Harriet looked up with an owlish expression and set her cup firmly down.

"This is insanity!" Victoria announced. "He has us trapped."

"Actually," Harriet said, "he only has you trapped. I could leave at any time, and he probably wouldn't notice."

"Oh, he'd notice," Victoria muttered. "He notices everything. I've never met a more stubborn, disgustingly organized—"

"I'm sure that's quite enough, dear," Madame Lambert cut in, aware that her shopgirl might be insulting her clientele. "After all, his lordship is Miss Brightbill's cousin."

"Oh, don't stop on my account," Harriet said enthusiastically. "I am enjoying myself immensely."

"Harriet!" Victoria suddenly exclaimed.

"Yes?"

"Harriet."

"I believe you said that already."

Victoria stared at the girl, her brain whirring at triple-speed. "Harriet, you might just be the answer to my prayers."

"I rather doubt I'm the answer to anyone's prayers," Harriet replied. "I'm forever getting into scrapes and speaking without thinking first."

Victoria smiled and patted her hand. "I find it most endearing."

"Do you really? How perfectly lovely. I shall adore having you as my cousin."

Victoria forced herself not to clench her teeth. "I shan't be your cousin, Harriet."

"I really wish you would. Cousin Robert isn't so bad once you get to know him."

Victoria forbore to point out that she already did know the man in question. "Harriet, if you could do me a favor?"

"I should be delighted."

"I need you to be a distraction."

"Oh, that will be easy. Mama is forever calling me a distraction."

"Would you mind terribly running out of the front of the store and distracting his lordship? So that I might slip out the back way?"

Harriet furrowed her brow. "If I do that he won't have a chance to court you."

Victoria thought herself the holiest kind of saint for not yelling out "Exactly!" Instead she said in gentle tones, "Harriet, I am not going to marry your cousin under any circumstances. But if I do not escape this store soon, we may very well be trapped here all through the night. Robert shows no sign of leaving."

Harriet appeared undecided.

Victoria decided to play a trump card and whispered, "Your mother might grow testy."

Harriet turned green. "Very well."

"Just give me a moment to get ready." Victoria hastily began to gather her things.

"What shall I say to him?"

"Whatever you like."

Harriet pursed her lips. "I am not certain that this is a sensible plan."

Victoria halted in her tracks. "Harriet, I am begging you."

With a loud sigh and a dramatic shrug of her shoulders, the younger girl pushed open the door to the dress shop and stepped outside.

"Brilliant, brilliant, brilliant," Victoria whispered, dashing through the back room. She pulled her cloak tightly around her shoulders and slipped through the back door.

Freedom! Victoria felt almost giddy.

She was aware that she was enjoying herself perhaps a touch too much; there was something incredibly satisfying about outwitting Robert. Eventually she would have to face her emotions and deal with the fact that the man who had broken her heart twice was back, but for now beating him at his own game would be enough.

"Ha!" she said, grinning like an idiot at the brick wall of a neighboring building. All she had to do was make her way down the rest of the alleyway, take a left, and she'd be out of his clutches. At least for today.

Victoria scurried down the back steps to the shop. But when her foot touched the cobblestones of the alley, she sensed a presence.

Robert! It had to be.

But as she turned she saw not Robert but a huge black-haired man with a frightening scar running down his cheek.

Then he reached for her.

Victoria dropped her satchel and screamed.

"Hush up, lassie," the villain said. "I'm not going to hurt you."

Victoria saw no reason to believe him, and she delivered a swift kick to his shin before taking off and trying to reach the end of the alleyway, where she prayed she could disappear into the London crowds.

But he was fast, or maybe she just didn't know how to kick hard enough, because he caught her around her waist and hauled her up until her feet no longer touched the ground. She thrashed, screamed, grunted; she wasn't about to let this thug carry her off without inflicting a bit of pain in the process.

She managed to land a sound whack on the side of his head, and he dropped her, letting out a loud expletive in the process. Victoria scrambled to her feet, but she'd only gained a few yards when she felt her assailant's hand close around some of the loose fabric of her cloak.

And then she heard the words she dreaded most.

"Your lordship!" the villain bellowed.

Lordship? Victoria's heart sank. She should have known.

The large man yelled out again. "If you dinna get yourself around the corner, I'll quit before you can dismiss me again!"

Victoria slumped, closing her eyes so she wouldn't have to see Robert's satisfied smile as he rounded the corner.

Chapter 12

B y the time Victoria opened her eyes, Robert was standing in front of her. "Are they coming after you?" he demanded.

"Who?"

"Them. The women," he said, sounding very much as if he were referring to a new breed of insect.

Victoria tried to yank her arm from his grasp. "They're still drinking tea."

"Thank the Lord."

"Your aunt invited me to come live with her, by the way."

Robert muttered something under his breath.

Silence reigned for a moment, and then Victoria said, "I really must be getting home, so if you would please release my arm . . ." She smiled tightly, determined to be polite if it killed her.

He crossed his arms, spread his feet until they were shoulder distance apart, and said, "I'm not going anywhere without you."

"Well, I'm not going anywhere *with* you, so I really don't see—"

"Victoria, do not strain my temper."

Her eyes bugged out. "What did you just say?"

"I said—"

"I heard what you said!" She smacked his shoulder with the heel of her hand. "How dare you even presume to tell me not to strain your temper. You sent a thug after me! A villain. I could have been injured."

The burly man who had grabbed her bristled. "Milord," he said, "I really must interrupt."

Robert's lips twitched. "Victoria, MacDougal objects to being called a villain. I believe you have hurt his feelings."

Victoria just stared at him, quite unable to believe the direction the conversation had taken.

"I was most gentle with her," MacDougal said.

"Victoria," Robert said. "Perhaps an apology is in order."

"An apology!" she screeched, having just been pushed a mile past her boiling point. "An apology! I think not."

Robert turned to his servant with a long-suffering expression. "I don't think she's going to apologize."

MacDougal sighed magnanimously. "The lassie has had a distressing day."

Victoria tried to figure out which one of them she wanted to punch first.

Robert said something to MacDougal, and the Scotsman quit the scene, presumably to ready the carriage waiting around the corner.

"Robert," Victoria said firmly. "I am going home."

"A fine idea. I'll escort you."

"*Alone.*"

"Much too dangerous for a woman by herself," he said briskly, obviously trying to keep his temper in check under a facade of efficiency.

"I have managed admirably for the last few weeks, thank you very much."

"Ah yes, the last few weeks," he said, a muscle starting to twitch in his cheek. "Shall I tell you how I have spent the last few weeks?"

"I'm sure I can't prevent you from doing so."

"I spent the last few weeks in a state of sheer terror. I had no clue as to your whereabouts—"

"I can assure you," she said acerbically, "that I had no idea you were looking for me."

"Why," he bit out, "didn't you inform anyone of your plans?"

"And just whom was I supposed to tell? Lady Hollingwood? Oh, yes, we were the *best* of friends. You? You, who have shown such regard for my well-being?"

"What about your sister?"

"I did tell my sister. I penned her a note just last week."

Robert thought back over the past month. He had gone to see Eleanor two weeks ago. She couldn't have heard from Victoria by then. He recognized that much of his temper was due to the fact that he'd been scared out of his mind for the past few weeks, and he tried to gentle his tone. "Victoria, would you please come with me? I'll take you to my home, where we might talk in private."

She stamped on his foot. "Is this another one of your horrid, insulting offers? Oh, I'm sorry, would you prefer to call them proposals? Disgusting, degrading—"

"Victoria," he drawled, "you're going to run out of adjectives very soon."

"Oh!" she burst out, quite unable to think of anything better, then threw up her arms in exasperation. "I'm leaving."

His hand closed around the collar of her cloak, and he reeled her back in. "I believe I told you," he said coolly, "that you are not going anywhere without me." He began to drag her around the corner to his carriage.

"Robert," she hissed. "You are causing a scene."

He cocked a brow. "Do I look as if I care?"

She tried a different tactic. "Robert, just what is it you want of me?"

"Why, to marry you. I thought I'd made that clear."

"What you made *clear*," she said furiously, "is that you want me to be your mistress."

"That," he said firmly, "was a mistake. Now I'm asking you to be my wife."

"Very well. I refuse."

"Refusal is not an option."

She looked as if she might go for his throat at any moment. "Last time I checked, the Church of England did not perform marriages without the consent of both parties."

"Torie," he said harshly, "do you have any idea how worried I have been about you?"

"Not a bit," she said with false brightness. "But I'm tired and really would like to be getting home."

"You fell off the bloody face of the earth. My God, when Lady Hollingwood told me she'd dismissed you . . ."

"Yes, well, we all know whose fault that was," she snapped. "But as it happens, I am now exceedingly happy with my new life, so I suppose I should thank you."

He ignored her. "Victoria, I found out . . ." He stopped and cleared his throat. "I spoke to your sister."

She went white.

"I didn't know your father had tied you up. I swear I didn't."

Victoria swallowed and looked away, painfully aware of the tears pricking her eyes. "Don't make me think about that," she said, hating the choked sound of her voice. "I don't want to think about it. I'm happy now. Please, let me have a bit of stability."

"Victoria." His voice was achingly soft. "I love you. I have always loved you."

She shook her head furiously, still not trusting herself to look at his face.

"I love you," he repeated. "I want to spend my life with you."

"It's too late," she whispered.

He whirled her around. "Don't say that! We are no better than animals if we cannot learn from our mistakes and move forward."

She lifted her chin. "It isn't that. I don't want

to marry you anymore." And she didn't, she realized. Part of her would always love him, but she'd found an intoxicating independence since she'd moved to London. She was finally her own woman, and she was discovering that having control over her life was a heady feeling, indeed.

He paled and whispered, "You're just saying that."

"I mean what I say, Robert. I don't want to marry you."

"You're angry," he reasoned. "You're angry, and you want to hurt me, and you have every right to feel that way."

"I'm not angry." She paused. "Well, yes, I am, but that's not why I'm refusing you."

He crossed his arms. "Why, then? Why won't you even listen to me?"

"Because I'm happy now! Is that so difficult for you to understand? I like my position and I love my independence. For the first time in seven years I am perfectly content, and I don't want to upset the balance."

"You're happy *here*?" He waved his hand at the storefront. "Here, as a shopgirl?"

"Yes," she said icily, "I am. I realize that this might be a bit much for your refined tastes to understand—"

"Don't be sarcastic, Torie."

"Then I suppose I cannot say anything." She clamped her mouth shut.

Robert began to pull her gently toward his waiting carriage. "I'm sure you'll be more comfortable if we can discuss this privately."

"No, you mean *you'll* be more comfortable."

"I mean we both will," he bit out, his temper showing signs of fraying.

She started to struggle against him, dimly aware that she was causing a scene but beyond caring about it. "If you think I'm going to get into a carriage with you . . ."

"Victoria, I give you my word that you will not come to harm."

"That depends on one's definition of 'harm,' don't you think?"

He abruptly let go of her and made a great show of holding his hands in the air in an unthreatening manner. "I give you my vow that I will not lay a hand upon your person."

She narrowed her eyes. "And why should I believe you?"

"Because," he growled, clearly losing patience with her, "I have never broken a promise to you."

She let out a snort, and not a particularly ladylike one at that. "Oh, please."

A muscle began to work in his throat. Honor had always been of paramount importance to Robert, and Victoria knew that she had just jabbed him right where it hurt.

When he finally spoke, his voice was low and intense. "I have never broken a direct promise to you or anyone. I might not have always treated you with the"—he swallowed convulsively—"respect you deserve, but I have never broken a vow."

Victoria exhaled, knowing that he spoke the truth. "You will deliver me home?"

He nodded curtly. "Where do you live?"

She gave him her address, which he repeated to MacDougal.

He reached for her, but Victoria pulled her arm away and instead circled around him and hoisted herself into the conveyance.

Robert exhaled raggedly, resisting the urge to plant his hands on her bottom and forcibly shove her into the carriage. Damn, but she knew how to try his patience. He took another deep breath—he rather thought he would need several of them before today's journey was through—and climbed into the carriage beside her.

He took great pains to avoid touching her as he entered, but her scent was everywhere. She always managed to smell like springtime, and Robert was struck by an overwhelming sense of nostalgia and desire. He took yet another deep breath, trying to collect his thoughts. Somehow he had been granted another chance at love, and he was determined not to muck things up this time.

"You wished to say?" she asked primly.

He closed his eyes for a moment. She certainly had no plans to make this easy on him. "All I wished to say is that I'm sorry."

Her eyes flew to his face in surprise. "You're sorry?" she echoed.

"For believing the worst of you. I let my father talk me into things I knew were not true."

She remained silent, forcing him to continue with his painful speech. "I knew you so well, Torie," he whispered. "I knew you like I knew myself. But when you didn't arrive at our assignation . . ."

"You thought I was an adventuress," she said, her voice flat.

He glanced out the window for a moment before returning his eyes to her pale, drawn face. "I didn't know what else to think," he said lamely.

"You might have remained in the district long enough to ask me what had happened," she said. "There was no need to jump to such unpleasant conclusions."

"I went to your window."

She gasped. "You did? I-I never saw you."

When Robert spoke, his voice was shaky. "Your back was to the window. You were lying in bed. You looked quite peaceful, as if you hadn't a care in the world."

"I was crying," she said in a hollow voice.

"I couldn't have known that."

A hundred emotions played across her face, and for a moment Robert was sure that she was going to lean forward and place her hand on his, but in the end she merely crossed her arms and said, "You behaved badly."

Robert forgot all his vows to control his temper. "And you didn't?" he returned.

She stiffened. "I beg your pardon."

"We are both guilty of mistrust, Victoria. You cannot lay all the blame at my door."

"What are you talking about?"

"Your sister told me what you thought of me. That I'd never intended anything more than seduction. That I had never been serious in my courtship of you." He leaned forward and stopped himself a split second before grabbing her hands with his. "Look into your heart, Victoria. You *know* I loved you. You know I love you still."

Victoria took a deep breath and exhaled. "I suppose I owe you an apology as well."

Robert let out a ragged sigh, exquisite relief surging through him. This time he let himself take her hands into his. "Then we can begin anew," he said fervently.

Victoria tried to tell herself to pull her hands away, but the feeling was too achingly tender. His skin was warm, and she was so tempted just to lean into his waiting embrace. It wouldn't be so dreadful to feel loved once again—to feel treasured.

She looked up at him. His blue eyes were staring at her with an intensity that both frightened and thrilled her. She felt something touch her cheek, then realized it was a tear. "Robert, I—" She stopped, realizing that she didn't know what to say.

He leaned forward, and Victoria saw that he meant to kiss her. And then, to her horror, she realized that she wanted his lips on hers. "No!" she burst out, as much for her own benefit as for his. She pulled her gaze away from him and then pulled her hands away, too.

"Victoria—"

"Stop." She sniffled and fixed her gaze on the window. "You don't understand me anymore."

"Then tell me what I need to know. Tell me what I need to do to make you happy."

"Don't you understand? You can't make me happy!"

Robert flinched, unable to believe how wounded he was by that one statement. "Would you care to explain yourself?" he said stiffly.

She let out a hollow laugh. "You gave me the moon, Robert. No, you did more than that. You picked me up and put me right on it." There was a long, painful pause, and then she said, "And then I fell. And it hurt so much when I landed. I don't want that again."

"It won't happen again. I am older and wiser now. We are both older and wiser."

"Don't you see? It has already happened twice."

"Twice?" he echoed, thinking that he very much didn't want to hear what she had to say.

"At the Hollingwoods," she said, her voice oddly flat. "When you asked me to be your—"

"Don't say it." His voice was curt.

"Don't say what? 'Mistress'? It's a fine time for you to suddenly develop scruples."

He paled. "I never knew you could be so vindictive."

"I'm not being vindictive. I'm being honest. And I didn't just fall off the moon that time. You pushed me."

Robert took a deep and ragged breath. It was not in his nature to beg, and part of him wanted desperately to defend himself. But he wanted Victoria more, and so he said, "Then let me make amends, Torie. Let me marry you and give you children. Let me spend every day of my life worshipping the ground you walk upon."

"Robert, don't." Her voice was shaky, and he knew he'd seen something flare in her eyes when he mentioned children.

"Don't what?" he tried to joke. "Worship the ground you walk upon? It's too late. I already do that."

"Don't make this so hard," she said, her voice only slightly more than a whisper.

His lips parted in amazement. "And why the hell should I not? You tell me why I should make it easy for you to walk out of my life again."

"I never walked out on you," she shot back. "*You* left. You."

"Neither of us is blameless. You were quick to believe the worst of me as well."

Victoria didn't say anything.

He leaned forward, his eyes intense. "I will not give up on you, Victoria. I'll haunt you day and night. I'll make you admit that you love me."

"I don't," she whispered.

The carriage came to a halt, and Robert said, "We seem to have arrived at your home."

Victoria immediately gathered up her belongings and reached for the door. But before she touched the polished wood, Robert's hand descended onto hers.

"Just one moment," he said, his voice hoarse.

"What do you want, Robert?"

"A kiss."

"No."

"Just one kiss. To get me through the night."

Victoria stared into his eyes. They were hot ice, burning straight into her soul. She licked her lips; she couldn't help it.

Robert's hand moved to the back of her head. His touch was achingly soft. If he had applied pressure or tried to force her, she knew she could have resisted. But his gentleness was disarming, and she couldn't pull away.

His lips touched hers, brushing back and forth until he felt her soften beneath him. His tongue moistened one corner of her mouth, then the other, then outlined the edge of her full lips.

Victoria thought she might melt.

But then he pulled away. His hands were shaking. Victoria looked down and realized that hers were, too.

"I know my limits," he said in a low voice.

Victoria blinked, realizing with despair that she didn't know her own. Another second of his sensual torture and she would have been on the floor of the carriage, begging him to love her. Shame colored her face and she left the carriage, letting MacDougal take her trembling hand in his to help her down. Robert followed immediately after her, and then swore viciously when he realized where he was.

Victoria didn't quite live in the worst part of town, but it came damn close. It took Robert a good ten seconds before he was calm enough to say, "Please tell me you don't live here."

She gave him an odd look and pointed to a fourth-story window. "Right there."

Robert's throat worked violently. "You . . . are not . . . going to remain here," he said, barely able to get the words out.

Victoria ignored him and began to walk toward her building. Robert had his arm around her waist within seconds. "I don't want to hear another word out of you," he barked. "You are coming home with me this instant."

"Let go of me!" Victoria struggled under his grasp, but Robert held firm.

"I will not permit you to remain in such a dangerous neighborhood."

"I can't imagine I'd be any safer with you," she retorted.

Robert softened his grip, but refused to relinquish his hold on her arm. Then he felt something on his foot and looked down.

"Bloody frigging hell!" He kicked his foot out wildly, sending a good-sized rat out into the street.

Victoria took advantage of his predicament by wrenching her arm from his grasp, and she ran to the relative safety of her building.

"Victoria!" Robert bellowed, following her. But when he yanked the door open, all he saw was a fat old lady with blackened teeth.

"And 'oo might you be?" she demanded.

"I am the earl of Macclesfield," he roared, "and get the hell out of my way."

The woman planted her hand against his chest. "Not so fast, yer lordship."

"Remove your hand from my person, if you please."

"Remove yer sorry ass from my house, if *you* please," she cackled. "We don't allow men in 'ere. This be a respectable house."

"Miss Lyndon," Robert bit out, "is my affianced bride."

"Didn't look that way to me. In fact, it looked like she didn't want anything to do with you."

Robert looked up and saw Victoria peering at him through a window. Rage poured through him. "I will not stand for this, Victoria!" he bellowed.

She merely shut the window.

For the first time in his life Robert truly learned the meaning of seeing red. When he'd thought Victoria had betrayed him seven years earlier, he'd been too pathetically heartbroken for this brand of fury. But now—God*damn* it, he'd been bloody frantic for more than two weeks, not knowing what the devil had happened to her. And now that he'd finally found her, not only had she thrown his proposal of marriage back in his face, but she insisted on living in a neighborhood peopled with drunks, thieves, and whores.

And rats.

Robert watched as a street urchin picked the pocket of an unsuspecting man across the street. He exhaled raggedly. He was going to have to get Victoria out of this neighborhood, if not for her safekeeping then for the sake of his sanity.

It was a miracle she hadn't been raped or murdered already.

He turned back to the landlady just in time to see the door slam in his face and hear a key turn in the lock. He crossed the short distance to the spot just below Victoria's window and started to eye the side of the building, looking for possible footholds for his ascent to her room.

"Milord." MacDougal's voice was soft but insistent.

"If I can get my foot up to that sill, I should be able to make it all the way up," Robert growled.

"Milord, she's safe enough for the night."

Robert whirled around. "Do you have any idea what kind of neighborhood this is?"

MacDougal stiffened at his tone. "Begging your pardon, milord, but I grew up in a neighborhood like this."

Robert's face immediately softened. "Damn. I'm sorry, MacDougal, I didn't mean—"

"I know you didna." MacDougal grasped Robert's upper arm and gently began to lead him away. "Your lady needs to stew on this for an evening, milord. Leave her be for a touch. You can talk to her on the morrow."

Robert gave the building one last scowl. "Do you really think she'll be all right for the night?"

"You heard the lock on that door. She's as safe as if she were tucked away in Mayfair with you. Probably safer."

Robert gave his next scowl to MacDougal. "I'm coming after her tomorrow."

"Of course you are, milord."

Robert put his hand on the carriage and exhaled. "Am I mad, MacDougal? Am I completely, utterly, incurably mad?"

"Well, now, milord, that's not my place to say."

"How delightfully ironic that now would be the time you finally decide to exercise a bit of verbal circumspection."

MacDougal only laughed.

Victoria sat on her narrow bed and hugged her arms to her body, as if curling herself into the tiniest ball possible would make all this confusion go away.

She had finally begun to carve out a life with which she could be content. Finally! Was it so much to want a bit of stability? Of permanence? She'd had seven years of rude employers threatening her with dismissal at every turn. She'd found security at Madame Lambert's dress shop. And friendship. Madame clucked about like a mother hen, always concerned about the welfare of her employees, and Victoria adored the camaraderie among the shopgirls.

Victoria swallowed as she realized she was crying. She hadn't had a friend in years. She couldn't count the number of times she'd fallen asleep clutching Ellie's letters to her chest. But letters couldn't give a gentle pat on the arm, and letters never smiled.

And Victoria had been so very lonely.

Seven years ago Robert had been more than the love of her life. He'd been her very best friend. Now he was back, and he said he loved her. Victoria choked on a sob. Why did he have to do this now? Why couldn't he leave well enough alone?

And why did she still have to care so much? She didn't want to have anything to do with him, much less marry him, and still her heart raced with every touch. She could feel his presence across a room, and one heavy-lidded gaze had the power to make her mouth go completely dry.

And when he kissed her . . .

Deep in her heart, Victoria knew that Robert had the power to make her happy beyond her wildest dreams. But he also had the power to crush her heart, and he'd already done so once—no, twice.

And Victoria was so tired of the pain.

Chapter 13

Robert was waiting on her doorstep when she left for work the next morning. Victoria wasn't particularly surprised; he was nothing if not stubborn. He'd probably been planning his return all night.

She let out a deep breath. "Good morning, Robert." It seemed infantile to pretend to ignore him.

"I've come to escort you to Madame Lambert's," he said.

"That is very kind of you, but wholly unnecessary."

He stepped directly in her path, forcing her to look up at him. "I beg to differ with you. It is never safe for a young woman to walk in London unescorted, but it is especially dangerous in this area."

"I have managed to get myself to the dress shop every day for the past month," she said.

His mouth settled into a grim line. "I can assure you that does not set my mind at ease."

"Setting your mind at ease has never been at the top of my list of priorities."

He clucked at her. "My, my, we have a pointy tongue this morning."

His condescending tone ate at her. "Have I ever told you how much I detest the use of the royal 'we'? It reminds me of all those odious employers I had over the years. Nothing like a good 'we' to put the governess in her place."

"Victoria, we are not discussing being a governess, nor are we discussing pronouns, either singular or plural."

She tried to push past him, but he stood firmly in her way.

"I am only going to repeat this one more time," he said. "I will not permit you to remain in this hellhole for another day."

She counted to three before she said, "Robert, you are not responsible for my welfare."

"Somebody damn well has to be. You obviously don't know how to take proper care of yourself."

She counted to five before she said, "I am going to ignore that comment."

"I cannot believe you took lodgings here. Here!" Robert gave his head a disgusted shake.

She counted to ten before she said, "This is all I can afford, Robert, and I am perfectly happy with it."

He leaned forward in an intimidating manner. "Well, I am not. Let me tell you how I spent last night, Victoria."

"Please do," she muttered. "As if I could stop you."

"I spent last night wondering how many men have tried to attack you in the last month."

"None since Eversleigh."

He either didn't hear her or didn't want to hear her. "Then I wondered how often you have to cross the street to avoid the prostitutes loitering on the street corners."

She smiled archly. "Most of the prostitutes are very nice. I had tea with one just the other day." That was a lie, but she knew it would needle him.

He shuddered. "Then I wondered how many damn rats share your room with you."

Victoria tried to force herself to count to twenty before responding, but her temper wouldn't allow it. She could take his insults and his overbearing attitude, but an attack on her housekeeping skills—well, that was really too much. "You could eat off the floor of my room," she hissed.

"I'm sure the rats do," he replied with an acerbic twist of his lips. "Really, Victoria, you cannot stay in this vermin-infested area. It isn't safe, and it isn't healthy."

She stood ramrod straight, holding her hands stiffly at her sides to keep herself from smacking him. "Robert, have you noticed that I am beginning to get just a trifle irritated with you?"

He ignored her. "I gave you one night, Victoria. That is all. You're coming home with me this evening."

"I think not."

"Then move in with my aunt."

"I value my independence above all things," she said.

"Well, I value your life and virtue," he exploded, "and you're going to lose them both if you insist upon living here."

"Robert, I am perfectly safe. I do nothing to attract attention, and people leave me alone."

"Victoria, you're a beautiful and obviously respectable woman. You can't help but attract attention every time you step foot out of the house."

She snorted. "You're a fine one to talk. Look at you!"

He crossed his arms and waited for an explanation.

"I was doing a fine job of keeping to myself before you came along." She waved her hand at his carriage. "This neighborhood hasn't seen such a grand vehicle in years, if ever. And I'm sure that at least a dozen people are already planning how to rid you of your wallet."

"So you do admit that this is an unsavory area."

"Of course I do. Do you think I'm blind? If nothing else, this should prove how very much I don't want your company."

"What the hell do you mean by that?"

"For God's sake, Robert, I'd rather stay here in this slum than be with you. Here! That ought to tell you something."

He flinched, and she knew she'd hurt him. What she didn't expect was how much it hurt herself to see his eyes fill with pain. Against her better judgment, she put her hand on his arm. "Robert," she said softly, "let me explain something to you. I am content now. I may not have much in the way of material comforts, but for the first time in years I have my independence. And I have my pride back."

"What are you saying?"

"You know I never liked being a governess. I was constantly insulted by my employers, both male and female."

Robert's mouth tightened.

"The customers at the dress shop aren't always polite, but Madame Lambert treats me with respect. And when I do a good job she doesn't try to take the credit. Do you know how long it has been since anyone has offered me any praise?"

"Oh, Victoria." There was a world of anguish in those two words.

"I have made lovely friends, too. I truly enjoy the time I spend in the dress shop. And no one makes any decisions for me." She shrugged helplessly. "They are simple pleasures, but they are dear to me, and I don't want to upset the balance."

"I had no idea," he whispered. "No idea."

"How could you?" Her words were not a retort, but a real and honest question. "You have always had complete control over your life. You have always been able to do whatever you wanted." Her lips curved into a wistful smile. "You and your plans. I always loved that about you."

His eyes flew to her face. He doubted that she even realized she'd used the word "love."

"The way you would attack a problem," she continued, her eyes growing nostalgic. "It was always so much fun to watch. You examined the situation from all four sides, and then from the

top and the bottom and upside down and inside
out. You would find the shortest route to a
solution, and then you went and did it. You
always figured out how to get what you
wanted."

"*Except you.*"

His words hung in the air for a long minute.
Victoria looked away, and then finally she said,
"I must be getting to work."

"Let me take you."

"No." Her voice sounded odd, as if she might
cry. "I don't think that is a good idea."

"Victoria, please don't make me worry about
you. I have never felt so helpless in all my life."

She turned to him with wise eyes. "I felt
helpless for seven years. Now I'm in control.
Please don't take that away from me." Straight-
ening her shoulders, she began to walk to the
dress shop.

Robert waited until she was about ten feet
away and then began to follow her. MacDougal
waited until Robert was about twenty feet away
and then began to follow him in the carriage.

All in all, it was a strange and solemn procession to Madame Lambert's.

Victoria was kneeling before a dressmaker's
dummy with three pins lodged between her
teeth when the bell over the door rang at noon.
She looked up.

Robert. She wondered why she was surprised.
He was holding a box in his hands and had a
familiar look on his face. Victoria knew that
look. He was up to something. He'd probably
spent the entire morning making plans.

He crossed the room until he was standing next to her. "Good day, Victoria," he said with a genial smile. "I must say you look rather frightening with pins hanging from your mouth like fangs."

Victoria found herself wanting to take one of those "fangs" and jab him with it. "Not frightening enough," she muttered.

"I beg your pardon?"

"Robert, why are you here? I thought we reached an understanding this morning."

"We did."

"Then why are you here?" she ground out.

He crouched beside her. "I think we reached different understandings."

What on earth was he talking about? "Robert, I'm very busy," she said.

"I brought you a gift," he said, holding out the box.

"I cannot accept a gift from you."

He grinned. "It's edible."

Victoria's traitorous stomach began to rumble. With a muttered curse she turned her back to him and began to attack the hemline of the gown she'd been working on.

"Mmmmm," Robert said tantalizingly. He opened the box and waved the contents before her. "Pastries."

Victoria's mouth watered. Pastries. Her biggest weakness. She supposed it would have been too much to hope that he'd forgotten.

"I made sure to get the kind without nuts," he said.

No nuts? The man never forgot a detail, blast him. Victoria looked up to see Katie craning her neck, examining the pastries over Robert's shoulder. Katie was eyeing the sweets with an expression that could only be called intense longing. Victoria didn't imagine that Katie often had occasion to partake of delicacies from London's most exclusive confectioner.

Victoria smiled at Robert and accepted the box. "Thank you," she said politely. "Katie? Would you like one?"

Katie was at her side in less than a second. Victoria handed her the entire box and went back to work on the hemline, trying to ignore the scent of chocolate that now pervaded the room.

Robert pulled up a chair and sat beside her. "That gown would look lovely on you," he said.

"Alas," Victoria replied, viciously jabbing a pin into the material, "but it is spoken for by a countess."

"I would tell you that I would buy you one just like it, but I don't think that would win me any points in my favor."

"How astute of you, my lord."

"You're annoyed with me," he stated.

Victoria's head swiveled slowly around until she faced him. "You noticed."

"Is it because you thought you'd rid yourself of me this morning?"

"It was a hope."

"You're eager for your life to return to normal."

Victoria let out a funny little sound that was part laugh, part sigh, and part snort. "You seem to be exceedingly proficient at stating the obvious."

"Hmmm." Robert scratched his head, looking for all the world like a man deep in thought. "Your logic is flawed."

Victoria didn't bother to reply.

"You see, you *think* this is normal."

Victoria jabbed a few more pins into the hemline, realized that her irritation was making her careless, and had to pull them out and reposition them.

"But this isn't a normal life. How could it be? You've only lived it for a month."

"I was only courted by you for two months," she was compelled to point out.

"Yes, but you spent the next seven years thinking about me."

Victoria didn't see any point in denying this, but she did say, "Weren't you listening to anything I said this morning?"

He leaned forward, his light blue eyes startlingly intense. "I listened to everything you said. And then I spent all morning thinking about it. I believe I understand your feelings."

"Then why are you here?" she ground out.

"Because I think you're wrong."

Victoria dropped her pins.

"Life isn't about crawling under a rock and watching the world go by, desperately hoping it won't touch us." He knelt down and began to help her gather the pins. "Life is about taking chances, about reaching for the moon."

"I took chances," she said flatly. "I lost."

"And you're going to let that rule your life forever? Victoria, you're only four and twenty. You have years ahead of you. Are you saying that you're going to take the safe road for the rest of your life?"

"As pertains to you, yes."

He stood. "I can see that I will have to give you some time to reflect on this."

She glared at him, hoping that he didn't notice how her hands were shaking.

"I will return at the end of the day to escort you home," he said, and she wondered whether he meant her home or his.

"I won't be here," she said.

He only shrugged. "I'll find you. I'll always find you."

Victoria was saved from having to ponder that ominous statement by the bell over the door. "I have to work," she muttered.

Robert executed a smart bow and waved his hand toward the door. His courtly gesture faltered, however, when he saw the dress shop's latest customers.

Mrs. Brightbill bustled in, pulling Harriet along behind her. "Ah, there you are, Miss Lyndon," she trilled. "And Robert, too."

"I had a feeling we might find you here, cousin," Harriet said.

Victoria bobbed a curtsy. "Mrs. Brightbill. Miss Brightbill."

Harriet waved a hand at her. "Please do call me Harriet. We are to be relations, after all."

Robert beamed at his cousin.

Victoria scowled at the floor. Much as she would have liked to scowl at Harriet, store policy did not allow her to make faces at customers. And she had just spent all morning trying to convince Robert that she wanted to keep her position at the dress shop, hadn't she?

"We have come to ask you to tea," Harriet announced.

"I'm afraid I must decline," Victoria said demurely. "It wouldn't be proper."

"Nonsense," Mrs. Brightbill declared.

"My mother is considered an authority on what is proper and what is not," Harriet said. "So if she says it is proper, you can be sure that it is."

Victoria blinked, needing an extra second to work through the maze of Harriet's words.

"I'm afraid I must agree with Harriet, much as it pains me to do so," Robert said. "I myself have often been on the receiving end of Aunt Brightbill's lectures on propriety."

"I don't find that particularly difficult to believe," Victoria said.

"Oh, Robert can be quite a rake," Harriet said. This earned her a disapproving look from her cousin.

Victoria turned to the younger girl with interest. "Is that so?"

"Oh, yes. I fear it was his broken heart that forced him to turn to other women."

A nasty feeling began to develop in Victoria's stomach. "Exactly how many other women are we talking about?"

"Scores," Harriet said earnestly. "Legions."

Robert began to chuckle.

"Don't laugh," Harriet hissed. "I am trying to make her jealous on your behalf."

Victoria coughed, hiding a smile behind her hand. Really, Harriet was such a dear.

Mrs. Brightbill, who had been conversing with Madame Lambert, rejoined the conversation. "Are you ready, Miss Lyndon?" Her tone clearly implied that she did not expect another refusal.

"It is very kind of you, Mrs. Brightbill, but I'm frightfully busy here at the dress shop, and—"

"I just spoke to Madame Lambert, and she assured me that she might spare you for an hour."

"You might as well give in gracefully," Robert said with a smile. "My aunt always gets her way."

"It must run in the family," Victoria muttered.

"I certainly hope so," he replied.

"Very well," Victoria said. "A cup of tea does sound rather nice, actually."

"Excellent," Mrs. Brightbill said, rubbing her hands together. "We have much to discuss."

Victoria blinked a few times and adopted an innocent expression. "His lordship won't be joining us, will he?"

"Not if you do not desire it, dear."

Victoria turned to the man in question and offered him an acidic smile. "Good day, then, Robert."

Robert merely leaned against the wall and smiled as she left, willing to let her believe she'd outwitted him. Victoria had said she craved normalcy, hadn't she? He chuckled. People didn't get more frighteningly normal than Aunt Brightbill.

Tea was actually a rather pleasant affair. Mrs. Brightbill and Harriet regaled Victoria with tales aplenty about Robert, few of which Victoria was inclined to believe. The way they extolled his honor, bravery, and kindness, one would think he was a candidate for sainthood.

Victoria wasn't entirely sure why they were so intent on welcoming her to their family; Robert's father certainly hadn't been enthusiastic about his son marrying a vicar's daughter. And now she was a common shopgirl! It was unheard of for an earl to marry someone such as her. Still, Victoria could only deduce from Mrs. Brightbill's frequent statements of, "My, but we'd quite given up on dear Robert marrying," and "You're the first respectable lady he's shown an interest in in years," that she was quite eager for a match.

Victoria didn't say much. She didn't feel she had very much to add to the conversation, and even if she had, Mrs. Brightbill and Harriet didn't give her many opportunities to do so.

After an hour the mother and daughter deposited Victoria back at the dress shop. Victoria poked her head through the door suspiciously, convinced that Robert was going to jump out at her from behind a dressmaker's dummy.

But he wasn't there. Madame Lambert said that he'd had business to attend to in another part of town.

Victoria was horrified to realize that she was feeling something that vaguely resembled a stab of disappointment. It wasn't because she missed him, she rationalized, she just missed the battle of wits.

"He did leave you this, though," Madame

said, holding out a fresh box of pastries. "He said he hoped you would deign to eat one."

At Victoria's sharp look, Madame added, "His words, not mine."

Victoria turned to hide the smile tugging at her lips. Then she forced her mouth back into a frown. He was not going to wear her down. She had told him that she valued her independence, and she'd meant it. He would not win her heart with romantic gestures.

Although, she thought pragmatically, one pastry really couldn't hurt.

Robert's smile spread into a full-fledged grin as he watched Victoria eat a third pastry. She obviously didn't know that he was watching her through the window, or she wouldn't have even so much as sniffed at one of the small cakes.

She then picked up the handkerchief he'd left with the box and examined the monogram. Then, after a quick scan to make sure that none of her co-workers were looking, she lifted the scrap of cloth to her face and inhaled its scent.

Robert felt tears prick his eyes. She was softening toward him. She'd die before she admitted it, but it was clear she was softening.

He watched as she tucked the handkerchief into her bodice. The simple gesture gave him hope. He would win her back; he was certain of it.

He smiled for the rest of the day. He couldn't help himself.

Four days later Victoria was ready to whack him over the head. And she rather relished the concept of doing so with an expensive box of sweets. Any one of the forty boxes he'd sent would suffice.

He'd also given her three romantic novels, a miniature telescope, and a small bouquet of honeysuckle, with a note reading, *I hope this reminds you of home.* Victoria had almost started to bawl right there in the dress shop when she read his words. The blasted man remembered everything she liked and disliked, and he was using it to try to bend her to his will.

He had become her shadow. He gave her enough time alone to get her work done at Madame Lambert's, but he always seemed to materialize by her side whenever she stepped foot outdoors. He didn't like it when she walked alone, he told her, especially in her neighborhood.

Victoria had pointed out that he followed her everywhere, not just to her neighborhood. Robert's mouth had tightened into a grim line and he had muttered something about personal safety and the dangers of London. Victoria was fairly certain that she'd heard the words "damn" and "fool" in the sentence as well.

She told him over and over that she valued her independence, that she wanted to be left alone, but he didn't listen. By the end of the week he wasn't speaking either. All he did was glower at her.

Robert's gifts continued to arrive at the dress shop with alarming regularity, but he no longer wasted words trying to convince her to marry him. Victoria asked him about his silence, and all he said was, "I am so goddamned furious with you that I am trying not to say anything for fear of biting your nitwit head off."

Victoria considered his tone of voice, noticed that they were trodding through a particularly unsavory area of town at the time, and decided not to say anything more. When they arrived at her boarding house, she slipped inside without a word of farewell. Up in her room she peeked out the window.

He stared up at her curtains for more than an hour. It was disconcerting, that.

Robert stood in front of Victoria's building and assessed it with the eye of a man who leaves nothing to chance. He had reached his boiling point. No, he had gone far, far beyond it. He had tried his best to be patient, had wooed Victoria not with expensive gifts but with thoughtful tokens that he felt would be more meaningful. He had tried to talk sense into her until he ran out of words.

But that night had been the straw that had broken the proverbial camel's back. Victoria didn't realize it, but every time Robert followed her home, MacDougal followed them both, about ten paces behind. Usually MacDougal waited for Robert to seek him out, but that night he had made his way to his employer's side the moment Victoria slipped into her boarding house.

A man had been stabbed, MacDougal said. It had happened the night before, right in front of Victoria's boardinghouse. Robert knew that her building had a sturdy lock, but that did little to ease his mind as he regarded the bloodstains on the cobblestones. Victoria had to walk back and forth to work every day; sooner or later someone was bound to try to take advantage of her.

Victoria didn't even like stepping on ants. How the devil was she supposed to defend herself against an attack?

Robert lifted his hand to his face, his fingers pressing against the muscle that was jumping spasmodically in his temple. Deep breaths did little to ease the fury or sense of impotence that was growing within him. It was becoming obvious that he would not be able to protect Torie properly, as long as she insisted on remaining in this hellhole.

Clearly the current state of affairs could not be allowed to continue.

Robert acted very strangely the next day. He was more silent and brooding than usual, but he seemed to have an awful lot to discuss with MacDougal.

Victoria grew suspicious.

He was waiting for her, as usual, at the end of the day. Victoria had long since given up arguing with him when he forced her to accept his escort. It required too much energy, and she hoped that eventually he'd give up and leave her alone.

Whenever she pondered that possibility, however, she felt an odd stab of loneliness in her heart. Like it or not, she'd grown accustomed to having Robert about. It would be quite odd once he was gone.

Victoria tightened her shawl around her shoulders for the twenty-minute walk home. It was late summer, but there was a chill in the air. When she stepped through the door and onto the street, however, she saw Robert's carriage parked outside.

"I thought we might drive home," Robert explained.

Victoria raised a questioning brow.

He shrugged. "It looks as if it might rain."

She looked up. The sky wasn't particularly overcast, but then again it wasn't particularly clear either. Victoria decided not to argue with him. She was feeling a bit tired; she'd spent the entire afternoon catering to an extremely demanding countess.

Victoria allowed Robert to help her up into the carriage, and she settled back against the plush squabs. She let out an audible sigh as her tired muscles relaxed.

"Busy day at the dress shop?" Robert inquired.

"Mmmm, yes. The Countess of Wolcott came in today. She was rather exacting."

Robert raised his brows. "Sarah-Jane? Good God, you deserve a medal if you managed to keep yourself from clouting her over the head."

"Do you know but I rather think I do," Victoria said, allowing herself a little grin. "A vainer woman I have never met. And so rude. She called me a clodhead."

"And what did you say?"

"I couldn't say anything, of course." Victoria's smile turned sly. "Out loud."

Robert chuckled. "What, then, did you say in your mind?"

"Oh, any number of things. I expounded upon the length of her nose and the size of her intellect."

"Small?"

"Very small," Victoria replied. "Her intellect, that is. Not her nose."

"Long?"

"Very long." She giggled. "I was quite tempted to shorten it for her."

"I should have liked to have seen that."

"I should have liked to have *done* it," Victoria retorted. Then she laughed, feeling giddier than she had in a long time.

"Goodness," Robert said wryly. "One might actually think you were enjoying yourself. Here. With me. Imagine that."

Victoria clamped her mouth shut.

"I am enjoying *my*self," he said. "It is good to hear you laugh. It has been a long time."

Victoria was silent, not sure how to respond. To deny that she had been having fun would clearly have been a lie. And yet it was so difficult to admit—even to herself—that his company brought her joy. So she did the only thing she could think to do, and yawned. "Do you mind if I nod off for a minute or two?" she asked, thinking that sleep was a good way to ignore the situation.

"Not at all," he replied. "I'll shut the curtains for you."

Victoria let out a sleepy sigh and drifted off, never noticing the wide smile that had broken out on Robert's face.

It was the quiet that woke her. Victoria had always been convinced that London was the noisiest place on earth, but she didn't hear a sound save for the clop-clop of the horses' hooves.

She forced her eyelids open.

"Good morning, Victoria."

She blinked. "Morning?"

Robert smiled. "Just an expression. You fell quite asleep."

"For how long?"

"Oh, about half an hour or so. You must have been very tired."

"Yes," she said absently. "I was quite." Then she blinked again. "Did you say half an hour? Shouldn't we be at my home now?"

He didn't say anything.

With an extremely ominous feeling in her heart, Victoria moved to the window and pulled back the curtain. Twilight hung in the air, but she could clearly see trees, and shrubs, and even a cow.

A cow?

She turned back to Robert, her eyes narrowing. "Where are we?"

He pretended to flick a piece of lint from his sleeve. "Well on our way to the coast, I imagine."

"The coast?" Her voice rose to a near shriek.

"Yes."

"Is that all you're going to say on the subject?" she ground out.

He smiled. "I suppose I could point out that I've abducted you, but I imagine you've already figured that out on your own."

Victoria went for his throat.

Chapter 14

Victoria had never thought of herself as a particularly violent person—indeed, she didn't even have much of a temper—but Robert's oh-so-casual statement pushed her right over the edge.

Her body reacted without any direction whatsoever from her brain, and she launched herself at him, her hands clutching perilously close to his neck. "You fiend!" she screamed. "You god-awful, bloody, blasted fiend!"

If Robert wanted to comment upon her less-than-ladylike language, he kept it to himself. Or perhaps his reticence had something to do with the way her fingers were pressing into his wind-pipe.

"How dare you?" she shrieked. "How dare you? All that time you were just pretending to listen to my talk of independence."

"Victoria," he gasped, trying to pry her fingers from his throat.

"Have you been plotting this all along?" When he didn't answer she began to shake him. "Have you?"

219

When Robert finally managed to get her off him, it required such force that Victoria was sent sprawling across the carriage. "For the love of God, woman," he exclaimed, still gasping for air, "were you trying to kill me?"

Victoria glared at him from her position on the floor. "It does seem a meritorious plan."

"You'll thank me for this someday," he said, knowing full well that such a condescending statement would enrage her.

He was right. He watched as her face grew redder by the half second. "I have never been so furious in my entire life," she finally hissed.

Robert rubbed his sore throat and said with great feeling, "I believe you."

"You had no right to do this. I can't believe you respect me so little that you would—you would—" She broke off and snapped her head around, a horrible thought occurring to her. "Oh my God! Did you poison me?"

"What the devil are you talking about?"

"I was very tired. I fell asleep so quickly."

"That was nothing but a lucky coincidence," he said with a little wave of his hand. "One for which I was most grateful. It really wouldn't have done for you to have been screaming your way through the London streets."

"I don't believe you."

"Victoria, I am not the villain you seem to think me. Besides, was I anywhere near your food today? I didn't even give you a box of pastries."

That much was true. The day before, Victoria had delivered a stinging diatribe on the wastefulness of one person being given so much food, and extracted a promise from Robert that he would donate any pastries he'd already purchased to a needy orphanage. And as furious as she was with him, she had to admit that he was not the sort to use poison.

"If it makes any difference," he added, "I had no plans to abduct you until yesterday. I had been hoping that you would come to your senses before drastic measures became necessary."

"Is it so very difficult for you to believe that I regard a life without you as sensible?"

"When such a life includes living in the worst sort of slum, yes."

"It isn't the 'worst' sort of slum," she said peevishly.

"Victoria, a man was stabbed to death in front of your building two nights ago!" he shouted.

She blinked. "Really?"

"Yes, really," he hissed. "And if you think I am going to stand by idly until the inevitable happens and you become the victim—"

"I beg your pardon, but it appears I *am* a victim. Of kidnapping at the very least."

He looked down at her with an irritated expression. "And at the very most?"

"Rape," she shot back.

He leaned back smugly. "It wouldn't be rape."

"I could never want you again after what you've done to me."

"You'll always want me. You might not want to want me just now, but you do."

Silence reigned for a moment. Finally, with eyes like slits, Victoria said, "You're no better than Eversleigh."

Robert's hand closed around her shoulder

with stunning force. "Don't you *ever* compare him to me."

"And why not? I think the comparison is most apt. You have both abused me, both used force—"

"I have not used force," he said between gritted teeth.

"I haven't seen you open the door to this carriage and give me the option of leaving." She crossed her arms in an attempt to appear resolute, but it was hard to maintain one's dignity while on the floor.

"Victoria," Robert said in an excruciatingly patient tone of voice, "we are in the middle of the Canterbury Road. It is dark, and there is no one around. I can assure you that you do not want to exit the carriage at this time."

"Goddamn you! Do you have any idea how much I hate it when you presume to tell me what I want?"

Robert gripped the seat of the carriage bench so hard his fingers shook. "Do you want me to stop the carriage?"

"You wouldn't do it even if I asked."

With a movement that spoke of barely leashed violence, Robert slammed his fist against the front wall three times. Within seconds the carriage came to a halt. "There!" he said. "Get out."

Victoria's mouth opened and closed like a dying fish.

"Would you like me to help you down?" Robert kicked open the door and jumped out. He held out his hand for her. "I live to be of service to you."

"Robert, I don't think—"

"You haven't been thinking all week," he snapped.

If she could have reached him, she would have slapped him.

MacDougal's face appeared next to Robert's. "Is aught amiss, my lord? Miss?"

"Miss Lyndon has expressed an interest in departing our company," Robert said.

"Here?"

"Not here, you idiot," Victoria hissed. And then, because MacDougal looked so affronted, she was compelled to say, "I meant Robert, not you."

"Are you getting down or not?" Robert demanded.

"You know I'm not. What I would like is for you to return me to my home in London, not abandon me here in—" Victoria turned to MacDougal. "Where the devil are we, anyway?"

"Near to Faversham, I would think."

"Good," Robert said. "We'll stop there for the night. We have made excellent time, but there is no sense exhausting ourselves by pushing on to Ramsgate."

"Right." MacDougal paused, then said to Victoria, "Wouldn't you be more comfortable on the bench, Miss Lyndon?"

Victoria smiled acidly. "Oh, no, I'm *quite* comfortable here on the floor, Mr. MacDougal. I prefer to feel every rut and bump in the road intimately."

"What she prefers is to be a martyr," Robert muttered under his breath.

"I heard that!"

Robert ignored her and gave some instructions

to MacDougal, who disappeared from view. He then climbed back into the carriage, shut the door, and ignored Victoria, who was still fuming on the floor. Finally she said, "What is in Ramsgate?"

"I own a cottage on the shore. I thought we might enjoy a bit of privacy there."

She snorted. "Privacy? Now there is a frightening thought."

"Victoria, you are beginning to try my patience."

"*You* are not the one who has been abducted, my lord."

He cocked a brow. "Do you know, Victoria, but I am beginning to think that you are enjoying yourself."

"You suffer from too much imagination," she shot back.

"I do not jest," he said, thoughtfully stroking his chin. "I think there must be something appealing in being able to vent one's offended sensibilities."

"I have every right to be outraged," she growled.

"I'm sure you think you do."

She leaned forward in what she hoped was a menacing manner. "I truly believe if I had a gun right now I would shoot you."

"I thought you were partial to pitchforks."

"I am partial to anything that would do you bodily harm."

"I do not doubt it," Robert said, chuckling.

"Don't you care that I hate you?"

He let out a long breath. "Let me make one thing clear. Your safety and well-being are my highest priorities. If removing you from that slum you insisted on calling home means that I must live with your hatred for a few days, then so be it."

"It won't be only a few days."

Robert didn't say anything.

Victoria sat there on the floor of the carriage, trying to collect her thoughts. Tears of frustration pricked at her eyes, and she started to take frequent and shallow breaths—anything to prevent her tears' mortifying spill down her cheeks. "You did the one thing . . ." she said, her words tinged with the nervous laughter of one who knows she has been beaten. "The one thing . . ."

He turned his head to face her. "Would you like to get up?"

She shook her head. "All I wanted was a bit of control over my own life. Was that so much to ask?"

"Victoria—"

"And then you did the one thing that would take that away from me," she interrupted, her voice growing louder. "The one thing!"

"I acted in your best int—"

"Do you have any idea what it feels like to have someone take your decisions away from you?"

"I know what it feels like to be manipulated," he said in a very low voice.

"It's not the same thing," she said, turning her head so he wouldn't see her cry.

There was a moment of silence as Robert tried to compose his words. "Seven years ago I had my life planned out to the very last detail. I was young, and I was in love. Madly, desperately in love. All I wanted was to marry you and spend the rest of my life making you happy. We'd have children," he said wistfully. "I always imagined them looking like you."

"Why are you saying this?"

He stared at her, drilling her with his eyes, even though she refused to return his gaze. "Because I know what it feels like to have one's dreams ripped away. We were young and stupid, and if we'd had any sense we would have realized what our fathers did to keep us apart. But it wasn't our fault."

"Don't you understand? I don't care about what happened seven years ago anymore. It doesn't matter to me."

"I think it does."

She crossed her arms and leaned against the wall. "I don't want to talk about it any longer."

"Very well." Robert picked up a newspaper and began to read.

Victoria sat on the floor and tried not to cry.

Twenty minutes later the carriage rolled to a halt in front of a small inn just off the Canterbury Road in Faversham. Victoria waited in the carriage while Robert went in to procure rooms.

A few minutes later he emerged. "Everything is arranged," he said.

"I hope you got me my own room," she said stiffly.

"Of course."

Victoria declined—somewhat forcefully—his offer of assistance, and she jumped down from the carriage on her own. Excruciatingly aware of his hand on the small of her back, she was led into the building. As they passed through the front room, the innkeeper called out, "I do hope you and your wife enjoy your stay, my lord."

Victoria waited just until they had turned the corner on the way to the staircase. "I thought you said we have separate rooms," she hissed.

"We do. I had no other option than to tell him you are my wife. It is clear that you are not my sister." He touched a lock of her sable hair with exquisite tenderness. "And I did not want anyone to think that you are my paramour."

"But—"

"I imagine the innkeeper simply thinks that we are a married couple who do not enjoy each other's company."

"At least part of that statement is true," she muttered.

He turned to her with a surprisingly radiant smile. "I always enjoy your company."

Victoria stopped in her tracks and just stared at him, utterly dumbfounded by his apparent good humor. Finally she said, "I cannot decide if you are insane, stubborn, or merely stupid."

"I opt for stubborn, if I get a vote."

She let out an exasperated breath of air and marched ahead of him. "I'm going to my room."

"Wouldn't you like to know which one it is?"

Victoria could positively feel his grin at her back. "Would you care to tell me," she said between clenched teeth, "the number of my room?"

"Three."

"Thank you," she said, and then wished that courtesy hadn't been so methodically drummed into her at a young age. As if he deserved her gratitude.

"I'm number four," he called out helpfully. "Just in case you want to know where to find me."

"I'm sure that won't be necessary." Victoria reached the top of the stairs, turned the corner, and began to look for her room. She could hear Robert a few paces behind her.

"One never knows." When she didn't comment, he added, "I can think of a host of reasons you may need to contact me." When she continued to ignore him, he added, "A thief might try to invade your room. You might have a nightmare."

The only bad dreams she might have, Victoria thought, would be about him.

"The inn might be haunted," he continued. "Just think of all the scary ghosts lurking about."

Victoria was quite unable to ignore that one. She turned slowly around. "That is the most implausible idea I have ever heard."

He shrugged. "It could happen."

She merely stared at him, looking very much as if she was trying to determine how to get him admitted to an asylum.

"Or," he added, "you might miss me."

"I rescind my earlier statement," she snapped. "*That* is the most implausible idea I have ever heard."

He clasped his heart dramatically. "You wound me, my lady."

"I am not your lady."

"You will be."

"Ah, look," she said with patently false brightness. "Here is my room. Good night." Without waiting for Robert to respond, Victoria entered her room and shut the door in his face.

Then she heard the key turn in the lock.

She gasped. The beast had locked her in!

Victoria indulged herself in a quick stamp of her foot, then flopped on her bed with a loud groan. She couldn't believe he had the gall to lock her in her room.

Well, actually, she *could* believe it. The man had abducted her, after all. And Robert never left a detail to chance.

Victoria fumed on her bed for several minutes. If she tried to escape Robert, she would have to do it that evening. Once he got her to his cottage by the sea, she doubted he'd let her out of his sight. And knowing Robert's penchant for privacy, she could safely assume that his cottage was isolated.

No, it would have to be now. Luckily Faversham was not so very far from Bellfield, where her family still lived. Victoria didn't particularly want to visit her father; she had never forgiven him for tying her up all those years ago. But the Reverend definitely seemed a lesser evil than Robert.

Victoria crossed the room to the window and peered out. It was a daunting distance to the ground. There was no way she'd make it without injury. Then her eyes fell on a door, and *not* the one to the hall.

A connecting door. She had a good idea to whose room it connected. How utterly ironic that the only way she would be able to escape was through his room.

She crouched down and squinted at the doorknob. Then she examined the door frame. It looked as if the door might stick. Opening it would be loud, and Robert would probably awaken. If he woke up before she even made it to the hall, she'd never escape. She would have to find a way to leave the connecting door slightly open without raising his suspicion.

Then it came to her.

Victoria took a deep breath and slammed the door open. "I might have known you'd have so little respect for my privacy!" she bellowed. She was aware that she was invading *his* privacy by barging into his room, but it seemed the only way to get the blasted door open without—

She gasped, forgetting whatever it was she'd been thinking about.

Robert was standing in the middle of the room, his chest bared. His hands were on the fastenings of his breeches. "Would you like me to continue?" he said mildly.

"No, no, that won't be necessary," she stammered, turning seven shades of red, from crimson to beet.

He smiled lazily. "Are you certain? I'd be happy to oblige you."

Victoria wondered why she couldn't seem to take her eyes off him. He was really quite magnificent, she thought in a bizarre burst of objectivity. His years in London had clearly not been inactive ones.

He took advantage of her dazed silence to hand her a small package.

"What is this?" she asked suspiciously.

"It occurred to me when I was making my plans that you might need something in which to sleep. I took the liberty of procuring you a nightgown."

The thought of him buying her lingerie was so startlingly intimate that Victoria nearly dropped the package. "Where did you get this?" she asked.

"I didn't get it from another woman, if that is what you want to know." He stepped forward and touched her cheek. "Although I must say that I'm touched to see you so jealous."

"I'm not jealous," she ground out. "It's just that—If you bought it at Madame Lambert's, I should be—"

"I didn't buy it at Madame Lambert's."

"Good. I should be quite angry to find out that one of my friends assisted you in this nefarious endeavor."

"I wonder how long you'll remain so angry with me," he said softly.

Victoria's head snapped up at his abrupt change of subject. "I'm going to bed." She took two steps toward the connecting door, then turned around. "I shan't be modeling this gown for you."

He offered her a seductive smile. "I never dreamed you would. However I'm quite pleased to hear that you at least contemplated the idea."

Victoria let out a low growl and stomped back into her room. She was so furious with him that she nearly slammed the door shut. But then, remembering her initial goal, she grasped the knob and closed the door so that it just touched the jamb. If Robert noticed that it was not closed properly, he would not think she had left it open as an invitation. She had made her anger too clear for him to jump to that conclusion. No, he would probably just assume that, in her distraction, she had overlooked a detail.

And if she was lucky he wouldn't notice the door at all.

Victoria tossed the offending package onto her bed and considered her plan for the rest of the night. She would have to wait several hours before attempting her escape. She had no idea how long it would take Robert to fall asleep, and since she had only one chance to flee, it seemed prudent to give him plenty of time to doze off.

She stayed awake by mentally reciting all her least favorite passages from the Bible. Her father had always insisted that she and Ellie commit large portions of the book to memory. An hour passed, then another, then another. Then yet another hour passed, and Victoria halted in mid-psalm as she realized that it was four in the morning. Surely Robert was sleeping soundly by now.

She took two tiptoed steps toward the door, then stopped. Her boots had nice hard soles on them and they clattered as she walked. She would have to remove them. Her bones let out a loud creak as she sat on the floor and unlaced her shoes. Finally, footwear in hand, she continued her silent trek toward the connecting door.

Heart pounding, she placed her hand on the

knob. Since she hadn't shut the door properly, she didn't have to twist it. She gave it a light tug, and then, with very controlled movements, pulled the door open.

She poked her face into the room first, then breathed a silent sigh of relief. Robert was sleeping soundly. The blasted man didn't appear to be wearing anything under the bed sheets, but Victoria quickly decided not to contemplate that fact just then.

She tiptoed toward his door, mentally thanking whomever it was who had decided to lay a rug in his room. It made her procession all the more quiet. Finally she reached the door. Robert had left the key in the lock. Ah, this would be the trickiest part. She had to get the door unlocked and slip out without waking him.

It occurred to her then that it was actually quite a good thing that Robert slept in the nude. If she did wake him up, she would be able to get quite a good head start while he pulled on his clothing. He might be determined to get her into his clutches, but she rather doubted that his determination extended to running through the streets of Faversham wearing nary a stitch.

She wrapped her fingers around the key and turned her head. The lock made a loud click. She caught her breath and looked over her shoulder. Robert made a sleepy, rumbling sort of noise and rolled over, but other than that he made no sign he was waking up.

With pent up breath, Victoria slowly pulled the door open, praying that the hinges wouldn't creak. It made a tiny noise, causing Robert to move a bit more and smack his lips in a curiously appealing manner. Finally she got the door halfway open and slipped through.

Escape! It was almost too easy; the triumph Victoria had expected to feel just wasn't there. She ran through the hall and made her way down the stairs. No one was on duty, so she was able to slip out the front door unnoticed.

Once out in the open, however, she realized that she had no idea where to go. It was about fifteen miles to Bellfield; not too far to walk when one was really determined, but Victoria didn't particularly relish the thought of walking along the Canterbury Road by herself at night. She would probably do better to find a place to hide near the inn and wait for Robert to depart.

Victoria eyed her surroundings as she put her shoes back on. The stables might do, and there were a few shops nearby that might have places to hide. Perhaps—

"Well, well, wot 'ave we 'ere?"

Victoria's heart sank into her instantly queasy stomach. Two large, dirty, and from the looks of it drunken men were closing in on her. She took a step backward—back toward the inn.

"Oy still got a few pennies left," one of them said. "Wot's yer price, missy?"

"I'm afraid you have the wrong idea," Victoria said, her words coming out terribly rushed.

"Come on now, lovey," the other said, reaching out and grabbing her arm. "We just want a bit of sport. Be a good lovey to us."

Victoria let out a surprised scream. The man's hand was biting into her skin. "No, no," she said, panic beginning to set in. "I'm not that kind of—" She didn't bother to finish the sentence; they didn't seem to be paying attention.

"I am a married woman," she lied, using a louder tone of voice.

One of them actually tore his eyes off her breasts for a moment and looked up. He blinked, then shook his head.

Victoria sucked in her breath. They obviously had no scruples concerning the sanctity of marriage. Finally, out of desperation, she burst out, "My husband is the earl of Macclesfield! If you touch a hair on my head, he'll have you killed. I swear he will."

That gave them pause. Then one of them said, "Wot's the wife of a bloody earl doing out by 'erself in the middle of the night?"

"It's a very long story, I assure you," Victoria improvised, still backing up toward the inn.

"I think she's making it up," the one holding her arm said. He yanked her closer to him with a movement surprisingly fast for one so inebriated. Victoria tried not to gag at his foul breath. Then she changed her mind and tried *to* gag. Vomit might be just the thing to dampen his ardor.

"We're just going to 'ave a bit of fun tonight," he whispered. "You and me and—"

"I wouldn't try it," drawled a voice Victoria knew all too well. "I don't like it when people touch my wife."

She looked up. Robert was standing next to the man—where had he come from so quickly?—and had a gun pressed up against his temple. He wasn't wearing a shirt, he wasn't even wearing shoes, and he had another gun tucked into the waistband of his breeches. He looked at the drunkard, smiled humorlessly, and said, "She makes me a bit irrational."

"Robert," Victoria said in a shaky voice, for once desperately glad to see him.

He jerked his head to the side, indicating for her to move into the doorway to the inn. She did so immediately.

"I'm going to start counting," Robert said in a deadly voice. "If the two of you aren't out of my sight by the time I get to ten, I'm going to shoot. And I won't aim for your feet."

The villains started to run before Robert even got to two. He counted all the way to ten, anyway. Victoria watched him from the doorway, tempted to run back up to her room and barricade herself inside while he ticked off the numbers. But she found herself rooted to the spot, quite unable to take her eyes off Robert.

When he was done he whirled around. "I suggest you don't provoke my temper any further this evening," he bit off.

She nodded. "No, I'll just be going to sleep. We can discuss this in the morning, if you like."

He didn't say anything, just let out a low growl as they mounted the steps back up to their chambers. Victoria wasn't particularly heartened by this reaction.

They reached his door, which had clearly been flung open in haste. Robert practically dragged her through the doorway and slammed the door shut. He let go of her to twist the key in the lock, and Victoria took advantage of this opportunity to run to the connecting door. "I'll just be going to bed," she said quickly.

"Not so fast." Robert's hand closed around her upper arm and he reeled her back in. "Do you really think I'm going to allow you to spend the rest of the night in there?"

She blinked. "Well, yes. I rather thought you were."

He smiled, but it was a dangerous sort of smile. "Wrong."

She thought her knees might give out. "Wrong?"

Before she knew what he was about, he'd scooped her up in his arms and dropped her on the bed. "You, my devious friend, are spending the night here. In my bed."

Chapter 15

"**Y**ou're insane," Victoria said, jumping off the bed with amazing speed.

He advanced on her with slow, menacing steps. "If I'm not, I'm damned close to it now."

That didn't reassure her. She took a few steps back, realizing with a sinking stomach that she was nearly to the wall. Escape did not look likely.

"Did I mention how much I enjoyed hearing you refer to me as your husband?" he asked in a deceptively lazy voice.

Victoria knew that tone. It meant he was furious and keeping it all inside. If she had been in a calmer and more reasonable frame of mind, she probably would have kept her mouth shut and done nothing to provoke his temper. But she was sufficiently concerned for her own welfare and virtue, so she snapped, "It's the last time you will ever hear it."

"Pity, that."

"Robert," she said in what she hoped was a gentling tone. "You have every right to be angry . . ."

He laughed at that. Laughed! Victoria was not amused.

"Angry does not begin to describe it," he said. "Allow me to tell you a story."

"Don't be facetious."

He ignored her. "I was sleeping in my bed, enjoying a particularly vivid dream . . . You were in it."

Victoria's cheeks flamed.

He smiled humorlessly. "I believe I had one hand in your hair, and your lips were . . . Hmmm, how do I describe it?"

"Robert, that's *enough!*" Victoria began to shake. Robert wasn't the sort to embarrass a lady by speaking to her in such terms. He must be far, far angrier than she'd dreamed.

"Now where was I?" he mused. "Ah, yes. My dream. Imagine, if you will, my distress when I was awakened from such delightful slumber by screams." He leaned forward, his eyes narrowing furiously. *"Your* screams."

Victoria couldn't think of anything to say. Well, that was not entirely true. She thought of several hundred things to say, but half of them were inappropriate and half were downright dangerous to her well-being.

"I have never before pulled on my breeches with such speed, do you know that?"

"I'm sure it will prove a useful talent," she improvised.

"And I have splinters in my feet," he added. "These floors were not meant to be traversed unshod."

She tried to smile, but found that her bravado

was sadly lacking. "I'd be happy to see to your injuries."

His hands descended upon her shoulders in a blindingly fast movement. "I wasn't walking, Victoria. I was running. I was running as if it were to save my own life. Except it wasn't." He leaned forward, his eyes glittering furiously. "I was desperate to save yours."

Her throat convulsed in a nervous swallow. What did he want her to say? Finally she opened her mouth and out tumbled, "Thank you?" It was more of a question than a statement.

He let go of her abruptly and turned away, clearly disgusted by her reaction. "Oh, for the love of Christ," he muttered.

Victoria fought against a choking feeling in the back of her throat. How had her life descended to this? She was dangerously close to tears, but she refused to cry in front of this man. He had broken her heart twice, pestered her for a week, and now he'd abducted her. Surely she was allowed a small measure of pride. "I want to go back to my own bed," she said, her voice small.

He didn't bother to turn around when he replied, "I already told you that I will not allow you to return to that hellhole in London."

"I meant in the next room."

There was a long silence. "I want you here," he finally said.

"Here?" she squeaked.

"I believe I have already said as much on two occasions."

She decided to try another tactic and appeal to

his deep sense of honor. "Robert, I know you are not the sort to take a woman against her will."

"It isn't that," he said with a disgusted scoff. "I don't trust you to stay put."

Victoria swallowed the stinging retort that formed on her lips. "I promise I shan't try to escape again this evening. I give you my most solemn vow."

"Pardon me if I'm not inclined to take you at your word."

That stung, and Victoria recalled the time she had snorted with disdain when he'd said he had never broken a promise to her. It was remarkable how unpleasant it was to receive a taste of one's own medicine. She grimaced. "I didn't promise not to try to escape before. I am doing so now."

He turned and stared at her with incredulous eyes. "You, my lady, should have been a politician."

"What is that supposed to mean?"

"Merely that you possess a stunning ability to use words to dance around the truth."

Victoria laughed. She couldn't help it. "And what exactly is the truth?"

He stepped forward purposefully. "You need me."

"Oh, *please*."

"You do. You need me in every way a woman needs a man."

"Don't say anything more, Robert. I would hate to be driven to violence."

He chuckled at her sarcasm. "Love, companionship, affection. You need all of that. Why do you think you were so miserable as a governess? You were alone."

"I could get a dog. A spaniel would be more intelligent company than you."

He laughed again. "Just look how quick you were to claim me as your husband tonight. You could have made up a name, but no, you chose me."

"I was using you," she spat out. "Using you and your name to protect myself. That is all!"

"Ah, but even that wasn't enough, was it, my sweet?"

Victoria didn't particularly like the way he said "my sweet."

"You needed the man, too. Those men didn't believe you until I arrived on the scene."

"Thank you ever so much," she ground out, not sounding particularly gracious. "You do have a flair for rescuing me from unpleasant situations."

He smirked. "Ah, yes, I am ever useful."

"Unpleasant situations that *you* cause," she shot back.

"Really?" he said, his voice dripping sarcasm. "I suppose that I rose out of bed—in my sleep, no less—dragged you from your room, pushed you down the stairs, and then left you in front of the inn to be accosted by two pox-ridden drunkards."

She pursed her lips in a prim expression. "Robert, you are behaving in a most unbecoming manner."

"Ah, the governess returns."

"You abducted me!" she nearly shrieked, completely losing hold of her temper. "You kidnapped me! If you had left me alone, as I have repeatedly asked you to, I would have been safe and sound in my own bed."

He stepped forward and jabbed her in the shoulder. "Safe and sound?" he repeated. "In your neighborhood? A bit of a contradiction of terms, I think."

"Ah, yes, and you magnanimously took it upon yourself to rescue me from my foolishness."

"Someone had to."

Her hand shot out to slap his cheek, but he caught her wrist easily. Victoria wrenched it from his grasp. "How dare you," she hissed. "How dare you condescend to me? You say you love me, but you treat me like a child. You—"

He cut her off by clamping his hand down on her mouth. "You'll say something you regret."

She stomped on his foot. Hard. He was trying to tell her what she wanted again, and she hated him for that.

"That is it!" he roared. "I have shown the patience of Job with you! I deserve a goddamn sainthood!" Before Victoria had a chance to react to his use of "goddamn" and "sainthood" in the same sentence, Robert picked her up and tossed her effortlessly onto the bed.

Victoria's mouth fell open. Then she started to slither off the mattress. Robert caught her ankle, though, and held firm. "Let go of me," she ground out, grabbing the far end of the bed with her hands and trying to pull herself from his grasp. She wasn't successful. "Robert, if you do not let go of my ankle . . ."

The lout actually had the nerve to laugh. "What will you do, Victoria? Do tell."

Seething with frustration and anger, Victoria stopped pulling and instead used her other foot to kick him soundly in the chest. Robert let out a grunt of pain and released his grip on her ankle, but before Victoria could scramble off the bed, he was on top of her, his weight pinning her against the mattress.

And he looked furious.

"Robert," she began, trying to use a conciliatory tone.

He stared down at her, his eyes burning with something that wasn't quite desire, although there was a good deal of that, too. "Do you have any idea how I felt when I saw those two men pawing at you?" he asked, his voice hoarse.

Mutely she shook her head.

"I felt rage," he said, his grip on her upper arms loosening into what could only be called a caress. "It was primitive, and it was hot, and it was pure."

Victoria's eyes widened.

"Rage that they should touch you. Rage that they should frighten you."

Her mouth went dry, and she realized that she was having a hard time taking her eyes off his lips.

"Do you know what else I felt?"

"No," she replied, her voice merely a whisper.

"Fear."

She brought her eyes up to his. "But you knew that I hadn't been injured."

He let out a hollow chuckle. "Not that, Torie. Fear that you're going to keep on running, that you will never admit what you feel for me. Fear that you'll always hate me so much that you'll run into danger to avoid me."

"I don't hate you." The words slipped out before she realized that she had just contradicted everything she'd told him in the last twelve hours.

He touched her hair, then cradled her head with his strong hands. "Then why, Victoria?" he whispered. "Why?"

"I don't know. I wish I did. I just know that I can't be with you right now."

His head lowered until they were nose to nose. Then his lips brushed up against hers, feather light and startlingly erotic. "Now? Or ever?"

She didn't answer. She couldn't answer, for his mouth had already taken fierce possession of hers. His tongue swooped into her mouth, tasting her with palpable hunger. His hips pressed gently into hers, reminding her of his desire. His hand ran up the length of her body and settled onto the curve of her breast. He kneaded and squeezed, the heat of his skin burning through the material of her dress. Victoria felt herself peaking beneath his touch.

"Do you know what I feel right now?" he whispered roughly.

She didn't answer.

"Desire." His eyes gleamed. "I want you, Victoria. I want to finally make you mine."

In a panic, Victoria realized that he was leaving the decision up to her. How easy it would be to let herself be swept up in the heat of the moment. How convenient to be able to tell herself the next day, *Passion made me do it; I wasn't thinking clearly.*

But Robert was forcing her to confront her feelings and to admit to the overwhelming desire that was racing through her body.

"You said you wanted to make your own decisions," he whispered into her ear. His tongue delicately traced its outline. "I won't make this one for you."

She let out a frustrated moan.

Robert trailed his hands down the length of her body, pausing ever so slightly at her gently rounded hips. He squeezed, and Victoria could feel the imprint of each and every one of his fingertips.

His lips curved into a masculine smile. "Perhaps I should help you clarify the issue," he said, touching his lips to the delicate skin of her neck. "Do you want me?"

She said nothing, but her body was arching up against his, her hips straining for him.

He slid his hands under her skirt and moved up her legs until they reached the warm skin at the tops of her stockings. One finger dipped beneath the edge, drawing lazy circles on her bare skin. "Do you want me?" he repeated.

"No," she whispered.

"No?" He moved his lips back up to her ear and softly nibbled. "Are you certain?"

"No."

"No, you're not certain or no, you don't want me?"

She let out a frustrated moan. "I don't know."

He contemplated her for a long moment, looking very much as if he wanted to crush her to him. His face was hungry, and his eyes burned in the candlelight. But in the end all he did was roll off her. He got to his feet and crossed the room, the evidence of his desire making his breeches tight. "I won't make this decision for you," he repeated.

Victoria sat up, utterly dazed. Her body was shaking with need, and in that moment she hated him for giving her the one thing she'd been asking for all along—control.

Robert stopped before the window and leaned on the sill. "Make your decision," he said in a low voice.

The only sound she made was a strangled cry. *"Make it!"*

"I-I don't know," she said, her words sounding lame and pathetic even to her own ears.

He whirled around. "Then get the hell out of my sight."

She flinched.

Robert strode to the bed and yanked her by the arm. "Tell me yes or tell me no," he bit out, "but don't demand that I give you a choice and then not make one."

Victoria was too startled to react, and before she knew it she had been pushed back into her own room, the connecting door slammed shut between them. She gasped for air, unable to believe how miserable and rejected she felt just then. God, she was such a hypocrite! Robert's words had cut to the quick. She had asked him over and over not to try to control her life, but when he finally put a decision into her hands, she was unable to act.

She sat on the bed for several minutes until

her eyes fell on the package she'd so carelessly thrown aside several hours earlier. It seemed a lifetime had passed since then. What, she wondered with a shaky laugh, was Robert's idea of appropriate nightwear?

She untied the strings holding the box together and lifted the lid. Even in the dim light of her single candle, she could see that the lingerie was made of the finest silk. With careful fingers Victoria lifted the garment out of the box.

It was dark blue—a shade hovering somewhere between royal and midnight. Victoria didn't think it was an accident that the silk was the exact color of her eyes.

She sat down on the bed with a sigh. Her mind held a picture of Robert, examining a hundred nightgowns until he found one he deemed perfect. He did everything with such care and precision.

She wondered if he made love with the same quiet intensity.

"Stop!" she said aloud, as if that would rein in her wayward thoughts. She rose to her feet and crossed the room to the window. The moon was high, and the stars were twinkling in a manner that could only be called friendly. Suddenly, more than anything, Victoria wanted another woman to talk to. She wanted her friends at the dress shop, she wanted her sister, she even wanted Robert's aunt Brightbill and cousin Harriet.

Most of all, she wanted her mother, who had died so many years earlier. She stared up into the heavens and whispered, "Mama, are you listening?" then scolded herself for foolishly hoping that a star would shoot through the night. Still, there was something soothing about talking to the darkened sky.

"What should I do?" she said aloud. "I think I might love him. I think I might have always loved him. But I hate him, too."

A star glinted sympathetically.

"Sometimes I think it would be so lovely to have someone to take care of me. To feel protected and loved. I went for so long without feeling that way. Without even a friend. But I also want to be able to make my own decisions, and Robert is taking that away from me. I don't think he means to. He just can't help it. And then I feel so weak and powerless. All the time I was a governess I was at the mercy of others. God, how I hated that."

She paused to brush a tear from her cheek. "And then I wonder—do all these questions mean anything, or am I just afraid? Maybe I am nothing but a coward, too scared to take a chance."

The wind whispered across her face, and Victoria took a deep breath of the clean, crisp air. "If I let him love me, will he break my heart again?"

The night sky made no response.

"If I let myself love him, can I still be my own person?"

This time a star twinkled, but Victoria wasn't sure how to interpret that gesture. She stood at the window for several minutes more, content to let the breeze caress her skin. Finally exhaustion claimed her and, fully clothed, she climbed into bed, not even realizing that she was still clutching the blue nightgown Robert had given her.

Ten feet away Robert stood at his own window, silently contemplating what he had overheard. The wind had carried Victoria's words to him, and, much as it went against his scientific nature, he couldn't help but believe that some benevolent spirit had pushed that wind along.

His mother. Or maybe Victoria's. Or perhaps both, working together from the heavens to give their children another chance at happiness.

He had been so close to giving up hope, but then he'd been given a gift more precious than gold—a brief glimpse into Victoria's heart.

Robert raised his eyes to the sky and thanked the moon.

Chapter 16

The next morning was almost surreal.

Victoria didn't wake up feeling particularly refreshed. She still felt drained, both emotionally and physically, and she was just as confused as ever about her feelings for Robert.

After she had washed her face and smoothed out her clothing, she knocked softly on his door. There was no answer. She decided to enter anyway, but she did so with a certain degree of apprehension. She well remembered his fit of temper the night before. Nibbling on her lower lip, she pushed open the door.

Only to be frightened out of her wits by MacDougal, who was dozing comfortably on Robert's bed.

"Good Lord!" she managed to say after she let out a shriek of surprise. "What are you doing here? And where is Lord Macclesfield?"

MacDougal smiled at her in a friendly manner as he rose to his feet. "He's seeing to the horses."

"Isn't that your job?"

251

The Scotsman nodded. "His lordship is rather particular about his horseflesh."

"I know," Victoria said, her mind traveling back seven years to when Robert had—unsuccessfully—tried to teach her to ride.

"Sometimes he likes to inspect the animals himself. Usually when he's thinking about something."

Probably how to most effectively flog me, Victoria thought. There was a beat of silence, and then she said, "Is there any particular reason why you came up to his room?"

"He wanted me to escort you to breakfast."

"Ah, yes," she said with a slight tinge of bitterness. "Keep the prisoner guarded at all times."

"Actually he mentioned something about your being accosted last night. He didn't want you to feel uncomfortable—a woman alone and all that."

Victoria smiled tightly, duly chastened. "Shall we be off, then? I am famished."

"Do you have anything you would like me to take down for you, my lady?"

Victoria was of half a mind to correct him and tell him that she wasn't anybody's lady, but she just didn't have the energy. Robert had probably already told his servant that they were as good as married anyway. "No," she replied. "His lordship didn't give me very much time to pack, if you recall."

MacDougal nodded. "Verra well, then."

Victoria took a couple of steps toward the door, and then she remembered the blue nightgown lying on the bed in the next room. She ought to leave it behind, she thought spitefully. She ought to have torn it into shreds the night before. But that artfully cut piece of silk gave her an odd sort of solace, and she didn't want to abandon it.

And, she rationalized, if she did, Robert would probably come up to retrieve it before they departed.

"Just one moment, MacDougal," she said, dashing back to the adjoining room. She bundled up the nightgown and tucked it under her arm.

She and MacDougal made their way downstairs. The Scotsman steered her toward a private dining room, where he said Robert would meet her for breakfast. Victoria was surprisingly hungry, and she put her hand against her stomach in a vain attempt to stop it from grumbling. Good manners dictated that she wait for Robert, but she doubted that any etiquette book had ever addressed the particularities of her uncommon situation.

Victoria waited for a minute or so, and then, when her stomach let out its third grumble, she decided not to bother with good manners, and reached for the plate of toast.

After a few minutes, two eggs, and a tasty slice of kidney pie, she heard the door open and Robert's voice. "Enjoying your meal?"

She looked up. He looked friendly, polite, and impossibly cheerful. Victoria was instantly suspicious. Wasn't this the same man who had forcibly ejected her from his room the night before?

"I'm famished," Robert declared. "How is the food? Is it to your liking?"

Victoria washed down a bite of toast with some tea. "Why are you being so nice to me?"

"I like you."

"Last night you didn't," she muttered.

"Last night I was, shall we say, misinformed."

"Misinformed? I suppose you stumbled on a wealth of information in the last ten hours?"

He grinned wickedly. "I did, indeed."

Victoria set her teacup on its saucer with slow, precise movements. "And would you care to share this with me? Your new fount of knowledge?"

He looked at her intently for a split second and then said, "Would you be so kind as to pass me a slice of that kidney pie?"

Victoria's fingers curled around the edge of the pie pan and she pulled the dish out of his reach. "Not just yet."

He chuckled. "You play dirty, my lady."

"I am not your lady, and I want to know why you're acting so bloody cheerful this morning. By all rights you should be frothing at the mouth."

"By all rights? Then you think my anger last night was justified?"

"No!" The word came out a touch more forcefully than Victoria would have liked.

He shrugged. "It's no matter, as I'm no longer angry."

Victoria stared at him, dumbfounded.

He motioned to the pie pan. "Would you mind?"

She blinked a few times and then snapped her

mouth closed when she realized it was hanging open. With an irritated little exhalation she pushed the pie pan in his direction and spent the next ten minutes watching him eat his breakfast.

The ride from Faversham to Ramsgate should have taken about four hours, but they had barely begun when Robert's face suddenly took on a what-a-marvelous-idea expression and he banged on the front of the carriage to signal MacDougal to stop.

The carriage rolled to a halt, and Robert hopped down with what Victoria deemed rather irritating energy and good cheer. He exchanged a few words with MacDougal and then reentered the carriage.

"What was that all about?" Victoria asked.

"I have a surprise for you."

"I rather think I've had a few too many surprises this past week," she muttered.

"Oh, come now, you must admit that I have made your life more exciting."

She snorted. "If one calls being abducted exciting, I suppose you have a point, my lord."

"I prefer it when you call me Robert."

"Pity for you, then, that I was not put on this earth to cater to your preferences."

He only smiled. "I do love sparring with you."

Victoria's hands clenched at her sides. Trust him to find joy in her insults. She peered out the window and realized that MacDougal had pulled off the Canterbury Road. She turned back to Robert. "Where are we going? I thought you said we were going to Ramsgate."

"We *are* going to Ramsgate. We are just making a slight detour to Whitsable."

"Whitsable? Whyever?"

He leaned forward and grinned rakishly. "Oysters."

"Oysters?"

"The best in the world."

"Robert, I do not want oysters. Please take me directly to Ramsgate."

He raised his brows. "I did not realize you were so eager for a few days alone with me. I shall have to instruct MacDougal to proceed to Ramsgate posthaste."

Victoria nearly jumped out of her seat in frustration. "That isn't what I meant, and you well know it!"

"So then we may continue on to Whitsable?"

Victoria felt rather like a cat who has found itself hopelessly entangled in a ball of string. "You won't listen to me no matter what I say."

Robert's face turned instantly grave. "That is not true. I always listen to you."

"Perhaps, and if you do, then you toss my opinions and requests over your shoulder and do what you please anyway."

"Victoria, the only time I have done that was in regard to your foolish desire to live in London's worst slum."

"It isn't the worst slum," she ground out, more out of habit than anything else.

"I refuse to discuss this further."

"Because you won't listen to what I have to say!"

"No," he said, leaning forward, "it is because

we have discussed that topic to death. I will not allow you to put yourself in constant danger."

"It isn't your place to 'allow' me anything."

"You are not usually so addlebrained as to endanger yourself out of spite." He crossed his arms, his mouth settling into a grim line. "I did what I thought was best."

"And so you kidnapped me," she said bitterly.

"If you recall I offered you the option of residing with my relatives. You refused."

"I want to be independent."

"One doesn't have to be alone to be independent."

Victoria couldn't think of a suitable rebuttal to that statement, so she remained silent.

"When I marry you," Robert said softly, "I want it to be a partnership in every sense of the word. I want to consult you on matters of land management and tenant care. I want us to decide together how to raise our children. I don't know why you are so certain that loving me means losing yourself."

She turned away, not wanting him to see the emotion welling up in her eyes.

"Someday you will realize what it means to be loved." He let out a weary sigh. "I just wish it would be soon."

Victoria pondered that statement the rest of the way to Whitsable.

They stopped to eat at a cheerful inn with outdoor dining. Robert scanned the sky and said, "It looks as if it might rain, but not, I think, in the next hour. Would you like to eat outside?"

She offered him a tentative smile. "The sun feels lovely."

Robert took her arm and escorted her to a little table with a view of the water. He was feeling very optimistic. He sensed that he had somehow gotten through to her in their conversation in the carriage. She wasn't ready yet to admit that she loved him, but he thought she might be a bit closer to it than she'd been the day before.

"The village of Whitsable has been famous for its oysters since the time of the Romans," he said as they sat down.

She plucked at her napkin with nervous fingers. "Really?"

"Yes. I don't know why we never came here when we were courting."

She smiled ruefully. "My father wouldn't have allowed it. And it would have been a long drive to the north Kent coast."

"Do you ever wonder what our lives might be like if we'd married seven years ago?"

Her eyes slid to her lap. "All the time," she whispered.

"We certainly would have dined here already," he said. "I wouldn't have let seven years go by without a meal of fresh oysters."

She didn't say anything.

"I would imagine we would have already had a child. Perhaps two or three." Robert knew he was being a touch cruel. Despite Victoria's distaste for the life of a governess, she had a maternal streak a mile wide. He was purposefully tugging on her heartstrings by mentioning the children they might have had together.

"Yes," she said, "you're probably correct."

She looked so forlorn that Robert didn't have the heart to continue. He planted a bright smile on his face and said, "Oysters, I understand, are supposed to have certain amorous properties."

"I'm sure you would like to believe that." Victoria looked visibly relieved that he'd changed the subject, even though the new topic was beyond racy.

"No, no, it's considered common knowledge."

"Much of what is considered common knowledge has no basis in fact," she countered.

"A good point. Being of a scientific bent myself, I don't like to accept anything as true unless it has been subjected to rigorous experimentation."

Victoria chuckled.

"In fact," Robert said, tapping his fork against the tablecloth, "I think that an experiment might be just the thing."

She eyed him suspiciously. "What are you proposing?"

"Simply that you eat some oysters this afternoon. Then I shall monitor you most closely"—he wiggled his eyebrows in a comical manner—"to see if you appear to like me any better."

Victoria laughed. She couldn't help herself. "Robert," she said, aware that she was beginning to enjoy herself despite her best intentions to remain a grouch, "that is the most harebrained scheme I have ever heard."

"Perhaps, but even if it doesn't work, I shall certainly enjoy the monitoring."

She laughed again. "Just as long as you don't partake of the oysters yourself. If you 'like' me any better, I may find myself being carted off to France."

"Now there is a thought." He pretended to give the matter serious consideration. "Ramsgate is a continental port, after all. I wonder if one can be married faster in France."

"Don't even think about it," she warned.

"My father would probably have a fit of apoplexy were I to be married in a Catholic ceremony," he mused. "We Kembles have always been rather militantly Protestant."

"Oh, goodness," Victoria said, tears of mirth forming in her eyes. "Can you imagine what *my* father would do? The good vicar of Bellfield? He would expire on the spot. I'm sure of it."

"He'd insist on remarrying us himself," Robert said. "And Eleanor would probably charge admission."

Victoria's face softened. "Oh, Ellie. I do miss her."

"Haven't you had a chance to visit with her?" Robert sat back to allow the innkeeper to place a platter of oysters on the table.

Victoria shook her head. "Not since—well, you know. But we write to each other regularly. She is the same as ever. She said she spoke to you."

"Yes, it was a rather serious conversation, but I could see that she was still completely irrepressible."

"Oh, indeed. Do you know what she did with the money she fleeced out of you when we were courting?"

"No, what?"

"First she invested it in an interest-bearing

account. Then, when she decided that she ought to be getting a better rate of return on her money, she studied the financial papers of the *Times* and began investing in stocks."

Robert laughed out loud as he put some oysters on a plate for Victoria. "Your sister never ceases to amaze me. I thought women weren't usually allowed to trade on the 'change."

Victoria shrugged. "She tells her man of business that she is acting on my father's behalf. I believe she said that Papa is something of a recluse and won't leave the house."

Robert was laughing so hard he had to set down the oyster he was about to eat. "Your father would have her head if he knew she was spreading such tales."

"No one is better at keeping a secret than Ellie."

A nostalgic smile crossed Robert's face. "I know. I should probably consult her on some financial matters."

Victoria looked up sharply. "You would do that?"

"Do what?"

"Ask her advice."

"Why not? I have never met anyone with a better knack for handling money than your sister. If she were a man she'd probably be running the Bank of England." Robert picked up the oyster he'd set down. "After we're married— No, no, no, don't even bother to remind me that you haven't accepted my suit, because I am well aware of it. I was merely going to say that you should invite her to stay with us."

"You would let me do that?"

"I am not an ogre, Victoria. I don't know why you seem to think that I will rule you with an iron fist once we are married. Believe me, I am more than happy to share with you some of the responsibilities of an earldom. It can be quite a chore."

Victoria regarded him thoughtfully. She had never realized that Robert's privilege could also be a burden. Although his title would be only an honorary one until his father died, he still had many responsibilities to his land and his tenants.

Robert motioned to her plate. "Do you not enjoy oysters?" He smiled wickedly. "Or perhaps you fear that my scientific experiment might prove successful?"

Victoria blinked herself out of her reverie. "I've never before tried an oyster. I haven't the faintest idea how to eat one."

"I had no idea you had such a gap in your culinary education. Here, let me prepare one for you." Robert picked up an oyster from the center platter, added a squirt of lemon juice and a dab of horseradish, and handed it to her.

Victoria eyed the mollusk dubiously. "Now what do I do?"

"You lift it to your lips and drink it down."

"Drink it? Without chewing?"

He smiled. "No, you chew a bit, too. But first we must make an oyster toast."

Victoria looked around. "I don't think they brought us any toast."

"No, no, a toast. Cheers. To happiness. That sort of toast."

"With an oyster?" She narrowed her eyes

suspiciously. "I am certain that this cannot be a custom."

"Then we'll make it our custom." Robert lifted his oyster in the air. "You, too."

Victoria held her oyster up. "I feel very foolish."

"Don't. We all deserve a bit of fun every now and then."

She smiled wryly. Fun. What a novel concept. "Very well. To what shall we toast?"

"Us, of course."

"Robert . . ."

"Such a spoilsport. Very well, to happiness!"

Victoria clinked her oyster shell against his. "To happiness." She watched as Robert ate his oyster, and then, after muttering "One only lives once, I suppose," she followed suit and sucked it down.

Robert watched her with an amused expression. "How did you enjoy it?"

Victoria came up spluttering. "My goodness, but that was the oddest culinary experience I have ever encountered."

"I'm finding it difficult to discern whether that is a positive or negative statement," Robert said.

"I am finding it difficult as well," she replied, looking a touch startled. "I cannot decide if that was the best food I have ever tasted or the absolute worst."

He laughed out loud. "Perhaps you should try another?"

"I don't suppose they serve beef stew?"

Robert shook his head.

"Well, then, I suppose I'll need another oyster

if I do not want to perish of starvation later in the day."

He prepared another for her. "Your wish is my command."

She shot him a disbelieving glance. "I'm going to pay you a small kindness and not make a suitable retort to that comment."

"I believe you just did."

Victoria ate another oyster, dabbed her lips with her napkin, and smiled archly. "Yes, I did, didn't I?"

Robert was silent for a moment, then he said, "I think it's working."

"I beg your pardon?"

"The oysters. I think you like me better already."

"I do not," she said, trying very hard not to smile.

He clutched at his chest. "I am heartbroken. Utterly bereaved."

"Stop being so silly."

"Or perhaps . . ." He scratched his head in an attempt to look serious and thoughtful. "Perhaps the reason you don't like me any better is because you liked me quite well to begin with."

"Robert!"

"I know, I know. I am having fun at your expense. But you are having fun, too."

She didn't say anything.

"Are you still angry we detoured to Whitsable?"

There was a long silence, and then Victoria shook her head.

Robert didn't realize he'd been holding his breath until it came out in a long whoosh. He reached across the table and placed his hand over hers. "It can always be like this," he whispered. "You can always be this happy."

She opened her mouth, but he didn't let her speak. "I saw it in your eyes," he said. "You enjoyed yourself more this afternoon than you have in the last seven years."

Victoria's head forced her reluctant heart to pull her hand away. "You weren't with me during the last seven years. You can't know what I did or did not feel."

"I know." He paused. "And it breaks my heart."

They didn't speak for the rest of the meal.

The ride to Ramsgate took just over three hours. Robert was surprised that Victoria fell asleep in the carriage. He'd thought her much too tense to drift into slumber, but then again maybe she was simply exhausted. He didn't much mind her inattention; he liked to watch her while she slept.

It also gave him the opportunity to carry her into the cottage when they arrived. She was warm and soft and everything he could ever want. He gently set her down on the bed in the cottage's second bedroom and pulled a quilt up over her. She might be uncomfortable sleeping in her clothing, but he rather thought she'd prefer that to being undressed by him.

He, of course, would have preferred . . . He shuddered and shook his head. Never mind what he would have preferred. He was getting hot just thinking about it, and his cravat suddenly felt uncommonly tight.

Robert left the room with a groan, firmly resolving to take a swim in the icy ocean as soon as possible.

Chapter 17

Victoria woke up to the smell of salt air. She yawned and blinked, momentarily confused by her surroundings. This must be Robert's cottage, she realized. She wondered when he had purchased it. He hadn't owned it when they had courted so many years before.

She sat up in bed and took stock of the room. It was quite lovely, actually, done in shades of blue and peach. It wasn't a particularly feminine room, but it wasn't masculine either, and she had no doubt that it was not Robert's chamber. She let out a sigh of relief. She hadn't *really* thought that he would be so bold as to put her in his bedroom, but it had been a niggling fear.

Victoria rose to her feet and decided to explore the cottage. The house was quiet—Robert was either asleep or out. Either way it afforded her a perfect opportunity to snoop. She padded out into the hall, not bothering to put on her shoes. It was a sturdy little house, with thick stone walls and a timbered roof. Its snug second floor housed only two rooms, but each had a fireplace. Victoria peeked into the other room and ascertained that it was Robert's. The four-poster bed was solid and masculine and faced a large window, open to a glorious view of the Strait of Dover. A telescope stood by the window. Robert had always loved to look at the stars.

She walked back into the hall and made her way downstairs. The house was nothing if not cozy. There was no formal dining room, and the sitting room looked comfortable and well loved. Victoria was making her way back through the dining area, intending to inspect the kitchen, when she spied a note on the table. She picked it up and instantly recognized Robert's handwriting.

V—

Have gone for a swim.

—R

A swim? Was the man batty? Granted, it was summer, but it was not a particularly sunny day, and the water had to be freezing. Victoria went to a window to see if she could see Robert in the surf, but the water was too far below her to make anything out.

She ran upstairs and put on her shoes. Because she didn't have a shawl—indeed, she didn't even have a change of clothing save the seductively cut blue silk nightgown that *he* had picked out for her—she took a thin blanket to wrap around her shoulders. The wind appeared to be picking up, and the sky was growing darker. She doubted her dress would be warm enough to brave the elements.

Victoria dashed back downstairs and out the front door. To her left she could see a path leading down the steep hill to the rocky beach. The path was very narrow, so she took careful steps as she began her descent, using one hand to hold the blanket around her shoulders and the other for balance. After several minutes of careful footwork, she reached the bottom and scanned the horizon for Robert.

Where was he?

She cupped her hands to her lips and bellowed his name. She heard no response save the swishing sound of the surf. She hadn't really expected him to yell back, but a wave or a motion to show that he was still alive would have been nice.

She clutched the blanket closer to her body, then arranged it so it would protect her clothing as she sat down.

The wind grew more fierce, and the salt air stung her cheeks. Her hair was beginning to grow stiff, her toes were freezing, and damn it, where was Robert? It couldn't be safe to be out swimming in this weather. She stood again, scanned the horizon, and yelled his name. Then, just when she decided that her situation could not get any worse, a sharp raindrop stabbed her cheek.

Victoria looked down, saw that her arms were shaking, and then realized that it wasn't because of the cold. She was terrified. If Robert drowned . . .

She couldn't even complete the thought. She was still angry with him for his high-handed behavior this past week, and she wasn't at all certain that she wanted to marry him, but the thought of him forever gone from this world was beyond comprehension.

The rain grew thicker. Victoria continued to yell Robert's name, but the wind refused to carry her words to sea. She felt helpless and impotent. There was absolutely no point in venturing into the water to save him—he was a much stronger swimmer than she was, and besides, she hadn't a clue where he was. So she just bellowed his name yet again. Not that he could hear her, but it was the only thing she could do.

And doing nothing was pure agony.

She watched as the sky darkened ominously, listened as the wind's shrieks grew more ferocious—and told herself to breathe evenly as her heart raced with panic. And then, just when she was sure she would explode with frustration, she saw a flash of pink on the horizon.

She ran to the water's edge. "Robert!" she screamed. A minute passed, and then she could finally make out that the object in the water was indeed a man.

"Oh, thank God, Robert," she breathed, running into the calf-deep water. He was still much too far away for her to be of any use, but she couldn't stop herself from moving toward him. Besides, it seemed silly to worry about her wet ankles when the rain had already soaked through her clothing.

She waded out farther until the waves smacked her knees. The current was strong, pulling her out toward the horizon, and she shook with fear. Robert was fighting that same current. She could see him more closely now; his strokes were still strong, but they were growing uneven. He was getting tired.

She yelled his name yet again, and this time he stopped and looked up while treading water. His mouth moved, and in her heart Victoria knew that he had said her name.

He put his head back down and swam forward. It might have been Victoria's imagination, but it looked as if he was moving a little faster now. She reached her arms out and took another step forward. Only ten yards or so separated them now. "You're almost there!" she shouted. "You can do it, Robert!"

The water was at her waist and then suddenly it was over her head, a giant wave crashing above her. She tumbled into a somersault, and for a moment she had no idea which way was up. And then, miraculously, her feet touched the ground, and her face found the air. She blinked, realized that she was now facing the shore, and turned around just in time to see Robert staggering into her. His chest was bare, and his breeches were plastered to his thighs.

He practically fell against her. "My God, Victoria," he gasped. "When I saw you go down . . ." Clearly unable to finish his sentence, he bent at the waist, gasping for air.

Victoria grabbed his arm and began to pull. "We've got to get to the shore," she pleaded.

"Are you—are you all right?"

She gaped at him through the driving rain. "You're asking that of *me*? Robert, you were miles from shore! I couldn't see you. I was terrified. I—" She stopped. "Why am I discussing this now?"

They stumbled to shore. Victoria was cold and weak, but she knew that he was weaker, so she forced her legs to pull them along. He clung to her, and she could feel his legs wobbling beneath him.

"Victoria," he gasped.

"Don't say anything." She concentrated on the shore, and when she reached it she concentrated on the path.

He ground to a halt, though, forcing her to stop. He took her face into his hands, ignoring the rain and the wind, and looked into her eyes. "Are you all right?" he repeated.

Victoria stared at him, unable to believe that he would pause in the middle of the storm to ask her that. She covered one of his hands with her own and said, "Robert, I'm fine. I'm cold, but I'm fine. We have to get you inside."

How they made it up the steep path, Victoria would never know. The wind and rain had loosened the earth, and more than once one of them stumbled and slipped, only to be pulled back upright by the other. Finally, her hands raw and scraped, Victoria pulled herself over the edge of the hill and landed on the green grass of the cottage's lawn. A second later Robert joined her.

The rain was torrential now, and the wind howled like a hundred furies. Together they staggered to the cottage's front door. Robert grabbed the knob and ripped the door open, shoving Victoria into the warmth of the interior.

Once they were both inside, they stood stock still, momentarily paralyzed with relief.

Robert was the first to recover, and he reached out and grabbed Victoria, crushing her to him. His arms were shaking uncontrollably, but they held her firm. "I thought I'd lost you," he whispered, pressing his lips to her temple. "I thought I'd lost you."

"Don't be silly, I—"

"I thought I'd lost you," he repeated, his grip on her remaining strong. "First I thought I was going to—that I wouldn't make it back, and I didn't want to—God, I didn't want to die, not when we were so close to—" His hands moved to her face, holding her still while he memorized every feature, every freckle, and every eyelash. "Then when you went under—"

"Robert, it was only for a moment."

"I didn't know if you could swim. You never told me if you could swim."

"I can swim. Not as well as you, but I can— It doesn't matter. I'm fine." She pried his hands from her face and tried to pull him toward the staircase. "We must get you into bed. You'll catch the death of you if we don't get you dry."

"You, too," he mumbled, letting her lead the way.

"I wasn't submerged in the Strait of Dover for God only knows how long. Once we take care of you, I promise I will change into dry garments." She practically pushed him up the stairs. He stumbled repeatedly, never seeming to lift his leg high enough to reach the next step. Once they reached the second story, she nudged him forward.

"I assume this is your room," she said, leading him inside.

He nodded briefly.

"Take off your clothes," she ordered.

Robert had just enough strength to laugh. "If you knew how many times I have dreamed of you saying that . . ." He looked down at his hands, which were shaking violently from the cold. His fingernails were purplish blue.

"Don't be silly," Victoria said sternly, running around the room to light the candles. It was only early evening, but the storm had taken away much of the sunlight. She turned around and saw that he hadn't made much headway on his clothing. "What is wrong with you?" she scolded. "I told you to undress."

He shrugged helplessly. "I can't. My fingers . . ."

Victoria's eyes fell to his hands, which were fumbling over the fastenings to his breeches. His fingers were shaking violently, and he couldn't seem to make them close around his buttons. With brisk determination reminiscent of her not so distant days as a governess, she closed the space between them and unfastened his breeches, trying not to look when she pulled them down.

"I'm usually a bit more impressive," Robert joked.

Victoria couldn't keep her eyes to herself after *that* comment. "Oh!" she said, startled. "That's not what I expected at all."

"It certainly isn't what I like to see, myself," he muttered.

She blushed and turned away. "Into the bed

with you," she said, trying for a normal voice but not quite succeeding.

He tried to explain as she herded him into the bed. "When a man gets cold, he—"

"That's quite enough, thank you. More than I need to know, I'm sure."

He smiled, but the chattering of his teeth marred the effect. "You're embarrassed."

"You noticed," she said, crossing to the wardrobe. "Have you any extra blankets?"

"There is one in your room."

"I took that down with me to the beach. I must have lost it in the water." She shut the wardrobe door and turned around. "What are you doing?" she nearly shrieked. He was sitting up in bed, having made no attempt to pull the quilts over him. He'd crossed his arms and was clutching himself.

He just stared at her, unblinking. "I don't think I've ever been this cold."

She yanked the covers up to his chin. "Well, you're not going to get any warmer if you don't use these blankets."

He nodded, still shivering uncontrollably. "Your hands are freezing."

"They're not nearly as bad as yours."

"Go change," he ordered.

"I want to make sure you—"

"Go." His voice was quiet, but it did not lack authority.

She paused, and then gave a brief nod. "Don't move."

"Wild horses couldn't—"

"I mean it!" she warned.

"Victoria," he said, sounding infinitely weary. "I couldn't move even if I wanted to, which, incidentally, I don't."

"Good."

"Go!"

She threw up her arms. "I'm going, I'm going."

Robert allowed himself to sink farther under the bed sheets once she left. Good Lord, he was cold. When he'd left for a swim, he'd never dreamed that the sky would whip up into such a ferocious storm. He clamped his teeth together, but they clattered anyway. He hated being so dependent on Victoria, especially when she had to be freezing cold herself. He'd always loved being her knight in shining armor—strong, brave, and true. Now he was wet, cold, and pathetic. And to add insult to injury, she'd finally seen him naked, and he did *not* have much to show for himself.

"Are you still under the covers?" Victoria yelled from the next room. "If you get out of bed, I'll—"

"I haven't moved!"

He heard a grunt that sounded something like "Good." He smiled. He might not like being dependent on Victoria, but there was something to be said for being fussed over.

He pulled the covers tighter around him and rubbed his feet against the sheets in a vain attempt to warm them up. He could barely feel his hands, so he shoved them under his buttocks, but as his rear was equally cold, this didn't do much to help. He pulled the blankets up over his head and breathed heavily on his hands. This brought some momentary relief.

Footsteps pattered in the hall for a moment before he heard Victoria say, "What are you doing under there?"

He poked his head out just far enough to see her. "It's warmer under here." Then he looked a little more closely. *"What* are you wearing?"

She made a face. "You might recall that I neglected to bring a change of clothing."

He wished his face was warm enough to smile.

"All I had," she continued, "was this nightgown you gave to me. And this quilt I pulled off the other bed, for the sake of decency." With a rather matronly sniff, she pulled the aforementioned quilt more closely around her body.

Robert's eyes rolled heavenward as he moaned, "I must be even more ill than I thought."

"What do you mean?" Victoria rushed to his side, perched on the edge of the bed, and brushed his hair aside as she placed her hand on his brow. "Are you feverish?"

He shook his head, his expression beyond pained.

"Then what is the matter?"

"It's you," he croaked.

Her eyes widened. "Me?"

"You. In that gown."

She frowned. "It's all I had."

"I know," he moaned. "It's my wildest fantasy come true. And I'm too damned miserable to even want you."

She leaned back and crossed her arms. "It serves you right, in my opinion."

"I had a feeling that would be your opinion," he muttered.

"Are you any warmer?" she asked, assessing him rather unsympathetically.

He shook his head.

Victoria stood. "I am going downstairs to prepare you some broth. I assume there is food in the kitchen?"

He looked at her blankly.

"Food?" she repeated. "In the kitchen?"

"I think so," he said, not sounding at all certain of himself.

She stared at him in disbelief. "You abducted me and forgot to stock the cottage with provisions?"

His lips stretched into a decidedly weak smile. "I might have."

"Robert, this is so stunningly unlike you, I don't know what to think. You've never forgotten a detail in your life."

"I sent word to the caretaker that I would be arriving, asking him to prepare the cottage. I'm sure he brought food." He paused and swallowed. "At least I hope he did."

Victoria stood, a stern, governess-worthy expression firmly in place on her face.

"Do you know how to cook?" Robert asked hopefully.

"I'm a wonder when I have food."

"You'll have food."

She didn't say another word as she left the room.

Robert remained in bed, shivering and feeling altogether sick. It hadn't been so bad when Victoria was there. She—and that devilish nightgown he was beginning to wish he hadn't purchased—took his mind off the fact that ten little icicles were attached to his feet and that he used to call them toes.

A few minutes later Victoria reappeared in his doorway, two steaming mugs in her hands. Robert's entire face lit up. "Broth?" he said. He couldn't remember a time when broth sounded so good.

Victoria smiled sweetly. A little too sweetly. "This is your lucky day, Robert."

Robert sniffed the air, searching for an aroma. "Thank you, Victoria, for—" He stopped when she handed him a mug. "What is this?"

"Hot water."

"You brought me hot water? Isn't one supposed to receive some sort of nourishment when one is ill?"

"You're not ill, just cold. And hot water is, by definition, hot. I'm sure it will warm you up."

He sighed. "There wasn't any food, was there?"

"Not even a biscuit."

He took a sip of the water, shuddering with delight as the heat traveled down his insides. Then, his mouth never leaving the rim of his mug, he looked up. "No tea?"

"Nary a leaf."

He drank some more, then said, "I never thought I'd see the day when an English household would be out of tea."

Victoria smiled. "Now do you feel warmer?"

He nodded and held out his empty mug. "I don't suppose there is more?"

She picked up his mug and stood, motioning to the window. Rain was still pelting the house furiously. "I don't think we're in any danger of running out of water. I have some heating on the stove and a bucket outside catching more."

He looked up sharply. "Surely you don't intend to go outside in this weather. I want you to stay dry."

She smiled and waved away his concern. "There is no need to worry about me. The overhang will keep me dry. Only my hand will get wet." She started to leave.

"Victoria, wait!"

She turned around.

"Are *you* still cold? You have done nothing but take care of me. I don't want to see you catch a chill."

"The water has helped. I—"

"Your hands are still shaking." It sounded almost like an accusation.

"No, I'm fine. Really. It just takes a bit of time for me to warm through and through."

He frowned, but before he could say anything more, she had darted from the room. She reappeared a few minutes later. The blanket around her shoulders slipped, and Robert tried to ignore the way the blue silk nightgown clung to her curves. It was the oddest thing he had ever encountered. His mind was racing with every sort of erotic fantasy, and his body refused to respond.

Robert cursed the cold with remarkable fluency.

As Victoria handed him his hot water, she asked, "Did you say something?"

"Nothing fit for your ears," he muttered.

She raised her brows, but other than that did not question him further. They sat in companionable silence for several minutes, Victoria perched on the opposite side of the bed from Robert.

Suddenly she sat up straight with such abruptness that Robert nearly dropped his mug. "Where is MacDougal?" she asked, tightening the blanket around her.

"I sent him back to London."

She relaxed visibly. "Oh. Good. I shouldn't like anyone to see me in this state."

"Mmm, yes. Of course, if MacDougal were here we could send him out for food."

Victoria's stomach growled loudly in response.

Robert shot her a sideways glance. "Hungry?"

"Oh, just a little," she said, patently lying.

"Still angry with me?"

"Oh, just a little," she said in the same tone.

He laughed. "I never intended to starve you, you know."

"No, I'm sure ravishment was at the top of your agenda."

"Marriage was my primary goal, as you well know."

"Hmmph."

"What is that supposed to mean? Surely you don't doubt my intentions."

She sighed. "No, I don't doubt you. You have been most enthusiastic."

There was a long silence. Robert watched her as she set her mug down on the bedside table and rubbed her hands together. "You're still cold, aren't you?" he asked.

She nodded, pulling her legs toward her body to conserve her heat.

"Get into the bed," he said.

Her head swiveled slowly in his direction. "Surely you jest."

"We will both be warmer if we pool the heat from our bodies."

To his surprise, she laughed. "I had no idea you'd grown so creative, Robert."

"I am not making this up. You know that I studied the sciences extensively at university. The dynamics of heat was one of my favorite subjects."

"Robert, I refuse to compromise my—"

"Oh, come now, Torie, you couldn't possibly compromise yourself any further." Wrong thing to say, he decided, once he saw the stricken expression on her face. "What I meant to say," he continued, "is that if anyone learns you have spent the night here with me, they will assume the worst. It doesn't matter whether or not we behave with propriety. No one will care."

"I will care."

"Victoria, I am not going to seduce you. I couldn't even if I tried. My body is so damned cold—trust me, I'm not exactly in optimum working order."

"You're still cold?" she asked.

He caught himself just before he smiled. Of

course! Victoria wouldn't snuggle in bed with him to warm herself, but she was bighearted enough to do it for his sake. "Freezing," he said, and then he clattered his teeth together a few times for effect.

"And my crawling into bed will help you get warmer?" She looked dubious.

He nodded, able to keep a sincere expression on his face because he wasn't technically lying. He *would* be warmer with the heat of another body in the bed beside him.

"And I'll be warmer, too?" She let out a shiver.

His eyes narrowed. "You have been lying to me, haven't you? You're still freezing. You have been running around the house tending to my needs without a thought to your own well-being." He scooted over a few inches, then reached out from under the covers. The blankets slipped, baring his firmly muscled chest.

"Robert!"

His hand closed around her bare foot. "My God!" he exclaimed. "You're colder than I am."

"It's really just my feet. The floorboards—"

"Now!" he roared.

Victoria scurried under the blankets. Robert's arm wrapped around her and hauled her onto his side of the bed.

"I'm sure this isn't necessary!" Victoria protested.

"Oh, it's necessary."

Victoria gulped as he pulled her closer. Her back was pressed up against his front, and the only thing between their bare skin was a thin layer of silk. She wasn't entirely certain how she'd ended up in this position. Robert had somehow manipulated her without her even realizing it. "I'm still cold," she said peevishly.

When he spoke, his words were hot against her ear. "Don't worry. We've all night."

Victoria elbowed him in the ribs. Hard.

"Ow!" Robert lurched backward and rubbed his midsection. "What was that for?"

"'We've all night,'" she mimicked. "Really, Robert, you're most insulting. I am doing you a favor by—"

"I know."

"—lying here next to you, and—" She looked up. "What did you say?"

"I said, 'I know.' You are doing me a wondrous favor. I am feeling warmer already."

That took some of the wind out of her sails, and all she could think to say was, "Grmmph." Not, she realized, her wittiest hour.

"Your feet, however, are still icicles."

Victoria grimaced. "They do radiate the cold, don't they?"

"One cannot radiate cold," he said, suddenly sounding very academic. "Cold objects suck in heat from the surrounding air, which makes it feel as if they are radiating cold, but in actuality one can only radiate heat."

"Oh," Victoria said, mostly just so that he would think she was listening.

"It's a common misconception."

That appeared to be the end of the conversation, which left Victoria right where she had started—lying in bed next to a man who was *not* wearing any clothing. And she in her scandalously low-cut nightgown—it was quite beyond anything. Victoria tried to pull herself at least a few inches away from him, but his arm, while cold, seemed admirably strong. Robert clearly had no intention of letting her scoot to the other side of the bed.

Victoria ground her teeth together so hard she thought her jaw might snap. "I am going to sleep," she declared firmly, then shut her eyes.

"Really?" Robert drawled, and it was clear from the tone of his voice that he didn't think she would be able to.

"Really," she said, eyes still closed. She doubted she'd fall asleep anytime soon, but she'd always been really good at faking it. "Good night."

Twenty minutes later Robert looked down at her in surprise. Her eyelashes rested lightly on her cheeks, and her chest rose and fell in an even, gentle rhythm. "I can't believe she nodded off," he muttered. He didn't want to relinquish his hold on her, but his arm was falling asleep, so he rolled over with a loud sigh and shut his eyes.

A few inches away, Victoria finally opened her eyes and allowed herself a small smile.

Chapter 18

When Victoria awakened the next morning, there was a naked arm thrown over her shoulder and an equally naked leg draped across her hip. The fact that both limbs were attached to a naked man immediately set her heart racing.

She carefully disentangled herself and climbed out of bed, pulling along a blanket to cover some of the skin the blue nightgown left bare. She'd just made it to the door when she heard Robert stir. Victoria grasped the knob, hoping that she could slip out before he opened his eyes, but before she could even twist her hand, she heard a groggy "Good morning" from behind her.

There was nothing for it but to turn around. "Good morning, Robert."

"I trust you slept well."

"Like a baby," she lied. "If you'll excuse me, I am going to change my clothing."

He yawned, stretched, and said, "I can't imagine that your dress wasn't ruined yesterday."

She swallowed, having forgotten the beating her one and only garment had taken the day before. The wind, rain, rocks, and saltwater had rendered it unmendable. Still, it was certainly more appropriate and respectable than what she was wearing now, and she told him so.

"Pity," he said. "The blue gown looks so fetching on you."

She snorted and wrapped the blanket more tightly around her. "It is indecent, and I'm sure that is exactly what you intended when you bought it."

"Actually," he said thoughtfully, "you fill it out even more delightfully than I'd dreamed."

Victoria took "delightful" to be a euphemism for something else altogether, and quickly left the room. She didn't want to be subject to Robert's double-entendres. Even worse, she was terrified that he was beginning to wear her down. She hated to think what she might do if he tried to kiss her again.

She'd probably kiss him back. What a nightmare.

She scooted into her room, where her ruined dress was laying on her bed. The saltwater had left it stiff, and she had to beat and stretch the material until it was pliable enough for her to put it on. She left the blue nightgown on as a chemise; her own itched like the devil and had a piece of seaweed tangled up in the strap.

When she finally stepped in front of the mirror, she couldn't suppress a loud groan. She looked a fright. Her hair was beyond hope. There was no way she would be able to style it properly without washing the salt away, and her cursory inspection of the cottage hadn't unearthed any soap. Her dress was unbearably wrinkled, torn in four places that she could see—no, make that five, she realized as she inspected her hem. Still, it covered her up better than what she'd been wearing before.

And if she wasn't precisely looking her best for Robert—well, the man had up and abducted her. It served him right.

Robert, plain-spoken man that he was, made no attempt to gloss over the fact that her appearance was not up to her usual standards. "You look as if you've been attacked by dogs," he said when they crossed paths in the hall. He had also gotten dressed, but unlike Victoria he looked immaculate. She supposed that he kept a change of clothing here at the cottage so he wouldn't have to pack for trips like these.

She rolled her eyes and said, "Flattery will get you nowhere," and then continued past him down the stairs.

He followed her into the kitchen with a cheerful expression. "Is that so? Then what is the path to your heart? I happily accept any and all advice."

Victoria didn't even miss a beat before she said, "Food."

"Food? Really? That is all it will take to impress you?"

It was difficult to remain grumpy when he was being so jovial, but she tried her best. "It would certainly be a start." Then, as if to punctuate her sentence, her stomach let out a loud roar.

Robert grimaced. "I feel much the same way myself," he said, patting his midsection. He looked down at his belly. It looked flat, but it felt concave. Last night he'd been too cold to attempt to seduce Victoria; this morning he was too damned hungry.

He moved his gaze back to her face. She was looking at him expectantly, as if she'd been saying something to him and he hadn't been listening. "Er, were you speaking to me?" he asked.

She scowled and repeated, "I can't possibly go out looking like this."

He blinked, still chuckling to himself over the image of himself and Victoria—finally making love and then passing out from hunger in the middle of the act.

"Robert," she said impatiently, "will you or won't you go to town? We need food, and I need something to wear."

"Very well," he said, somehow grumbling and smiling at the same time. "I'll go. But I must demand payment."

"Are you mad?" she exclaimed, her voice rising halfway to a shriek. "First you abduct me, completely ignoring my wishes, then I nearly drown trying to save you, and now you have the nerve to tell me that I must pay to eat?"

One side of his mouth lifted into a lazy smile. "Just a kiss," he said. Then, before she had a chance to react, he pulled her against him and kissed her soundly. He had meant it to be a teasing kiss, a nothing-but-fun sort of kiss, but the minute his lips touched hers, he was captured by a hunger that far eclipsed anything his stomach had felt all morning. She was perfect in his arms, small and soft and warm and everything he'd ever dreamed a woman could be.

He touched his tongue to hers, marveling at

the soft heat of it. She was yielding to him—no, she had already yielded, and now she was returning his affections.

Robert felt that kiss in his very soul. "You'll love me again," he whispered. And then he rested his chin on her head and just held her close. Sometimes that was enough. Sometimes just feeling her in his arms was all he needed. His body didn't race with desire, his loins didn't harden and throb. He just needed to hold her.

They stayed that way for a full minute. Then he pulled away and saw the wary confusion on her face. Before she could say something he didn't want to hear, he gave her a jaunty grin and said, "Your hair smells like seaweed."

That earned him a whack on the side of his head with an empty sugar sack she'd been holding. Robert only laughed, thankful that she hadn't been carrying a rolling pin.

About an hour after Robert left to go shopping, Victoria realized that they had both overlooked an important point. MacDougal had taken the carriage back to London. As far as she knew, there wasn't even a mount for Robert to ride into town. She hadn't inspected the property very carefully the day before, but she certainly hadn't seen any building in which one could stable a horse.

Victoria wasn't particularly perturbed that Robert would have to walk into town. It was a perfectly lovely day outside, with no sign of yesterday's storm, and the exercise would probably do him good. But she did wonder how he would be able to carry his purchases home. They

were both famished—he would need to buy a
lot of food. And, of course, she needed a new
dress or two.

With a shake of her head she decided not to
worry about it. Robert was nothing if not resourceful, and he loved to plan. She couldn't
imagine that he wouldn't figure out how to solve
this little dilemma.

She wandered aimlessly about the house, giving it a closer inspection than she'd been able to
the day before. The cottage was charming, and
she didn't understand how Robert could bear to
live anywhere else. She supposed he was used to
grander lodgings. Victoria let out a regretful
sigh. A cottage such as this was all she would
ever want. Neat, tidy, homey, with a beautiful
view of the water. How could anyone want
anything else?

Aware that she was growing maudlin, Victoria
snapped herself back to attention and continued
her inspection. She knew she was invading
Robert's privacy by rifling through his drawers
and cabinets, but she didn't feel particularly
guilty about it. He had abducted her, after all.
She had a few rights as the victim in this little
scenario.

And, much as she didn't enjoy admitting it to
herself, she knew that she was looking for pieces
of herself. Had Robert saved memories of their
courtship, mementos of their love? It was unre-
alistic to think that he would have moved them
to this cottage even if he had, but she couldn't
stop herself from looking.

She was falling in love with him again. He was
wearing her down, just as he said he would. She

wondered if there was any way to reverse the tide. She certainly didn't *want* to love him.

She headed back up to his bedroom and opened the door to what she assumed was his dressing room. In the corner was a tub, and in the tub—could it be? She looked a little more closely. Sure enough, stuck to the bottom of the tub was a half-melted bar of soap that someone—probably Robert—had forgotten to clean up. Victoria had never in her life been so thankful for someone else's lack of housekeeping skills. The last time she had tried to run her hand through her hair, it had gotten stuck there. Being able to wash the salt out was about the closest thing to heaven she could imagine.

Robert would surely be gone for several hours. She would have plenty of time to enjoy a hot bath. With a grunt of exertion, Victoria pulled the tub out of the dressing room and into Robert's room, where sunlight streamed through the windows. Then, suddenly feeling very uncomfortable at the thought of bathing in his private chamber, she pulled the tub down the hall to her room. She tried to pry the soap from the metal, but it felt as if it had been bonded. She decided to leave it. The hot water would probably loosen it up.

It took nearly half an hour and several trips up and down the stairs, but eventually Victoria had the tub full of steaming water. Just the sight of it had her shivering with anticipation. She stripped out of her clothing as fast as could be and stepped into the bathwater. It was hot enough to sting her skin, but it was wet and it was clean and it felt like heaven.

Victoria sighed contentedly as she slowly lowered herself into the metal tub. She watched as the white patches of salt that clung to her skin dissolved in the hot water, then she dunked under the surface to wet her hair. After quite a while of happy soaking, she used her left foot to nudge against the soap still stuck to the bottom.

It wouldn't move.

"Oh, come now," she muttered. "You've had a good twenty minutes." It occurred to her that she was talking to a bar of soap, but after what she'd been through in the past forty-eight hours, she thought she had a right to act a bit oddly if she pleased.

She switched to her right foot and pushed harder. Surely the thing would have loosened by now. "Move!" she ordered, jamming her heel up against the side of it. It was slick and slippery, and all that happened was that her foot slid right over the top.

"Oh, blast," she muttered, sitting up. She was going to have to use her hands to pry it loose. She dug her fingernails in and pulled. Then she got a better idea and twisted. Finally she felt the soap begin to move, and after a few more seconds of twisting and yanking, she had at least some of the bar in her hands.

"Aha!" she yelled, feeling triumphant even if her enemy was only a silly old bar of soap. "I win. *I* win. I *win*."

"Victoria!"

She froze.

"Victoria, to whom are you speaking?"

Robert. How on earth could he have traveled to town and back in such a short time? Not to mention do all of his shopping. He'd only been gone an hour. Or was it two?

"Just to myself!" she yelled back, stalling. Dear Lord, he was back, and she hadn't even washed her hair yet. Drat. She *really* wanted to wash her hair.

Robert's footsteps sounded on the stairs. "Don't you even want to know what I bought?"

There was nothing for it. She would have to come clean. Wincing at her mental pun, Victoria fairly screamed, "Don't come in here!"

The footsteps halted. "Victoria, is everything all right?"

"Yes, I'm . . . I'm just . . ."

After a long beat, Robert said from just behind the door, "Do you have any plans to complete that sentence?"

"I'm taking a bath."

More silence, then, "I see."

Victoria gulped. "I would rather you didn't."

"Didn't what?"

"See. Me, that is."

He let out a loud groan that Victoria heard right through the door and clear across the room. It was impossible not to think about him thinking about her in the tub, and—

"Do you need a towel?"

Victoria exhaled, more than thrilled that he'd interrupted her thoughts, which were taking her in a most dangerous direction. "No," she replied. "I have one here."

"How unfortunate," he muttered.

"I found it with the bed linens," she said, mostly because she felt as if she had to say something.

"Do you need soap?"

"It was stuck to the tub."

"Do you need food? I brought back a half dozen pasties."

Victoria's stomach rumbled, but she said, "I'll have one later, if you don't mind."

"Do you need *anything?*" He sounded almost desperate.

"No, not really, although—"

"Although what?" he said, very quickly. "What do you need? I'd be happy to bring it to you. Ecstatic. Anything to make you more comfortable."

"Did you happen to buy me a new dress? I'm going to need something to change into. I suppose I could put this one back on, but it's terribly itchy with the salt."

She heard him say, "Just one moment. Don't move. Don't go anywhere."

"As if I had anywhere to go like this," she said to herself, looking down at her naked body.

A moment later she heard Robert running up the hall. "I'm back!" he said. "I have your dress. I hope it fits."

"Anything would be an improvement over—" Victoria gasped as she saw the doorknob turning. "What are you doing?" she shrieked.

Mercifully the doorknob froze in place. She supposed even Robert knew when he was going too far. "Bringing you your dress," he said. But there was a hint of a question in his voice.

"Just open the door a few inches and drop it in," she instructed.

A moment of silence, and then: "I don't get to come inside?"

"No!"

"Oh." He sounded like a disappointed schoolboy.

"Robert, surely you didn't think I would allow you to come in here while I am bathing."

"I was hoping . . ." His words trailed off into a big heartfelt sigh.

"Just drop the dress inside."

He did as she asked.

"Now close the door."

"Would you like me to drop a pasty inside, too?"

Victoria judged the distance between the tub and the door. She would have to get out of the bath in order to get the food. Not an appealing concept, but then again her stomach was roaring at the thought of a meat pasty. "Could you scoot it across the floor?" she asked.

"Won't it get dirty?"

"I don't care." And she didn't. That's how hungry she was.

"Very well." His hand came into sight, about an inch above the floor. "In which direction?"

"I beg your pardon?"

"In which direction should I push the pasty? I wouldn't want to send it out of your reach."

Victoria thought that what should have been a very simple task was turning into a most complicated endeavor, and she wondered if he'd found some insidious peephole. Maybe he was stalling as he watched her. Maybe he could see her naked body. Maybe—

"Victoria?"

Then she thought of the scientific precision

with which he approached everything he did. The crazy man probably did want to know which way to scoot the pasty. "I'm at about one o'clock," she said, lifting her left hand from the tub and shaking it dry.

Robert's hand twisted slightly to the right, and he sent the pasty careening across the wood floor. It came to a halt when it smacked into the side of the metal tub. "Bull's eye!" Victoria called out. "You can close the door now."

Nothing.

"I said you can close the door now!" she said, her voice a little more stern.

Another heartfelt sigh, and then the door shut. "I'll just wait in the kitchen," he said, his voice small.

Victoria would have answered him, but her mouth was full.

Robert lowered himself onto a stool and let his head drop dejectedly onto the wooden kitchen table. First he'd been cold. Then he'd been hungry. But now—well, to be frank, now his body was in perfect working order, and Victoria was naked in a tub, and he was—

He groaned. He was *not* comfortable.

He busied himself in the kitchen, putting away some of the food he'd brought home. He wasn't accustomed to the chore, but he rarely brought many servants with him to the Ramsgate cottage, so he was a bit more at home here than he would have been at Castleford or in London. Besides, there wasn't much to unpack; he'd made arrangements for the shopowners to deliver most of his purchases. He'd only brought with him what was ready-made and could be eaten immediately.

Robert finished his chores by popping two rolls into the bread box, and he settled back down onto the stool, trying very hard not to imagine what Victoria was doing right then.

He wasn't successful, and he started feeling so warm he had to open a window.

"Keep your mind off her," he muttered. "No need to think about Victoria. There are millions of people on this planet, and she's just one of them. And there are a number of planets, too. Mercury, Venus, Earth, Mars . . ."

Robert ran out of planets in short order and, desperate to keep his mind on anything but Victoria, started in on the Linnaean system of taxonomy. "Kingdom, phylum, then . . ."

He paused. Was that a footstep he'd heard? No, he must have imagined it. He sighed, then resumed. ". . . class, order, family, and then . . . and then . . ." Damn it, what came next?

He started pounding the table with his fist in an attempt to jog his memory. "Damn, damn, damn," he said, punctuating each pound. He was well aware that he getting a bit too upset over his inability to remember a simple scientific term, but the task had taken on almost desperate proportions. Victoria was upstairs in the tub, and—

"Genus!" he fairly yelled out. "Genus and then species!"

"I beg your pardon?"

He whipped his head around. Victoria was standing in the doorway, her hair still damp. The dress he'd bought her was a hair too long and dragged on the floor, but other than that it fit her quite well. He cleared his throat. "You look—" He had to clear his throat again. "You look fetching."

"Thank you very much," she said automatically. "But what were you yelling about?"

"Nothing."

"I could have sworn you were saying something about the genius of the three seas."

He stared at her, certain that his loins had sapped some of the energy from his brain, because he truly had no idea what she was talking about. "What does that mean?" he asked.

"I don't know. Why did you say it?"

"I didn't say it. I said, 'genus and species.'"

"Oh." She paused. "That would explain everything, I suppose, if I knew what it meant."

"It means . . ." He looked up. She had an expectant and slightly amused expression on her face. "It's a scientific term."

"I see," she said slowly. "And was there any reason you were shouting it at the top of your lungs?"

"Yes," he said, focusing on her mouth. "Yes, there was."

"Was there?"

He took a step toward her, and then another. "Yes. You see, I was trying to keep my mind off something."

She nervously wetted her lips and blushed. "Oh, I see."

He moved ever closer. "But it didn't work."

"Not even a little bit?" she squeaked.

He shook his head, so close to her now that his nose nearly brushed hers. "I still want you." He shrugged apologetically. "I can't help it."

She did nothing but stare at him. Robert decided that was better than an outright rejection and moved his hand to the small of her back. "I searched the door for a peephole," he said.

She didn't look surprised when she whispered, "Did you find one?"

He shook his head. "No. But I have a very good imagination. Not"—he leaned forward and brushed the lightest of kisses onto her mouth—"as good as the real thing, I'm afraid, but it was enough to lead to my current state of extreme and prolonged discomfort."

"Discomfort?" she echoed, her eyes growing wide and unfocused.

"Mmm-hmm." He kissed her again, another light touch intended to arouse, not invade.

Again she made no move to pull away. Robert's hopes soared, as did his arousal. But he held his desire in check, sensing that she needed to be seduced by words as well as actions. He touched her cheek as he whispered, "May I kiss you?"

She looked startled that he'd asked. "You just did."

He smiled lazily. "Technically I suppose that this"—he brushed another of those feather light kisses across her mouth—"qualifies as a kiss. But what I want to do to you is so different it seems a crime against words to call them the same thing."

"Wh-what do you mean?"

Her curiosity thrilled him. "I think you know," he said, smiling. "But just to refresh your memory . . ."

He slanted his mouth against hers and kissed her deeply, nibbling on her lips and exploring her with his tongue. "That is more along the lines of what I intended."

He could sense her being swept away on the tide of his passion. Her pulse was racing and her breath was coming faster and faster. Beneath his hand he could feel her skin burning through the thin fabric of her dress. Her head fell back as he kissed her neck, trailing hot fire along the line of her throat.

She was melting. He could feel it.

His hands moved down and curved around her backside, pulling her firmly against him. There was no denying his arousal, and when she didn't move immediately away, he took it as a sign of acquiescence. "Come upstairs with me," he whispered in her ear. "Come and let me love you now."

She didn't quite freeze in his arms, but she did go uncommonly still.

"Victoria?" His whisper had grown harsh.

"Don't ask me to do this," she said, turning her face away.

He cursed under his breath. "How long are you going to make me wait?"

She didn't say anything.

His grip on her tightened. "How long?"

"You're not being fair to me. You know I can't simply . . . It's just not right."

He let go of her so abruptly that she stumbled. "Nothing has ever been more right, Victoria.

You just don't want to see it." He looked at her for one last hungry moment, feeling too angry and rejected to care about her anguished expression. Then he turned on his heel and left the room.

Chapter 19

Victoria had closed her eyes against his bitterness, but she couldn't close her ears. His angry footsteps pounded through the house, ending with the loud slam of his bedroom door.

She leaned against the kitchen wall. What was she so afraid of? She could no longer deny that she cared for Robert. Nothing had the power to lift her heart like one of his smiles. But letting him make love to her was so permanent. She would have to let go of that little piece of anger she'd been holding inside for so many years. At some point that anger had become a part of who she was, and nothing terrified her more than losing her sense of herself. That was all she'd been able to hold on to when she was a governess. *I am Victoria Lyndon,* she would tell herself after a particularly trying day. *No one can ever take that from me.*

Victoria covered her face with her hands and exhaled. Her eyes were still closed, but all she could see was Robert's warm expression. She could hear his voice in her mind, and he kept saying, over and over, "I love you." And then she breathed in. Her hands smelled like him, like sandalwood and leather. It was overwhelming.

"I need to get out of here," she muttered, then crossed the room to the door leading to the cottage's back garden. Once outside, she took a deep breath of the fresh air. She knelt in the grass and touched the flowers. "Mama," she whispered. "Are you listening?"

Lightning didn't crash through the sky, but a sixth sense told her to turn around, and when she did she saw Robert in the window of his room. He was perched on his windowsill with his back to her. His posture looked desolate and bleak.

She was hurting him. She was clutching onto her anger because it was all she could depend on, but all she was doing was hurting the one person she—

The flower in her hand snapped in two. Had she been about to say loved?

Victoria felt herself rising to her feet as if lifted by some invisible force. There was something else in her heart now. She wasn't sure it was love, but it was something gentle and good, and it had pushed the anger aside. She felt freer than she had in years.

She looked back up to the window. Robert's head was in his hands. This wasn't right. She couldn't keep hurting him this way. He was a good man. A bit domineering at times, she thought with a wobbly smile, but a good man.

Victoria reentered the house and quietly made her way to her room.

She sat motionless on her bed for a full

minute. Could she really do this? She closed her eyes and nodded. Then, taking a deep breath, she moved her shaking hands to the fastenings of her dress.

She slipped into the blue nightgown, sliding her hands down its silky length. She felt transformed.

And she finally admitted to herself what she had known all along—she wanted Robert. She wanted him, and she wanted to know that he wanted her. The question of love was still too scary for her to confront, even in her own mind, but her desire was strong and impossible to deny. With a steadiness of purpose she hadn't felt in some time, Victoria walked to his chamber door and turned the knob.

He'd locked it.

Her mouth fell open. She tried the knob again, just to be sure. It was definitely locked.

She nearly fell to the ground in frustration. She had made one of the most momentous decisions in her life, and he had gone and locked the damn door.

Victoria had half a mind to turn around and head back to her own room, where she could sulk alone. He would never know what he had missed, the blasted man. But then she realized that she would never know, either. And she wanted to feel loved again.

She raised her hand and knocked on the door.

Robert's head shot up in surprise. He thought he'd heard the doorknob rattle, but he'd assumed that it was merely the creaking of an old building. Not in his wildest dreams did he imagine that Victoria would come to him of her own volition.

But then he heard something different. A knock. What could she possibly want?

He crossed the room in swift, long strides and pulled open the door. "What do you—" He sucked in his breath. He didn't know what he'd been expecting, but it certainly wasn't this. Victoria had donned the seductive gown he'd given her, and this time she wasn't covering herself up with a quilt. The blue silk clung to her every curve, the neckline plunged to reveal her delicate cleavage, and one of her legs was visible though a long slit in the side.

Robert's body went instantly taut. Somehow he managed to utter her name. It wasn't easy; his mouth had gone dry as death.

She stood before him, her bearing proud but her hands shaking. "I've made a decision," she said in a low voice.

He inclined his head, not trusting himself to speak.

"I want you," she said. "If you'll still have me."

Robert froze, so unable to believe what he was hearing that he couldn't move.

Her face fell. "I'm sorry," she said, misinterpreting his inaction. "How ill-bred of me. Please forget I—"

The rest of her sentence was lost as Robert crushed her to him, his hands roving wildly up and down the length of her body. Robert wanted to devour her—he wanted to wrap himself around her and never let go. So all encompassing was his reaction that he was afraid he'd frightened her with his passion. With a ragged breath he pulled himself a few inches away from her.

She looked up at him with huge, questioning blue eyes.

He managed a shaky smile. "I'll still have you," he said.

For a second she didn't react. Then she laughed. The sound was almost musical, and it did more for his soul than the Church of England ever had. He took her face in his hands with reverent gentleness. "I love you, Torie," he said. "I will always love you."

She didn't say anything for a long moment. Finally she stood on her tiptoes and brushed a feathery kiss across his lips. "I can't talk of 'always' yet," she whispered. "Please don't—"

He understood, and he saved her from having to finish her sentence by claiming her mouth once again in a fiercely possessive kiss. He didn't mind that she wasn't yet ready for "always." Soon she would be. He would prove to her that their love was a forever emotion. He would do it with his hands and lips and words.

His hands slid up the length of her body, the silk of her gown bunching under his fingers. He could feel her every curve through the thin material. "I'm going to show you what love is," he whispered. He leaned down and pressed his lips against the soft skin of her breast. "I'm going to love you here."

He moved his lips to her neck. "And here."

His hands squeezed her buttocks. "And here."

She moaned in reaction, a hoarse, sensual sound that came from deep within her throat.

Robert suddenly doubted his ability to remain standing. He swooped her into his arms and carried her to the bed. As he laid her down, he said, "I'm going to love you everywhere."

Victoria sucked in her breath. His eyes were burning into her, and she felt terribly exposed, as if he could see into her very soul. Then he came down beside her, and she was lost in the heat of his body and the passion of the moment. He was hard and strong, hot and overwhelming. Her senses were swimming.

"I want to touch you," she whispered, barely able to believe her own boldness.

He grasped her hand and guided it to his chest. His skin burned, and she could feel his heart pounding under her fingers. "Feel me," he murmured. "Feel what you do to me."

Overcome by curiosity, Victoria sat up, tucking her legs underneath her. She saw the question in Robert's eyes, smiled, and murmured a soft "Shhh."

She let her fingers slide down to the taut skin of his abdomen, mesmerized by the way his muscles leaped at her touch. She sensed that he was exerting incredible control. It was an awesomely powerful feeling to know that she could make him like this, his breathing hard and ragged, his every muscle straining and tense.

Victoria felt daring. She felt wild and reckless. She wanted the whole world, and she wanted it that afternoon. She swayed forward, teasing him with her nearness, then pulled back, feeling giddy and off-balance. Her hand dipped lower until it brushed against the waistband of his breeches.

Robert gasped, and his hand flew to cover hers. "Not yet," he said hoarsely. "I can't control— Not yet."

Victoria lifted her hand. "Tell me what to do," she said. "Whatever you want."

He stared at her, quite unable to utter a word.

She swayed toward him. "Anything you want," she whispered. "Anything."

"I want to feel your hands on me again," he finally managed to say. "Both of them."

She reached out, but then stopped when her hand was an inch away from his shoulder. "Here?"

He nodded, sucking in his breath when her hand slid from his shoulder to his upper arm. She wrapped her hand around his biceps. "You're very strong."

"You make me strong," he said. "Everything in me that is good—you make me that way. With you, I become more than I am." He shrugged helplessly. "I'm not making sense. I don't how to explain it. I don't know the words."

Tears filled Victoria's eyes, and emotions she didn't want to feel pressed against her heart. She moved her hand to the back of his neck. "Kiss me."

He did. Oh, how he did! He was soft at first, teasing her mercilessly, leaving her body straining for more. And then, just when Victoria was certain she couldn't withstand another second of his sensual torture, his arms snaked around her back and bound her to him in a steely grip.

He grew wild, his movements uncontrolled. He pushed the silk of her gown up until it was bunched around her midriff. He separated her legs with one of his powerful thighs, and Victoria could feel the fabric of his breeches rubbing against her womanhood. It was so overwhelming that she was certain she would have fallen over if he hadn't been holding her so close to his body.

"I want you," he groaned. "Lord, how I want you."

"Please," she begged.

He continued to push the silky gown up until it slid over her head and landed in a forgotten heap on the floor next to the bed. Victoria was struck by a sudden shyness, and she looked away, unable to watch him watching her. She felt his fingers touch her chin, and with gentle pressure he turned her head until she faced him again.

"I love you," he said, his voice low but fervent.

She didn't say anything.

"You'll tell me soon enough," he said, drawing her into his arms and lowering her down. "I'm not worried. I can wait. For you I can wait forever."

Victoria wasn't sure how he did it, but within seconds she no longer felt his breeches between them. It was just skin against skin, and she felt so exquisitely close to him.

"God, you're beautiful," Robert said, lifting himself up on his arms to gaze down at her.

She touched his cheek. "So are you."

"Beautiful?" he said, his voice tinged with a smile.

She nodded. "I used to dream about you, you know. All those years."

"You did?"

Victoria inhaled sharply as his hand closed around her breast and gave it a loving squeeze. "I couldn't stop," she admitted. "And then I realized I didn't want to stop."

Robert made a ragged sound in the bottom of his throat. "I dreamed about you, too. But it was never like this, never this good." He lowered his head until his lips were scant inches from her breast. "I couldn't taste you in my dreams."

Her hips bucked off the bed as his mouth closed around her nipple, loving her with tantalizing thoroughness. Without realizing what she was about, her fingers sank themselves into his thick hair. "Oh, Robert," she moaned.

He whispered something against her breast. She couldn't make out the words, then realized it didn't matter. His tongue traced patterns on her skin, his breath devilishly ticklish and seductive. He dragged his mouth along her neck, murmuring, "I want more, Torie. I want it all."

He nudged her legs apart, and she could feel him settling against her. He was hard and hot, intimidating and oddly comforting at the same time. His hands were underneath her, squeezing her backside, pulling her closer to him.

"I want to go slowly," he whispered. "I want it to be perfect."

Victoria heard the ragged emotion in his voice and knew instantly what it had cost him to utter those words. She reached up and smoothed her thumbs along his eyebrows. "It can't help but be perfect," she whispered. "No matter what you do."

Robert stared down at her, his body shaking

with need and near to bursting with love. He couldn't believe how unreservedly she was accepting him into her embrace. She was honest and open and everything he had ever wanted, not just in a woman but out of life.

Hell, she *was* his life. And he didn't care who knew it. He felt like shouting it to the rafters, right then, right before he finally made her his own. *I love this woman,* he wanted to yell. *I love her!*

He positioned himself at the edge of her womanhood. "This may hurt a little," he said.

She touched his cheek. "You won't hurt me."

"I don't want to, but I—" He couldn't finish the sentence. He'd pushed forward into her—just an inch, but it felt so perfect that he lost the power of speech.

"Oh, my," Victoria breathed.

Robert just grunted. It was all he could manage. Intelligent speech was clearly beyond his capabilities. He forced himself to hold still, waiting to feel her muscles relax around him before sinking himself deeper into her. It was damned near impossible to hold himself back; every nerve in his body was screaming for release. It took clenched teeth, clenched muscles, clenched *everything* to keep his passion in check, but he did it.

All because he loved her. It was an awesome feeling, that.

Finally he moved that last inch and let out a shudder of complete and total pleasure. It was the sweetest of embraces. He was overcome by the most intense desire in his life, yet at the same time he had never felt more protected and content. "We are one now," he whispered, brushing a sweaty strand of hair from her forehead. "You and I. We are one person."

Victoria nodded and took a deep breath. She felt very strange. Strange, and somehow complete at the same time. Robert was *inside* her; she could scarcely fathom that. It was the oddest and yet the most natural feeling she had ever experienced. She felt as if she would surely burst if he moved even a quarter of an inch, and yet she was hungry for something more.

"Did I hurt you?" he whispered.

She shook her head. "It's so . . . odd."

He let out a little laugh. "It will get better. I promise."

"Oh, it isn't bad," she said, trying to reassure him. "Please don't think—"

He chuckled again as he pressed a gentle finger to her lips. "Shhh. Just let me show you." He replaced his fingers with his mouth, distracting her so she wouldn't notice when he started to move within her.

She noticed. The first brush of exquisite friction made her cry out, and before she knew it she had wrapped her legs around his.

"Oh, Victoria," he moaned. But it was a very happy moan. He moved forward again, then pulled back, slowly creating a rhythm as beautiful as it was primitive.

Victoria moved with him, instinct carrying her along where experience could not. Something began to build within her—a mounting pressure. She didn't know if it was pain or if it was pleasure, and at that moment she didn't particularly care which. All she knew was that she was on a road to *some*where, and if she didn't get there soon, she would surely explode.

And then she reached her destination and she exploded anyway, and then, for the first time in her life, she knew what it meant to be totally at peace with the world.

Robert's movements grew frenzied and then he, too, shouted his release and collapsed on top of her. Several minutes passed before either was able to speak.

Robert rolled to his side, pulling Victoria along with him. He kissed her gently on the lips. "Did I hurt you?"

She shook her head.

"Was I too heavy?"

"No. I liked feeling your weight." She blushed, feeling very risqué. "Why did you lock the door?"

"Hmm?"

"The door. It was locked."

He turned and looked at her, his blue eyes warm and thoughtful. "Habit, I suppose. I've always locked my door. I certainly didn't intend to keep you out." His lips spread into a lazy, contented smile. "I rather enjoy your company."

She giggled. "Yes, I believe you've demonstrated that."

His face grew serious. "There won't be any more locked doors between us. Barriers have no place in our relationship, be they doors or lies or misunderstandings."

Victoria swallowed, feeling too emotional to speak. All she did was nod.

Robert slid a leg over her, drawing her close.

"You won't leave, will you? I know it's the middle of the day, but we can take a nap."

"Yes," she said softly. Then she curled up in his arms, closed her eyes, and drifted off into peaceful sleep.

Chapter 20

When Victoria woke from her nap an hour later, Robert's beaming face was only a few inches from her own. He was propped up on his elbow, and she suspected that he'd spent the entire nap time watching her.

"Today," he announced with great cheer, "is a superb day to be married."

Victoria was certain she'd misheard him. "I beg your pardon?"

"Married. Man and wife."

"You and me?"

"No, actually I think that the hedgehogs out in the garden need to be joined in holy matrimony. They have been living in sin for years. I can no longer stand for it."

"Robert," Victoria said, giggling despite herself.

"And all those little illegitimate hedgehogs. Think of the stigma. Their parents have been breeding like rabbits. Or like hedgehogs, as the case may be."

"Robert, this is a serious matter."

The levity left his eyes, and they burned hot

and intense into hers. "I have never been more serious."

Victoria was silent for a moment while she chose her words. "Don't you think today is a bit sudden? Marriage is a very serious matter. We must give it sufficient thought."

"I have been thinking of little else for the better part of a month."

Victoria sat up, pulling the sheet along with her to cover her nakedness. "But I have not. I'm not ready to make this kind of decision just yet."

His face hardened. "You might have thought of that before you knocked on my door this afternoon."

"I wasn't thinking beyond—"

"Beyond what?" he asked, his voice sharp.

"I'd hurt your feelings," she whispered. "And I wanted to—"

He was out of the bed and on his feet in under a second. He planted his hands on his hips and stared down at her furiously, oblivious to the fact that he wasn't wearing a stitch of clothing. "You made love to me out of *pity*?" he spat.

"No!" She, however, was not oblivious to the fact that he was naked, and so her denial was directed to his knees.

"Look at me!" he ordered, his anger making his voice terribly harsh.

She raised her eyes a few inches, then lowered them again. "Would you please put on some clothing?"

"It's a little late for modesty," he bit out, but he pulled his breeches off the floor and put them on.

"I didn't do this out of pity," she said, finally

raising her eyes to his face, even though she'd much rather look at the ceiling or the walls or even at the chamber pot in the corner. "I did it simply because I wanted to do it, and I wasn't thinking much beyond today."

"I find it difficult to believe that you, a person who craves stability and permanence, would embark on a short-term affair."

"I wasn't thinking of it as such."

"Then how were you thinking of it?"

Victoria looked into his eyes, saw the vulnerability he was trying to hide beneath his anger, and realized just how important her answer was to him. "I wasn't thinking with my head," she said softly. "I was thinking with my heart. I looked up at your window, and you looked so sad—"

"As you have so kindly pointed out," he said bitterly.

Victoria fell silent for a moment to let him speak. Then she continued with, "It wasn't just for you. It was for myself as well. I suppose I just wanted to feel loved."

Hope flared in his eyes. "You *are* loved," he said fervently, reaching forward to take her hands in his. "And you can feel that way every day of the rest of your life if you'd only let yourself. Marry me, Victoria. Marry me and make me the happiest man in the world. Marry me and give yourself peace and contentment. And," he added, his voice dropping to a husky whisper, "love. For surely there has never been a woman loved more deeply and truly than I do you."

Victoria fought against the tears that were

pricking her eyes, but his words were too powerful, and she felt her cheeks grow salty and wet. "Robert," she began, not at all certain what she was trying to say, "for so very long I have—"

"You might be with child," he cut in. "Have you considered that?"

"I had not," she admitted with a convulsive swallow. "But I—"

"Marry me," he repeated, tightening his grip on her hands. "You know it is the right thing to do."

"Why did you have to say that?" she said. "You know I hate it when you try to tell me what I want."

Robert let out an exasperated breath. "That wasn't what I meant, and you know it."

"I know, it's only that . . ."

"It's only what?" he said softly. "What is holding you back, Torie?"

She looked away, feeling rather stupid. "I don't know. Marriage is so permanent. What if I make a mistake?"

"If it's a mistake then you've already made it," he said with a glance toward the bed. "But it isn't a mistake. Marriage won't always be easy, but life without you—" He ran his hand through his hair, his face showing his inability to put his thoughts into words. "Life without you would be impossible. I don't know how else to say it."

Victoria chewed on her lower lip, aware that she was coming to feel the same way. For all that he'd put her through during this past month, she couldn't quite imagine life without his lopsided smiles, the twinkle in his eyes, or the way his hair never quite looked as if he'd brushed it properly. She looked up at him, her eyes locking with his. "I have a few reservations," she began.

"You wouldn't be human if you didn't," he said reassuringly.

"But I can see that there are several reasons why marriage might be a good idea." She spoke slowly, working her words out in her head as she spoke. She shot a quick glance at Robert, half expecting him to yank her into another crushing embrace. But he remained still, clearly understanding that she needed to speak her mind.

"First of all," Victoria said, "as you pointed out, there is the matter of a child. It was very irresponsible of me not to consider it, but I didn't and there is nothing for it now. I suppose I could simply wait a few weeks and see—"

"I wouldn't recommend that particular course of action," Robert said quickly.

She bit back a smile. "No, I don't imagine you're going to let me go back to London, and I don't imagine that if I stay here—"

"I can't keep my hands off you," he said with an unapologetic shrug. "I freely admit it."

"And I won't try to lie and say that I do not"—she blushed—"enjoy your attentions. You know that I always have, even seven years ago."

He smiled knowingly.

"But there are other reasons why we should or should not marry."

"Should."

She blinked. "I beg your pardon?"

"We *should* marry. Not should not."

Victoria was finding it hard not to laugh.

When he was eager for something, Robert was more adorable than a puppy. "I do worry that you will not let me make my own decisions," she warned.

"I shall try to abide by your wishes," he said, his expression solemn. "If I become an overbearing ass, I give you leave to whack me over the head with your reticule."

Her eyes narrowed. "May I have that in writing?"

"Certainly." He crossed the room to his writing table, opened a drawer, and whipped out a quill, a piece of paper, and a bottle of ink. Victoria stared at him openmouthed as he scribbled a sentence, then signed the bottom with a flourish. He walked back to her, handed her the paper, and said, "There you are."

Victoria looked down and read, "If I become an overbearing ass, I give my beloved wife, Victoria Mary Lyndon Kemble—" She looked up. "Kemble?"

"It will be Kemble. Today, if I have any say." He pointed to a scrawl at the top of the note. "I postdated the note, however, for next week. You'll be a Kemble by then."

Victoria forebore to comment on his amazing confidence and continued reading. "Let's see . . . Victoria Mary Lyndon, ahem, Kemble . . . leave to whack me over the head with whatever object she chooses." She glanced up questioningly. "Any object?"

Robert shrugged. "If I become a *really* overbearing ass, you might want to hit me with something sturdier than your reticule."

Her shoulders shook as she turned back to the

note. "Signed, Robert Phillip Arthur Kemble, Earl of Macclesfield."

"I'm not a scholar of the law, but I think it is legal."

Victoria's face broke into a watery smile. With an impatient hand she brushed her tears away. "This is why I'm going to marry you," she said, holding the slip of paper in the air.

"Because I have told you that you may hit me at your discretion?"

"No," she said, sniffling loudly, "because I don't know what will happen to me if I don't have you to tease me. I've grown too serious, Robert. I wasn't always this way."

"I know," he said gently.

"For seven years I wasn't allowed to laugh. I forgot how."

"I'll remind you."

She nodded. "I think I need you, Robert. I think I do."

He sat on the end of the bed and gathered her into a tender embrace. "I know I need you, darling Torie. I know I do."

After several moments of enjoying the warmth of his arms, Victoria pulled just far enough away to ask, "Were you serious about getting married today?"

"Absolutely."

"But that's impossible. We have to post banns."

He smiled wickedly. "I procured a special license."

"You did?" She gaped at him. "When?"

"Over a week ago."

"A bit prematurely certain of yourself, don't you think?"

"It all worked out in the end, didn't it?"

Victoria tried to adopt a suspicious expression, but she couldn't do anything about the laughter in her eyes. "I think, my lord, that some might deem you an overbearing ass for this type of behavior."

"An overbearing ass, or a *really* overbearing ass? I should like to know, as the welfare of my skull depends upon it."

Victoria melted into a pool of giggles. "Do you know, Robert, but I think that I might actually like being married to you."

"Does that mean you forgive me for abducting you?"

"Not just yet."

"Really?"

"Yes, I shall have to withhold forgiveness until I have milked the situation for all it is worth."

This time it was Robert's turn to explode with laughter. While he was catching his breath, Victoria poked him in the shoulder and said, "We cannot marry today in any case."

"And why is that?"

"It is well past noon. A proper marriage must take place in the morning."

"A silly rule."

"My father always abided by it," she said. "I know, for I was always forced to pound away at the organ at every wedding at which he offici- ated."

"I didn't know we had an organ at our village vicarage."

"We didn't. This was in Leeds. And I believe you're changing the subject."

"No," he said, nuzzling her neck. "Merely a temporary digression. As for morning weddings, I believe that the early hour is required only for conventional marriages. With a special license we can do whatever we please."

"I suppose I should be thankful that I am cleaving unto a man who is so supremely organized."

Robert let out a happy sigh. "I shall take my compliments in any form you wish."

"Do you really want to get married this evening?"

"I can think of nothing else as appealing. We've no playing cards, and I have already read most of the books in the library."

She swatted him with a pillow. "I am serious."

It took only a second for him to pin her down onto her back, his weight flattening her bare breasts, his eyes gleaming into hers. "So am I," he said.

She caught her breath, then smiled. "I believe you."

"Besides, if I do not marry you tonight, I shall have to ravish you again."

"Is that so?"

"Indeed. But you are a good churchgoing woman, daughter of a vicar no less, so I know that you will want to keep your premarriage ravishments to a minimum." His expression turned suddenly serious. "I always swore that when I made love to you, it would be as man and wife."

She grinned and touched his cheek. "Well, we ruined that vow."

"Once, I suppose, is not so very great a sin," he said, turning his attention to her earlobe. "But I should like to get my ring on your finger before I am overcome with lust again."

"You're not overcome now?" she asked with a disbelieving expression. It wasn't very difficult to feel the imprint of his desire on her hip.

Robert laughed against the underside of her chin. "I'm going to enjoy being married to you, Torie."

"I-I suppose that is a good reason to propose," she gasped, trying to ignore the spasms of pleasure he was stirring within her.

"Mmmm, yes." He moved back to her mouth and kissed her deeply, teasing her until she was quivering beneath him. Then, abruptly, he rolled off her and onto his feet. "I'd better stop now," he said with a wicked smile, "for in another moment I won't be able to."

Victoria wanted to shout out that she didn't care, but she contented herself with tossing a pillow at him instead.

"I wouldn't want to compromise you any further," Robert continued, easily dodging her attack. "And I wanted to remind you of"—he leaned down and dropped one last kiss on her mouth—"this. Just in case you were having second thoughts."

"I'm having them *now*," she retorted, certain that she looked just as frustrated as she felt.

Robert laughed as he crossed the room. "I'm sure you'll be pleased to know that my little

reminder has left me feeling every bit as uncomfortable and unfulfilled as you."

"I'm perfectly fine," she said, lifting her chin
in the air.

"Yes, of course you are," he teased as he
reached into the traveling case he'd left carelessly on the desk. Victoria was about to let out a
stinging retort when his countenance turned
quite black and he let out a loud "Damn!"

"Is something amiss?" she asked.

His head whipped up to face her. "Have you
been in this bag?"

"No, of course not, I wouldn't—" She colored
as she remembered that she'd been looking
through his things. "Well, actually I *would* snoop
in your belongings, I admit, but I found the tub
before I found your case."

"I don't care if you want to pull up the
floorboards," he said distractedly. "What's mine
is yours. But I had important papers in this case,
and now they're gone."

A unexpected bubble of mirth welled up in
Victoria's chest. "What sort of papers?" she
asked carefully.

Robert let out another low curse before reply-
ing, "The special license."

Victoria had a feeling that it wasn't an appropriate time to burst into loud and raucous laughter, but she did so anyway.

Robert planted his hands on his hips as he
turned to face her. "This is not funny."

"I'm sorry," she said, not sounding particularly apologetic. "It is simply that you— Oh,
my!" Victoria collapsed into another round of
giggles.

"It must be in my other case," Robert said. "Damn."

Victoria wiped her eyes. "Where is your other case?"

"London."

"I see."

"We'll have to leave within the hour."

Her mouth fell open. "Leave for London? Right now?"

"I don't see any other option."

"But how will we get there?"

"MacDougal stabled my carriage just a quarter mile away before leaving for London. The local squire has always been most accommodating. I'm sure he can spare a groom to drive us back."

"You let me believe that I was stranded here?" she yelled.

"You never asked," he said, shrugging. "Now then, I suggest you get dressed. As delightful as you are in your current attire, there is a slight chill in the air."

She held the bed sheets tightly against her body. "My dress is in the next room."

"You're going to be modest now?"

Her mouth twisted into an offended frown. "I'm sorry I can't be as cosmopolitan as you are, Robert. I don't have much experience with this sort of thing."

He smiled and dropped an affectionate kiss on her forehead. "I'm sorry, I'm sorry. You're simply too much fun to tease. I'll get your dress right away. And," he added as he opened the door, "I shall leave you to your privacy to change into it."

* * *

Thirty minutes later they were on their way to London. Robert was having a difficult time keeping himself from breaking out into song. On his way back from retrieving the carriage, he had actually belted out a rather off-key version of Handel's "Hallelujah Chorus." He probably would have finished the piece if the horses hadn't whinnied in aural agony. Robert quieted down, thinking it best not to offer similar torture to his betrothed's ears—his betrothed! He loved saying that. Hell, he loved just thinking it.

Still, his happiness was so great that he couldn't quite keep it all inside, and thus, every so often he forgot himself, and then he'd realize he was whistling.

"I didn't know you liked to whistle," Victoria said after about the fifth time he caught himself.

"I certainly cannot sing," he replied. "So I whistle."

"I don't think I've heard you whistling in—" She paused and thought. "I can't remember the last time."

He grinned. "I haven't been this happy in a great many years."

A pause, and then she said, "Oh." She looked ridiculously pleased, and Robert felt ridiculously pleased that she looked that way. He whistled atonally for another few minutes, and then he looked up and said, "Do you realize how wonderful it is to feel spontaneous again?"

"I beg your pardon?"

"When I first met you, we used to run through the woods at midnight. We were wild and carefree."

"It was lovely," Victoria said softly.

"But now . . . Well, you know how ordered my life is. I am, as you like to say, the most organized man in Britain. I always have a plan, and I always follow it. It feels quite nice to do something spontaneous again."

"You abducted me," Victoria pointed out. "That was spontaneous."

"Not at all," he replied, waving away her comment. "I planned that quite carefully, I assure you."

"Not carefully enough to *feed* us," she responded just a touch acerbically.

"Ah, yes, the food," he mused. "A small oversight."

"It didn't seem small at the time," she muttered.

"You didn't perish of hunger, did you?"

She swatted him playfully on the shoulder. "And you forgot the special license. When one considers the fact that the entire purpose of the abduction was to marry me, that constitutes a large gap in the plan, indeed."

"I didn't forget to plan for the special license. I just forgot to bring it. I certainly meant to."

Victoria peered out the window. Twilight hung in the air, as it would for several hours. They would not make it to London that evening, but they would get more than halfway there. "Actually," she said, "I'm rather glad you forgot the license."

"You want to put off the inevitable as long as possible, I gather?" he said. He was clearly teasing, but Victoria sensed that her answer was important to him.

"Not at all," she replied. "Once I make a

decision I like to carry it out immediately. It's just that it is nice to see you do something wrong every now and then."

"Excuse me?"

She shrugged. "You're nearly perfect, you know."

"Why doesn't that sound like a compliment? And more importantly, if I'm so damned perfect why has it taken me so long to convince you to marry me?"

"It's *because* you're perfect," she said with a sly smile. "It can grow annoying. Why should I do anything if you're going to do it better?"

He grinned devilishly and pulled her against him. "I can think of many things that you do better."

"Oh, really?" she murmured, trying not to get too aroused by the way his hand was stroking her hip.

"Mmm. You kiss better." To prove his point, he let his lips drift down onto hers.

"You taught me."

"You look much better without any clothes on."

She blushed, but she was growing comfortable enough with him that she dared to say, "That is a matter of opinion."

He pulled back with a loud sigh. "Very well. You sew better."

She blinked. "You're right."

"And you certainly know more about children," he added. "When we are parents I shall constantly have to defer to your better judgment. I'm liable to launch into a lecture on Newton's three laws of motion before they're out of the cradle. Most inappropriate. You'll have to teach me all the nursery rhymes."

Victoria's heart soared at his words. Her brief life as a seamstress had shown her the joy of being able to make important decisions for herself. More than anything she was afraid that marriage would mean she would lose all of this. But now Robert was telling her that he valued her judgment.

"And you have a bigger heart," he said, touching her cheek. "I often get swept up in myself. You always notice the needs of others first. It's a rare and lovely gift."

"Oh, Robert." She leaned toward him, eager for the warmth of his arms. But before she reached him, the carriage hit a deep rut in the road, and she slipped.

"Oh!" she called out—in surprise.

"Aargh!" Robert grunted—in pain.

"Oh dear, oh dear," Victoria said, her words rushed. "What is wrong?"

"Your elbow," he gasped.

"What? Oh, I'm sorry—" The carriage jolted again, and her elbow slid deeper into his midsection. Or at least she thought it was his midsection.

"Please . . . move . . . it . . . *NOW!*"

Victoria scrambled and managed to disentangle her limbs from his. "I'm so sorry," she repeated. Then she looked at him more closely. He was doubled over, and even in the dim light she could tell that his skin looked quite green. "Robert?" she asked in a hesitant voice, "are you going to be all right?"

"Not for several minutes."

She watched him for a few seconds and then ventured, "Did I hit you in the stomach? I assure you it was an accident."

He remained hunched over as he said, "It's a *male* sort of pain, Victoria."

"Ohhhh," she breathed. "I had no idea."

"I wouldn't have expected you to," he muttered.

Another minute went by, and then Victoria suddenly got a horrible thought. "This isn't permanent, is it?"

He shook his head. "Don't make me laugh. Please."

"I'm sorry."

"Stop saying you're sorry."

"But I am."

"Cold, hunger, and then mortal injury," Robert said under his breath. "Was ever a man as plagued as I?"

Victoria didn't see any reason to reply. She kept her gaze scrupulously on the window, watching as Kent rolled by. There was no sound out of Robert for at least ten minutes, and then, just when she was certain he must have fallen asleep, she felt a tap on her shoulder. "Yes?" she said, turning around.

He was smiling. "I'm feeling better now."

"Oh. Well, I'm so happy for you," she replied, not really certain what type of comment passed for appropriate in this situation.

Robert leaned closer, a hungry look in his eyes. "No, I meant that I'm feeling *much* better."

Victoria wished he'd stop speaking so cryptically. "Well, then," she said, "I'm *very* happy for you."

"I'm not certain you understand," he murmured.

Victoria wanted to say that she was certain she *didn't* understand, but before she could get a word out, Robert had yanked her legs onto the seat, and she was lying on her back. She gasped his name, but he silenced her with a kiss.

"I'm much improved," he said against her mouth. "Very"—kiss—"very"—kiss—"much improved." He raised his head and gifted her with the slowest and most languorous of smiles. "Would you care for a demonstration?"

Chapter 21

H ere?" Victoria croaked. "In the carriage?"
"Why not?"

"Because . . . Because . . . It's indecent!" She tried to pull herself away, then muttered, "It must be."

Robert lifted his head a fraction of an inch. His blue eyes twinkled mischievously. "Is it? I don't recall your father ever delivering a sermon on the topic."

"Robert, I am certain that this is most irregular."

"Of course it is," he said, nuzzling the underside of her chin. She was soft and warm and still smelled like his sandalwood soap. "Normally I would not indulge here in the carriage, but I did want to set your mind at rest."

"Oh, so this is for my benefit?"

"You were so concerned about possible permanent effects of my injury . . ."

"Oh, no," she said, trying to catch her breath. "I am confident of your recovery, I assure you."

"Ah, but I want to make certain you have no lingering doubts." His hands wrapped around

334

her ankles and began to slide up her legs, leaving twin trails of fire that burned right through her stockings.

"None, I assure you."

"Shhh, just kiss me." He nibbled at her lips, his hands sliding up and over the soft curve of her hips. Then he rounded them behind her, cupping her soft backside.

"I thought—" She cleared her throat. "I thought you didn't want to do this again until we were married."

"That," he said, moving to the corner of her mouth, "was when I still thought we could be married this evening. I have discovered that there is a time and a place for scruples."

"And this isn't one of them?"

"Most definitely not." He found the bare skin of her upper thighs and squeezed, eliciting a gasp of delight. He groaned, loving the sounds of her desire. Nothing had the power to inflame his passion quite so much as the sights and sounds of her pleasure. He felt her arching beneath him, and his hands moved to her back, where they furiously worked at her buttons. He needed her. . . . God, he needed her *now*.

He pushed down the bodice of her gown. She was still wearing the blue nightdress as a chemise. Too impatient to unfasten that as well, he instead captured her breast with his mouth, dampening the fabric around her peaking nipple with his tongue.

Victoria was thrashing beneath him, incoherent mumblings escaping her lips. He lifted his head for a moment to look at her. Her sable hair was wild and free on the bench cushions, and her dark blue eyes were nearly black with desire. Robert's throat filled with an incomprehensible choking sensation, and he was overcome by a feeling so strong that he couldn't possibly contain it. "I love you," he whispered. "I will always love you."

He saw her inner struggle and knew she wanted to say it, too. But whatever was holding her back still had a grip on her heart, and she couldn't. He didn't care; he knew she'd eventually come to understand her love for him. But he couldn't bear to see her so torn, so he pressed a gentle finger against her lips. "Don't speak," he whispered. "We don't need words right now."

He kissed her anew, his mouth hungry and wild. His hands found her drawers and within seconds the garment was on the floor of the carriage. He touched her intimately, his knowing fingers teasing the folds of her womanhood.

"Oh, Robert!" she gasped. "What— Last time you didn't—"

"There's more than one way to love you," he murmured. He felt her more deeply, marveling at how responsive she was beneath his touch. Her body moved against him, drawing his finger in more deeply. She was whipping him deeper and deeper into his desire, and he felt himself straining against his breeches. He pressed his lips roughly against the pulse point in her temple and whispered, "Do you want me?"

She looked at him in disbelief.

"I want to hear you say it," he said, his voice hoarse.

Gasping for air, she nodded.

Robert decided that that was good enough,

and he fumbled with the fastenings of his breeches. He was too hot, too ready to get the damned garment off his legs. Instead, he just pulled himself out and nudged his way between her thighs, where his fingers were still tickling their way to heaven.

One of Victoria's legs slid off the bench, giving him more room to probe her womanhood. He pressed forward, sheathing just his tip within her. Her muscles turned hot and convulsed around him, and his entire body shuddered in reaction. "I want more, Torie," he rasped. "More."

He felt her nod, then he pushed farther, moving closer and closer to the very center of her being, until finally he was fully embedded within her. Robert pulled her tightly against him, silently savoring their union. His lips trailed across her cheek to her ear, and he whispered, "I'm home now." Then he felt her tears on his face, tasted the salt as they rolled to his lips, and he was undone. Animal desire overtook him, and his mind and body separated. He pumped into her relentlessly, somehow managing to hold back his release until he felt her stiffen and cry out beneath him.

With a loud groan he thrust one last time, pouring himself into her. He collapsed almost instantly, every muscle exquisitely weary. A thousand thoughts collided in his mind in that instant—was he too heavy for her? Did she have any regrets? *Had they made a baby?*—but his mouth was so busy gasping for air that he couldn't have spoken if his life depended on it.

Finally, when he was able to hear something

other than their hearts thudding in unison, he lifted himself onto his elbow, unable to believe what he'd done. He'd taken Victoria in a cramped, moving carriage. They were half dressed, rumpled—hell, he hadn't even managed to remove his boots. He supposed he should say he was sorry, but he wasn't. How could he be sorry when Victoria—no, Torie—was lying beneath him, her breathing still uneven with the last vestiges of her climax, her cheeks hot and flushed with pleasure.

Still, he felt he should say something, so he offered her a lopsided smile and said, "That was certainly interesting."

Her mouth opened, her jaw moved slowly forward as if she was trying to say something. But no sound emerged.

"Victoria?" he asked. "Is something wrong?"

"Two times," she said, blinking dazedly. "Two times before the ceremony." She closed her eyes and nodded. "Two times is quite all right."

Robert threw back his head and laughed.

As it happened, "two times" was not quite accurate. By the time Robert managed to slide a gold band onto the fourth finger of Victoria's left hand, she had been thoroughly made love to not twice but four times. They had had to stop at an inn on the way to London, and he didn't even bother to consult her before informing the innkeeper that they were man and wife, and requesting a chamber with a large and comfortable bed.

And then he'd pointed out that it would be a sin to let such a nice big bed go to waste.

They were married almost immediately on their arrival in London. Much to Victoria's amusement, Robert left her waiting in the carriage as he ran into his house to retrieve the special license. He returned in under five minutes, and then they made their way to the residence of the Reverend Lord Stuart Pallister, the youngest son of the marquess of Chippingworth, and an old school chum of Robert's. Lord Pallister married them in a trice, completing the ceremony in less than half the time Victoria's father had usually taken to do the job.

Victoria was terribly self-conscious when they finally arrived at Robert's home. It wasn't that it was imposingly grand; with his father still living, Robert had adopted one of the family's smaller holdings. Still, his stately town house was impeccably elegant, and Victoria had a feeling that living in the family quarters of such a residence would be much different than a governess's top-floor cubbyhole.

She was also afraid that all the servants would immediately recognize her as a sham. A vicar's daughter—a governess!—They wouldn't like to receive orders from her. It was imperative that she start out on the right foot with Robert's staff—a bad first impression could take years to correct. She just wished she knew which of her feet was the right one.

Robert seemed to understand her dilemma. As they rode in the carriage from Lord Pallister's home to his, he patted her on the hand and said, "Now you shall be a countess when you are introduced to your new home. It shall be much better that way."

Victoria agreed, but that didn't stop her hands from shaking as they walked up the front steps. She tried to keep them still, but she wasn't successful, and her wedding band suddenly felt very heavy on her finger.

Robert paused before opening the door. "You're trembling," he said, taking her gloved hand in his.

"I'm nervous," she admitted.

"Why?"

"I feel as if I'm at a masquerade."

"And your costume would be . . ." he prompted.

Victoria let out a nervous laugh. "A countess."

He smiled. "It's not a costume, Victoria. You *are* a countess. My countess."

"I don't feel like one."

"You'll get used to it."

"That is easy for you to say. You were born to this sort of thing. I haven't the slightest idea how to go about it."

"Didn't you spend seven years as a governess? Surely you must have observed a thing or two from Lady— No, I take that back," he said, frowning. "Contrive *not* to emulate Lady Hollingwood. Just be yourself. There is no rule that a countess must be haughty and stern."

"Very well," she said doubtfully.

Robert reached for the doorknob, but the door was pulled open before he touched it. A butler swept into a deep bow, murmuring, "My lord."

"I think he watches out the window for me," Robert whispered into Victoria's ear. "I have never once managed to grasp the doorknob."

Victoria let out a little giggle despite herself. Robert was trying so hard to set her at ease. She decided then and there that she would not disappoint him. She might be terrified, but she was going to be a perfect countess if it killed her.

"Yerbury," Robert said, handing the man his hat, "may I present my new wife, the Countess of Macclesfield."

If Yerbury was surprised it certainly did not show on his face, which Victoria was sure was made of granite. "My deepest congratulations," he said, then turned to Victoria and added, "My lady, it will be my pleasure to serve you."

Victoria almost giggled again at that. The thought of someone serving her was so utterly foreign. But, determined to act properly, she managed to stifle her laugh into a friendly smile and said, "Thank you, Yerbury. I'm delighted to become a part of your household."

Yerbury's pale eyes glowed just a touch warmer when she said "*Your* household." Then the unthinkable occurred. Yerbury sneezed. "Oh!" he exclaimed, looking as if he wanted to melt into the ground. "My lady, I am so dreadfully sorry."

"Don't be silly, Yerbury," Victoria said. "It is only a sneeze."

He sneezed again, just as he was saying, "A good butler never sneezes." Then he let out four more sneezes in rapid succession.

Victoria had never seen a man look more distressed. With a quick glance at Robert, she went forward and laced her arm through the butler's. "Come now, Yerbury," she said warmly, before he had a chance to faint at such intimate contact with the new countess. "Why don't you show me to the kitchens? I know of an excellent remedy. We shall have you cured in no time."

And then Yerbury, his face betraying more emotion than he'd let show in forty years, led her to the back of the house, thanking her profusely all the while.

Robert only smiled as he was abandoned in the front hall. It had taken less than two minutes for Victoria to charm Yerbury. He predicted she would have the rest of the household eating from her hand by nightfall.

A few days passed, and Victoria slowly grew comfortable with her new position. She didn't think she would ever be able to order servants around like most of the nobility; she had spent far too long in their ranks not to realize that they were all people, too, with hopes and dreams much like her own. And although the servants were never told of Victoria's background, they seemed to sense that she had a special affinity for them.

Victoria and Robert were breakfasting one day when a particularly devoted maid insisted that she reheat her mistress's morning chocolate because it wasn't quite warm enough. As the maid scurried off with the pot, Robert remarked, "I do think they would give their lives for you, Torie."

"Don't be silly," she said with a scoff and a smile.

Robert added, "I'm not at all certain they would do the same for me."

Victoria was about to repeat her earlier comment when Yerbury entered the room. "My lord, my lady," he said, "Mrs. Brightbill and Miss Brightbill have come calling. Shall I tell them you are not at home?"

"Thank you, Yerbury," Robert said, turning back to his newspaper.

"No!" Victoria exclaimed. Yerbury immediately halted in his tracks.

"Who is supposed to be in charge here?" Robert muttered, watching as his butler blatantly disregarded his wishes in deference to those of his wife.

"Robert, they are family," Victoria said. "We must receive them. Your aunt's feelings will be terribly bruised."

"My aunt has an amazingly thick skin, and I would like some time alone with my wife."

"I am not suggesting that we invite all of London for tea. Merely that you spare a few minutes to greet your aunt." Victoria looked back up at the butler. "Yerbury, please show them in. Perhaps they might like to share our meal."

Robert scowled, but Victoria could see that he wasn't really upset. In a few seconds Mrs. Brightbill and Harriet bustled into the room. Robert immediately rose to his feet.

"My dear, dear nephew!" Mrs. Brightbill trilled. "You have been a naughty boy."

"Mother," Harriet added, throwing a sheepish look Robert's way, "I don't think one can still call him a boy."

"Nonsense, I can call him whatever I wish." She turned to Robert and fixed a stern expression on her face. "Have you any idea how upset your father is with you?"

Robert sat back down once the two women had taken their seats. "Aunt Brightbill, my father has been angry with me for seven years."

"You didn't invite him to your wedding!"

"I didn't invite anyone to my wedding."

"That is entirely beside the point."

Harriet turned to Victoria and said behind the back of her hand, "My mother does love a good cause."

"And what cause is this?"

"Righteous indignation," Harriet replied. "She loves nothing better."

Victoria glanced over at her new husband, who was enduring his aunt's scolding with remarkable patience. She turned back to Harriet. "How long do you think he'll be able to withstand it?"

Harriet furrowed her brow as she pondered that question. "I would have to say that he must be nearing his limit."

As if on cue Robert's hand came crashing down on the table, rattling all the dishes. "Enough!" he boomed.

In the doorway to the kitchen, the maid hovered in terror. "You don't want any more chocolate?" she whispered.

"No!" Victoria cut in, jumping to her feet. "He wasn't speaking to you, Joanna. We would love some chocolate, wouldn't we, Harriet?"

Harriet nodded enthusiastically. "I'm certain my mother would as well. Isn't that so, Mother?"

Mrs. Brightbill twisted in her seat. "What are you blithering on about, Harriet?"

"Chocolate," her daughter replied patiently. "Wouldn't you like some?"

"Of course," Mrs. Brightbill said with a sniff. "No sensible woman would refuse chocolate."

"My mother has always prided herself on being very sensible," Harriet said to Victoria.

"Of course," Victoria said loudly. "Your mother is all that is sensible and true."

Mrs. Brightbill beamed. "I shall forgive you, Robert," she said with a great huff, "for neglecting to include Harriet and me in your nuptials, but only because you have finally exhibited the sense that God gave you and chosen the lovely Miss Lyndon as your wife."

"The lovely Miss Lyndon," Robert said firmly, "is now Lady Macclesfield."

"Of course," Mrs. Brightbill replied. "Now then, as I was saying, it is imperative that you introduce her to society as soon as you can."

Victoria felt her stomach grow queasy. It was one thing to win over the hearts of Robert's servants. His peers were another matter altogether.

"The season is nearing its end," Robert said. "I see no reason why we cannot wait until next year."

"Next year!" Mrs. Brightbill screeched—and she knew how to screech better than most. "Are you mad?"

"I shall introduce Victoria to my closer friends at dinner parties and the like, but I see no reason to subject her to an odious *ton* ball when all we really want is a bit of privacy."

Victoria found herself fervently hoping that Robert won his point.

"Nonsense," Mrs. Brightbill said dismissively. "The entire world knows that you are in London now. To hide her would be to give the impression that you are ashamed of your new wife, that perhaps you *had* to marry her."

Robert bristled with anger. "You know that is not the case."

"Yes, of course. I know it, and Harriet knows it, but we are only two of many."

"Perhaps," Robert said smoothly, "but I have always held your ability to disseminate information in the highest of esteem."

"He means she talks a lot," Harriet said to Victoria.

"I know what he means," Victoria shot back, and then was immediately ashamed of herself because she'd just called her new aunt a gossip.

Harriet caught Victoria's embarrassed expression and said, "Oh, don't worry yourself over that. Even Mother knows she's the worst sort of gossip."

Victoria bit back a smile and turned to the sparring match that was taking place on the other side of the table.

"Robert," Mrs. Brightbill was saying, one hand splayed dramatically over her heart, "even *I* am not that efficient. You will have to introduce your new wife to society before the season is out. This is not my opinion. It is fact."

Robert sighed and looked over at Victoria. She tried very hard to keep the terror out of her eyes, and she feared that she must have succeeded, for he let out another sigh—this one infinitely more weary—and said, "Very well, Aunt Brightbill.

We will make one appearance. But just one, mind you. We are still newly wed."

"This is so romantic," Harriet whispered, fanning herself with her hand.

Victoria grabbed her cup of chocolate and lifted it to her mouth in an attempt to hide the fact that she absolutely could not manage to pull her lips into a smile. But this action only served to show how badly her hands were shaking, so she set the cup back down and looked at her lap.

"Naturally," Mrs. Brightbill said, "I shall have to take Victoria shopping for a new wardrobe. She will need the guidance of one who is familiar with the ways of society."

"Mother!" Harriet interjected. "I am certain that Cousin Victoria will be more than able to choose her own wardrobe. After all, she worked for many weeks at Madame Lambert's, the most exclusive dressmaker in London."

"Euf!" Mrs. Brightbill said by way of reply. "Do not remind me. We shall have to do our best to hide that little episode."

"I am not ashamed of my work," Victoria said quietly. And she wasn't. Of course this didn't mean she wasn't terrified of Robert's social peers.

"And you shouldn't be," Mrs. Brightbill said. "There is nothing wrong with a hard day's work. We just needn't speak of it."

"I do not see how it would be possible to avoid it," Victoria pointed out. "I assisted a great many ladies at the shop. Madame always liked to have me out in front because my accent is gentle. Someone is bound to recognize me."

Mrs. Brightbill let out a long-suffering sigh. "Yes, it will be unavoidable. What am I to do? How to avoid a scandal?"

Robert, who was clearly feeling somewhat henpecked, turned back to his breakfast and ate a bite of his omelet. "I am certain you are up to the task, Aunt Brightbill."

Harriet cleared her throat and said, "Surely everyone will understand once they realize what a romantic past Robert and Victoria have." She sighed. "Young lovers, separated by a cruel father—even the best of my French novels cannot compare."

"I do not intend to drag the marquess's name through the gutter," Mrs. Brightbill said.

"Better his name than Victoria's," Robert put in caustically. "He is more to blame for our separation than we are."

"We are all equally to blame," Victoria said firmly. "As is my own father."

"It matters not who is to blame," Mrs. Brightbill stated. "I am only interested in minimizing the damage. I do think that Harriet has the right idea of it."

Harriet beamed.

"Just inform me where I have to be and when," Robert said with a bored expression.

"You can be sure I shall also tell you what to say," Mrs. Brightbill returned. "As for particulars, I believe that the Lindworthy bash tomorrow evening shall suit our purposes."

"Tomorrow?" Victoria mouthed, her stomach suddenly feeling so fluttery that she couldn't manage to make her voice work properly.

"Yes," Mrs. Brightbill replied. "Everyone will be there. Including my dear, dear, dear Basil."

Victoria blinked. "Who is Basil?"

"My brother," Harriet replied. "He's not often in London."

"The more family the better," Mrs. Brightbill said briskly. "Just in case Victoria is not received favorably and we have to close ranks."

"No one would dare cut Victoria," Robert growled. "Not unless they want to answer to me."

Harriet gaped at her cousin's uncharacteristic ferocity. "Victoria," she said, "I think he really does love you."

"Of course I love her," Robert snapped. "Do you think I would have gone to the trouble of abducting her if I didn't?"

Victoria felt something warming in her chest—something that felt suspiciously like love.

"And no one would want to cross my dear, dear, dear Basil, either," Mrs. Brightbill added.

Victoria turned to her husband with a secret smile and whispered, "I'm afraid Basil is closer to her heart than you, darling. He gets three 'dears,' whereas you only received two."

"A fact for which I thank my maker every day of my life," Robert muttered.

Mrs. Brightbill's eyes narrowed suspiciously. "I don't know what you two are saying, but I vow I do not care. Unlike some of those present, I am able to keep my thoughts focused on the goals at hand."

"What *are* you talking about?" Robert said.

"Shopping. Victoria will have to come with me this very morning if she is to have a proper gown for tomorrow evening. Madame is likely to have a fit at such short notice, but there is nothing to do about it."

"Aunt Brightbill," Robert said, eyeing her over his cup of coffee, "you might want to *ask* Victoria if she is free."

Victoria stifled a smile at the way he stood up for her. Robert showed her in so many ways how much he loved her. From his passionate kisses to his unflagging support and respect, he couldn't have made his love more clear if he shouted it out. Which he did, actually. The thought made her grin.

"What is so funny?" Robert asked, looking a trifle suspicious.

"Nothing, nothing," Victoria said quickly, realizing in a flash that she really did love this man. She wasn't sure how to tell him, but she knew it was true. Whatever he had been as a boy, he was ten times more as a man, and she couldn't imagine life without him.

"Victoria?" Robert prodded, breaking into her thoughts.

"Oh, yes." She flushed with embarrassment at having let her mind wander off. "Of course I shall go shopping with Mrs. Brightbill. I always have time for my new favorite aunt."

Mrs. Brightbill sniffled back a sentimental tear. "Oh, my darling girl, I should be so honored if you would call me Aunt Brightbill, just as my dear, dear Robert does."

Her dear, dear Robert just then looked as if he had had just about enough.

Victoria placed her hand atop the older lady's.
"I should be honored."

"See?" Harriet chirped. "I knew we would be
family. Didn't I say so?"

Chapter 22

Mrs. Brightbill turned out to be almost frighteningly organized, and Victoria found herself bustled from shop to shop with the precision of a master. It was easy to see where Robert had gotten his ability to devise a plan and then single-mindedly execute it. Aunt Brightbill was a woman on a mission, and nothing was going to get in her way.

Normally they wouldn't have been able to buy a suitable gown on such short notice, but this time Victoria's working class past worked to her advantage. The staff at Madame Lambert's was thrilled to see her again, and they worked around the clock to make certain that her dress would be beyond compare.

Victoria suffered through the preparations somewhat absentmindedly. Now that she had finally decided she truly loved Robert, she was at a complete loss as to how to tell him. It should have been easy—she knew he loved her and would be delighted no matter how she said it. But she wanted it to be perfect, and it was difficult to do anything perfectly when four seamstresses were poking pins in one's side. And it was even more difficult with Aunt Brightbill snapping off orders like an army general.

There was, of course, the night, but Victoria didn't want to tell him while in the heat of passion. She wanted it to be clear that her love for him was based on more than desire.

And so, by the time she was preparing for the ball, she still hadn't told him. She was sitting at her vanity table, pondering this while a maid dressed her hair. A knock sounded at the door, and Robert entered without waiting for a reply. "Good evening, darling," he said, leaning down to drop a kiss on the top of her head.

"Not the hair!" Victoria and her maid yelled in unison.

Robert stopped his descent about an inch above her head. "I knew there was a reason why I agreed to attend only one function. I do so like to muss your hair."

Victoria smiled, about ready to blurt out her love for him then and there, but not wanting to do it in front of the maid.

"You look exceedingly lovely this evening," he said, sprawling on a nearby chair. "The dress is most becoming. You should wear that color more frequently." He blinked distractedly. "What is it called?"

"Mauve."

"Yes, of course. Mauve. I cannot fathom why women must devise so many silly names for colors. Pink would have done just as well."

"One might suppose that we need something with which to occupy our time while you men are off running the world."

He smiled. "I thought you might need a little something to go with your new dress. I wasn't certain what would match with mauve"—he pulled a jeweler's box from behind his back and snapped it open—"but I have been told that diamonds go with everything."

Victoria gasped.

Her maid gasped even louder.

Robert actually flushed, looking a bit embarrassed.

"Oh, Robert!" Victoria said, almost afraid to reach out and touch the glittering necklace and matching earrings. "I have never seen anything more lovely."

"I have," he murmured, touching her cheek.

The maid, who was French and very discreet, quietly left the room.

"They are much too precious," Victoria said, but she was reaching out to touch them with an air of wonder in her eyes.

Robert picked the necklace up and made to put it around her neck. "May I?" At her nod he moved behind her. "What else, pray tell, should I spend my money on?"

"I-I don't know," Victoria stammered, really liking the feel of the gemstones on her breastbone despite her protestations. "I'm sure there must be something more worthy."

Robert held out the earrings for her to put on. "You are my wife, Victoria. I like to buy you presents. Expect many more in the future."

"But I have nothing for you."

He leaned over her hand and kissed it gallantly. "Your presence in my life is enough," he murmured. "Although . . ."

"Although?" she prompted. She did so want to give him what he needed.

"A child might be nice," he said with a sheepish smile. "If you could give me one of those . . ."

Victoria blushed. "At the rate we've been going, I don't foresee any problem with that."

"Good. Now then, if you could further endeavor to make her a girl who looks just like you—"

"I have no control over that," she said, laughing. Then her face sobered. It was on the tip of her tongue to say that she loved him. Every muscle in her body was poised to throw herself in his arms and say "I love you" over and over and over. But she didn't want him to think that she confused love and gratitude, so she decided to wait until later that night. She would light a scented candle in their room, wait until the mood was just right . . .

"Why do you suddenly look so dreamy?" Robert asked, touching her chin.

Victoria smiled secretively. "Oh, no reason. Just a little surprise I have for this evening."

"Really?" His eyes lit with anticipation. "During the ball or afterward?"

"After."

His gaze grew heavy lidded and sensual. "I can hardly wait."

An hour later they were poised to enter the Lindworthy mansion. Mrs. Brightbill and Harriet were standing directly behind the newlyweds; they had decided that it would be easier for all four of them to take one carriage.

Robert looked down at his new wife with concern in his eyes. "Are you still nervous?"

She glanced up at him in surprise. "How did you know I was nervous?"

"Yesterday when Aunt Brightbill declared her intention to bring you out immediately, I thought you might lose your breakfast."

She smiled weakly. "Was I that transparent?"

"Only to me, darling." He brought her hand to his lips and left a lingering kiss on her knuckles. "But you haven't answered my question. Are you still nervous?"

Victoria gave her head a tiny shake. "I wouldn't be alive if I weren't a little bit nervous, but no, I am not afraid."

Robert was so full of pride for her in that moment that he wondered if his family could see his chest expand with it. "Why the change of heart?"

She looked deeply into his eyes. "You."

It was all he could do not to pull her to him in a crushing embrace. God, how he loved this woman. It felt as if he had loved her since before he was born. "What do you mean?" he asked, knowing that his heart was in his eyes and not even caring.

She swallowed, then softly said, "Just knowing that you're with me, that I have you by my side. You would never let anything bad happen to me."

His grip on her hand grew fervent. "I would protect you with my life, Torie. Surely you know that."

"And I you," she returned softly. "But such

talk is silly. I am certain we are destined to live happy, uneventful lives."

He stared at her with single-minded intensity. "Nonetheless, I would—"

"The Earl and Countess of Macclesfield!"

Robert and Victoria jumped apart as the Lindworthys' butler boomed their names, but the damage had already been done. It would be talked about for years to come—society's first glimpse of the new couple was of them practically devouring each other with their eyes. A hush fell over the crowd, and then some old biddy cackled, "Well, that's a love match if ever I saw one!"

Robert cracked a smile as he held his arm out to his wife. "I suppose there are worse reputations we could acquire."

Her answer was a barely stifled grin.

And then the evening began.

Three hours later Robert was not feeling so cheerful. Why? Because he'd had to spend the last three hours watching the *ton* watching his wife. And they seemed to be watching her with great affection. Especially the men.

If one more damned Corinthian came along and kissed her hand . . . Robert growled to himself, trying to stifle the urge to yank at his cravat. It was utter hell to stand back and smile serenely as the duke of Ashbourne—who was universally acknowledged as society's reigning rake—murmured his greetings to Victoria.

He felt his aunt's restraining hand on his arm. "Do try to contain yourself," she whispered.

"Will you look at the way he's looking at her?" he hissed. "I have half a mind to—"

"*Half* a mind is exactly right," Mrs. Brightbill returned. "Victoria is behaving beautifully, and Ashbourne has never been the sort to dally with married women. Besides, he's dangling after some American. Now stop complaining and smile."

"I am smiling," he said through clenched teeth.

"If that's a smile, I shudder to see you laugh."

Robert offered her a sickly sweet grin.

"Do stop worrying," Mrs. Brightbill said, patting his arm. "Here comes dear Basil. I shall have him take Victoria out for a dance."

"*I* shall dance with her."

"No, you won't. You have already danced with her three times. Tongues are wagging."

Before Robert could reply, Basil appeared at their sides. "Hullo Mother, Cuz," he said.

Robert only nodded at him, his eyes never leaving Victoria.

"Enjoying your first social engagement with your lovely wife?" Basil asked.

Robert eyed his cousin, conveniently forgetting that Basil had always been one of his favorite relations. "Shut up, Brightbill," he bit out. "You know damned well I'm having a hellish time."

"Ah yes, the curse of a beautiful wife. Isn't it curious how a maid is protected from lechers by her innocence, but a married woman—who has vowed before God to remain faithful to one man only—is considered fair game?"

"Just what are you getting at, Brightbill?"

Robert looked at his hands, then at his cousin's throat, assessing how well the former would fit around the latter.

"Nothing," Basil said with a mild shrug. "Merely that your plan to retire from society for a time is probably a wise one. Have you noticed the way men are staring at her?"

"Basil!" Mrs. Brightbill exclaimed. "Stop teasing your cousin." She turned to Robert. "He is only joking with you."

Robert looked about ready to explode. It was a testament to Mrs. Brightbill's courage that she didn't remove her hand from his arm.

Basil merely smiled, obviously thrilled at having so successfully baited Robert. "If you'll excuse me, I must pay my respects to my favorite cousin."

"I thought I was your favorite cousin," Robert said sarcastically.

"As if you could compare," Basil said with a slow, almost regretful shake of his head.

"Basil!" Victoria said warmly when he reached her side. "How nice to see you again this evening."

Robert gave up all pretense of normal, sane behavior and crossed to her side in two steps.

"Robert!" she said, and he rather thought her voice was twice as warm as it had been with Basil. He grinned stupidly.

"I was just enjoying your wife's company," Basil said.

"Contrive not to enjoy it so much," Robert barked.

Victoria's mouth fell open. "Why, Robert, are you jealous?"

"Not at all," he lied.

"Don't you trust me?"

"Of course I do," he snapped. "I don't trust *him*."

"Me?" Basil said with an amazingly straight face.

"I don't trust any of them," Robert growled.

Harriet, who had been standing silently by Victoria's side, nudged her and said, "See, I told you he loves you."

"Enough already!" Robert said. "She knows. Trust me."

"We all love her," Basil said, grinning.

Robert groaned. "I am plagued with relations."

Victoria touched his arm and smiled. "And I am plagued with fatigue. Would you mind if I darted off to the retiring room for a moment?"

His eyes immediately clouded with concern. "Are you ill? If you are, I'll call for—"

"I'm not ill," Victoria said under her breath. "I just need to go to the retiring room. I was trying to be polite."

"Oh," Robert replied. "I'll escort you."

"No, don't be silly. It's just down the hall. I'll be back before you notice I'm gone."

"I always notice when you're gone."

Victoria reached out to touch his cheek. "You say the sweetest things."

"Stop touching him!" Mrs. Brightbill gasped. "People will say you're in love!"

"What the devil would be wrong with that?" Robert demanded, turning on her.

"In principle, nothing. But love is not at all fashionable."

Basil chuckled. "I fear you're trapped in a very bad farce, Cuz."

"With no escape in sight," Harriet quipped.

Victoria took advantage of this exchange to slip away. "If you'll all excuse me," she murmured. She scooted along the perimeter of the ballroom until she reached the double doors leading to the hall. Mrs. Brightbill had pointed out the washroom to her earlier that evening, and Victoria found it again with ease.

The ladies' retiring room was actually in two parts. Victoria slipped through the mirrored antechamber and entered the actual washroom, locking the door behind her. She heard someone else enter the antechamber as she did her business, and hurried up, assuming that the other lady would need to relieve herself as well. Victoria quickly smoothed down her skirts and unlocked the door, a society smile pasted on her face.

Her smile lasted less than a second.

"Good evening, Lady Macclesfield."

"Lord Eversleigh!" she gasped. The man who had attacked her at the Hollingwoods' house party. Victoria suddenly found herself fighting the urge to retch. Then she redirected her efforts, deciding that if she was going to empty her stomach, she might as well aim for his feet.

"You remember my name," he murmured. "I'm honored."

"What are you doing here? This room is for ladies."

He shrugged. "Any lady who attempts to enter will find only a locked door. Lucky for them that the Lindworthys set up another retiring room on the other side of the house."

Victoria rushed past him and tried the door. It didn't budge.

"I invite you to look for the key," he said insolently. "It's on my person."

"You're mad!"

"No," he said, pinning her against the wall. "Just furious. No one makes a fool out of me."

"My husband will kill you," she said in a low voice. "He knows where I am. If he finds you here—"

"He will assume you are cuckolding him," Eversleigh finished for her, stroking her bare shoulder with a revolting brand of tenderness.

Victoria knew that Robert would never believe the worst of her, especially in light of Eversleigh's past behavior. "He will kill you," she repeated.

Eversleigh's hand slipped down to the crook of her waist. "How did you manage to trap him into marriage, I wonder. What a devious little governess you turned out to be."

"Get your hands off me," she hissed.

He ignored her, cupping the curve of her hip. "Your charms are obvious," he mused, "but you're not precisely marriage material for the heir to a marquessate."

Victoria tried to ignore the revulsion rolling in her stomach. "I will tell you one more time to remove your hands from my person," she warned.

"Or you'll do what?" he said with an amused smile, clearly not believing that she could be any kind of threat to him.

Victoria slammed her foot down on his with all the force she could muster, and then, while he was howling with surprise, she brought her knee up and jammed it into his groin. Eversleigh immediately collapsed onto the floor. He hissed something. Victoria thought he might be calling her a bitch, but he was in so much pain that his words were unclear. She brushed her hands together and allowed herself a satisfied smile. "I've learned a thing or two since our last encounter," she said.

Before she could say any more, someone started pounding on the door. Robert, she thought, and then was proved correct when she heard him bellow her name in the hall.

She grabbed the doorknob, but the door wouldn't budge. "Damn," she muttered, remembering that Eversleigh had locked it. "Just one moment, Robert," she called out.

"What the devil is going on in there?" he demanded. "You've been gone for hours."

It certainly hadn't been hours, but Victoria didn't see any point in arguing the issue. She wanted to remove herself from the washroom just as badly as he did. "I'll be right out," she said to the door. Then she turned around and regarded the pathetic heap on the floor. "Give me the key."

Eversleigh, even in his emasculated state, somehow managed a snicker.

"Who are you talking to?" Robert yelled.

Victoria ignored him. "The key!" she demanded, fixing a furious stare on Eversleigh. "Or I swear I'll do it again."

"Do what again?" Robert said. "Victoria, I insist that you open this door."

Exasperated, Victoria planted her hands on her hips and yelled back, "I would if I had the bloody key!" She turned to Eversleigh and ground out, "The key."

"Never."

Victoria flexed her foot. "I'll kick you this time. I wager I could do more damage with my foot than I did with my knee."

"Stand clear of the door, Torie!" Robert yelled. "I'm breaking it down."

"Oh, Robert, I really wish you—" She jumped back in time to avoid a splintering crash.

Robert stood in the doorway, heaving with exertion and seething with anger. The door swung drunkenly on one of its hinges. "Are you all right?" he said, rushing to her side. Then he looked down. His face turned nearly purple with rage. "What is he doing on the floor?" he asked, his words chillingly even.

Victoria knew it wasn't the right time to laugh, but she couldn't help it. "I put him there," she said.

"Would you care to elucidate further?" Robert requested, kicking Eversleigh onto his stomach and planting the sole of his boot on the man's back.

"Do you remember our carriage ride up from Ramsgate?"

"Intimately."

"Not that part," Victoria said quickly, blushing. "When I . . . Ah . . . When I accidentally nudged you—"

"I remember," he cut in. His voice was

clipped, but Victoria thought she could detect the beginnings of humor in it.

"Right," she replied. "I do try to learn from my mistakes, and I could not help but remember how incapacitated you were. I thought the same might work on Eversleigh."

Robert started to shake with laughter.

Victoria shrugged and stopped trying to hold back her smile. "He had the requisite parts," she explained.

Robert held up his hand. "No further explanation is needed," he said, chuckling all the while. "You are ever resourceful, my lady, and I love you."

Victoria sighed, completely forgetting Eversleigh's presence. "And I love you," she sighed. "So very much."

"If I might interrupt this touching scene," Eversleigh said.

Robert kicked him. "You may not." His eyes flew back to his wife. "Oh, Victoria, do you really mean it?"

"With all my heart."

He reached out to embrace her, but Eversleigh was in the way. "Is there a window in there?" he asked, flicking his head toward the washroom.

Victoria nodded.

"Big enough for a man?"

Her lips twitched. "I'd say so."

"How utterly convenient." Robert picked up Eversleigh by his collar and the seat of his pants, and shoved him halfway out the window. "Last time you attacked my wife, I believe I told you I'd tear you from limb to limb if you repeated your insults."

"She wasn't your wife then," Eversleigh spat out.

Robert slugged him in the stomach, then turned to Victoria and said, "It's amazing how good that feels. Would you like give it a try?"

"No, thank you. I would have to touch him, you see."

"Very wise," Robert murmured. Turning his attention back to Eversleigh, he said, "My marriage has left me in remarkable good humor, and it is for that reason alone that I do not kill you right now. But if you should approach my wife ever again, I will not hesitate to put a bullet between your eyes. Do I make myself clear?"

Eversleigh may have tried to nod, but it was hard to tell as he was hanging upside down outside the window.

"Do I make myself clear?" Robert roared. Victoria actually took a step back. She'd had no idea he was still so furious; he'd been keeping such a firm control on his emotions.

"Yes, damn you!" Eversleigh yelled.

Robert dropped him.

Victoria rushed to the window. "Was it very far to the ground?" she asked.

Robert looked out. "Not so far. But do you happen to know if the Lindworthys have dogs?"

"Dogs? No, why?"

He smiled. "It looks a little messy out there. I was just curious."

Victoria clapped her hand over her mouth. "Did you . . . ? Did we . . . ?"

"We certainly did. Eversleigh's valet is going to have a devil of a time washing his hair."

There was no holding in her laughter at that

one. Victoria doubled over with giggles, managing to catch her breath only long enough to gasp, "Move, so I can see!" She peered out the window just in time to catch Eversleigh shaking his head like a dog as he quit the scene, vicious invective streaming from his mouth all the while. She pulled her head back in the window. "It certainly smelled noxious," she said.

But Robert's face had grown serious. "Victoria," he began awkwardly, "what you said . . . Did you . . ."

"Yes, I meant it," she said, taking his hands in hers. "I love you. I just wasn't able to say it before now."

He blinked. "You needed to knee a man in the groin before you could tell me you loved me?"

"No!" Then she thought about his words. "Well, yes, in a way. I've always been so fearful that you would run my life. But I've learned that having you with me doesn't mean that I can't take care of myself just as well."

"You certainly made short work of Eversleigh."

Her chin lifted a notch and she allowed herself a satisfied smile. "Yes, I did, didn't I? And do you know, but I think I couldn't have done it without you."

"Victoria, you did this all on your own. I wasn't even present."

"Yes, you were." She picked up his hand and placed it over her heart. "You were here. And you made me strong."

"Torie, you're the strongest woman I know. You always have been."

She didn't even try to put a halt to the tears

rolling down her cheeks. "I'm so much better with you than I am without you. Robert, I love you so much."

Robert leaned down to kiss her, then realized that the door to the retiring room was still hanging on its hinge. He shut the connecting door and locked it. "There," he murmured in what he hoped was his best rakish voice. "Now I have you all to myself."

"You certainly do, my lord. You certainly do."

Many minutes later, Victoria pulled her mouth a fraction of an inch away from his. "Robert," she said, "do you realize—"

"Hush, woman, I'm trying to kiss you, and there's damned little room to maneuver in here."

"Yes, but do you realize—"

He cut her off with his mouth. Victoria surrendered to his kiss for another minute, but then she pulled away again. "What I wanted to tell you—"

He let out a dramatic sigh. "What?"

"Someday our children are going to ask us what the most meaningful moment of our lives was. And they're going to want to know where it happened."

Robert lifted his head and regarded the cramped washroom, then chuckled. "Darling, we're just going to have to lie and say we traveled to China, because no one would believe this."

Then he kissed her again.

Epilogue

S everal months later Victoria was watching snowflakes through the window of the Macclesfield carriage as she and Robert returned home from supper at Castleford. Robert hadn't wanted to visit his father, but she had insisted that they needed to make peace with their families before they could think about beginning a family of their own.

Victoria's reunion with her own father had occurred two weeks earlier. It had been difficult at first, and Victoria still wouldn't say that their relationship was completely repaired, but at least the healing process had begun. After this visit to Castleford, she felt that Robert and his father had reached a similar point in their own relationship.

She let out a soft sigh and turned back to the carriage's interior. Robert had dozed off, his dark lashes sinfully long against his cheeks. She reached out to brush away a lock of his hair, and his eyelids fluttered open.

He yawned. "Did I fall asleep?"

369

"Just for a moment," Victoria said. Then she yawned, too. "Goodness, it must be catching."

Robert smiled. "Yawns?"

Victoria nodded, still yawning.

"I didn't expect that we'd be there so late," Robert said.

"I'm glad we were. I wanted you to have time with your father. He is a good man. A bit misguided, but he loves you, and that is what is important."

Robert pulled her closer to him. "Victoria, you have the biggest heart of anyone I have ever met. How can you possibly forgive him for the way he treated you?"

"You forgave my father," she pointed out.

"Only because you ordered me to."

Victoria swatted at his shoulder. "If nothing else, we can learn from their mistakes. For when we have our own children."

"I suppose if one must find a silver lining," he muttered.

"I would hope we could learn *soon*," she said pointedly.

Robert was clearly still sleepy, because he didn't catch her hint and just gave her a dutiful nod.

"Very soon," Victoria repeated. "Maybe by early summer."

He wasn't such a dolt that he missed her meaning twice. "What?" he gasped, sitting up straight.

She nodded and placed his hand on her abdomen.

"Are you certain? You haven't been queasy. I

would have noticed if you had morning sickness."

Victoria gave him an amused smile. "Are you disappointed that I am not having trouble keeping my breakfast down?"

"No, of course not, it's just . . ."

"Just what, Robert?"

His throat worked, and Victoria was surprised to see a tear forming in his eye. She was even more surprised when he didn't move to brush it away.

He turned to her and kissed her lightly on the cheek. "When we finally married I never thought I could be happier than I was at that very moment, but you've gone and proved me wrong."

"It's nice to prove you wrong from time to time." She laughed. Then Robert suddenly stiffened, startling her. "What is it?"

"You're going to think I'm mad," he said, sounding a bit baffled.

"Perhaps, but only in the nicest possible way," she teased.

"The moon," he said. "I could swear it just *winked* at me."

Victoria twisted her head to look back out the window. The moon hung heavy and low in the night sky. "It looks perfectly normal to me."

"It must have been a tree branch," Robert muttered, "crossing in front of our window."

Victoria smiled. "Isn't it interesting how the moon follows one wherever one goes?"

"There is a scientific explanation for—"

"I know, I know. But I prefer to think it follows me."

Robert looked back up at the moon, still dumbstruck over the winking incident. "Do you remember when I promised you the moon?" he asked. "When I promised you everything and the moon?"

She nodded sleepily. "I have everything I need right here in this carriage. I don't need the moon anymore."

Robert watched as the moon followed their carriage, winking at him once again. "What the devil?" He craned his head to look for a tree branch. He didn't see one.

"What is it?" Victoria mumbled, burrowing into his side.

Robert stared at the moon, silently daring it to wink again. It remained mockingly full. "Darling," he said distractedly, "about the moon . . ."

"Yes?"

"I don't think it matters whether you want it or not."

"What are you talking about?"

"The moon. I think it's yours."

Victoria yawned, not bothering to open her eyes. "Fine. I'm glad to have it."

"But—" Robert shook his head. He was growing fanciful. The moon didn't belong to his wife. It didn't follow her, protect her. It certainly didn't *wink* at anybody.

But he stared out the window the rest of the way home, just in case.

*Watch out
for the following titles by
Julia Quinn,
now available
from
Piatkus!*

BRIGHTER THAN THE SUN

Eleanor Lyndon was minding her own business when a lord of the realm fell – quite literally – into her life.

When Charles Wycombe, the dashing and incorrigible Earl of Billington, toppled out of a tree and landed at Ellie's feet, neither suspected that such an inauspicious meeting would lead to marriage. But Charles must find a bride before his thirtieth birthday or her father's odious fiancée will choose one for her. And so they agree to wed, even though their match appears to have been made somewhere hotter than heaven . . .

Ellie never dreamed she'd marry a stranger, especially one with such a devastating combination of rakish charm and debonair wit. She tries to keep him at arm's length, at least until she discovers the man beneath the handsome surface. But Charles can be quite persuasive – even tender – when he puts his mind to it, and Ellie finds herself slipping under his seductive spell. And as one kiss leads to another, this unlikely pair discovers that their marriage is not so inconvenient after all . . . and just might lead to love.

978-0-7499-0892-8

TO CATCH AN HEIRESS

When Caroline Trent is kidnapped by Blake
Ravenscroft, she doesn't even try to elude this
dangerously handsome agent of the crown. Yes, he
believes she's a notorious spy named Carlotta De Leon
but she's tired of running from unwanted marriage
proposals and hiding out in the titillating company of a
mysterious captor is awfully convenient – especially as,
in six weeks, when she turns twenty-one, she'll gain
control of her fortune.

Blake Ravenscroft's mission is to bring 'Carlotta' to
justice, not to fall in love. His heart has been hardened
by years of intrigue, but this little temptress proves
oddly disarming and thoroughly kissable. And suddenly
the unthinkable becomes possible – this mismatched
couple might actually be destined for love.

978-0-7499-0882-9